Regards,

Barish
One Rainy Day

Punitha Muniandy

iUniverse, Inc.
Bloomington

Barish
One Rainy Day

iUniverse books may be ordered through booksellers or by contacting:

iUniverse
1663 Liberty Drive
Bloomington, IN 47403
www.iuniverse.com
1-800-Authors (1-800-288-4677)

ISBN: 978-1-4620-3095-8 (sc)
ISBN: 978-1-4620-3097-2 (hc)
ISBN: 978-1-4620-3096-5 (e)

Printed in the United States of America

iUniverse rev. date: 8/23/2011

For Reuben, the man who made it happen.

Characters

The Sharmas:
Ajay Sharma
Menaka Sharma (His wife)
Kaveri (Their older daughter) – Married to Raj Dhillon
Gangga (Their middle daughter) – Engaged to Subash Mehta
Jamuna (Their youngest daughter) – Dating Jason Broughton

Devika – Menaka's sister married to Siva Bose
Priya – Devika's daughter

The Kumars:
Chandi Kumar -Ajay's Sister
Mahesh Kumar - Her husband
Vikram Kumar - Their older son
Johan & Karan - Their twins

The Dhillons
Mr & Mrs Dhillon - Kaveri's in-laws

Chapter one – Ajay

The tent *wallahs* were coming at eight. So were the caterers, the cleaners and the rest of the help. The flowers would be arriving around the same time. All the house-guests would be up plus the guests who'd be showing up for the *big breakfast*. Ajay hoped Menaka, for once, had planned the breakfast menu.

The bed creaked softly as Ajay Sharma pushed himself up. He crossed the room and gazed out of the water spotted window at the indolent drops of rain that fell to the ground. Usually Ajay liked the rain, especially the loud and heavy ones with the booming sound of thunder in between. He found it therapeutic. He liked the noise it made on the roof, as if someone were dropping thousands of marbles. It lulled him, took him to times he thought of fondly, of lost times. But the rain here, in Canada, could never compare to the ones in India, dripping idly like water from a loose tap. The Monsoon rain was what Ajay missed most about India.

But that day, the rain annoyed him. It added to his anxiety. His insides curled up in one tight big knot every time he thought of the day ahead.

"Go to bed, Ajay," Menaka's voice startled him. He turned to look at his wife. All that was visible was the mob of messy hair at the end of the earthy brown duvet.

"How can you sleep when there's so much to do today?"

"It's five in the morning, Ajay. The wedding's not for another twelve hours. Please go to sleep or let me sleep." The mass of black hair didn't even budge as she grumbled.

"Fine."

Ajay draped an old robe around him and exited the bedroom. The hallway from his bedroom to the kitchen was dark. Ajay groped the wall and found the familiar rectangle shape of the switch. As the oval shaped lamp brightened the hallway, Ajay's eyes fell on the framed pictures adorning the narrow wall; their glass frames reflecting the newly lit light. His lips curved upward when he saw the pictures, mostly the smiling faces of his three daughters.

Ajay's gaze lingered on his middle daughter Gangga. His fingers traced the contour of Gangga's moon-shaped face and his eyes moistened. In a little more than twelve hours she'd be someone's wife. Where had all the time gone? When did his daughters grow out of their cribs? Wasn't it only recently he was teaching them how to drive around the block? And shopping for prom dresses?

First it had been his eldest daughter Kaveri who got married two years ago.

"To a useless fellow!" he shook his head.

Ajay had his reservations when it came to Raj – Kaveri's husband. He still remembered telling Kaveri to re-think her decision, but she had been adamant, as she had been in everything else in her life. And now look at where they were. Only two years of marriage and it was already on the rocks. It was as if those two didn't care about each other anymore. He wondered if they ever did.

Ajay wished Kaveri had listened to him. But it didn't help that his wife had been on her daughter's side as well. She had fought Kaveri's battle, defying Ajay along the way. It was Raj's parents The Dhillons came over with their proposal that Ajay finally gave in. With parents that polite surely the son would have inherited some of the goodness. Now looking back, Ajay sighed. What goodness? All Raj had inherited were the father's good looks and arrogance that went with being a Dhillon. He hoped Gangga's fate to be different. He *knew* it would be different. Gangga's fiancé, Subash, was the son of Ajay's childhood friend.

He had grown up with Subash's father in India. They went to the same school. They had both migrated to Canada at different times, each following his destiny and belief that life would be better in the foreign land. And fate brought them together a year ago when they had bumped into each other at a wedding. That was when Subash's father had suggested both their children meet. Ajay was happy with Subash and he knew Gangga would be happy too. She obviously liked Subash, agreeing to the arranged marriage. He only had Jamuna, the youngest daughter, to worry about after this. Then he could finally rest. Maybe go back to India for a long vacation.

Thinking of India made his heart flutter like a teenager meeting his first love. He breathed deeply in anticipation of his journey back to India. Already the spicy smell of pungent dried chilies on the verandah of his childhood house filling his nose, the cooling sweetness of sugar-cane juice from the road-side vendor lingering on his tongue.

His eyes fell on another face, a younger one than Jamuna's, a face not very unlike his three daughters, a face that held so much resemblance to his children but yet one that caused much turmoil within him.

"Priya – " he whispered.

But that was for another day. Ajay forced his gaze and mind away from Priya and proceeded to the kitchen, but not before glancing at his image on the full length mirror by the door. The mirror was placed there to make the narrow hallway look wider. But it was often used for self grooming in his household. Ajay stood tall in the image behind the mirror, with broad shoulders and a slim waist. His still thick hair combed back neatly displayed streaks of black and white. Ajay smiled and rubbed his cheeks, the morning stubble pricking his palm mildly. Not bad for a middle aged man, thought Ajay with a smug. He knew he looked good for his age. If not for the pair of glasses, his face would probably look much younger. With a slight bow of his head, as if acknowledging himself, Ajay walked into the kitchen.

He put the kettle on to boil and, out of habit, brought the round orange pekoe tea-bag to his nose before dropping it into a mug. The bitter fragrance of black tea always woke him up in the morning, especially the smell of orange pekoe, with no added aroma like some of the more refined teas. It was the only tea he had come to like, the only one that came close to tasting like the tea from India. He spent many years in Canada finding the right tea for his palate - but nothing came close. Orange pekoe was not his first choice but the taste grew on him, like many other things in his life, many other things that were not his first choice, including Menaka. Only Menaka didn't grow on him, like orange pekoe did.

He worked quietly, lest he wake the household. He glanced at the old grandfather clock by the dining table, hoisted against the pale yellow wall that its rich cherry brown wood stood out prominently in contrast. It was his only possession from India, a material linkage that chained him to his past. The needles were pointing at half past five now. Ajay had a little more than two hours to himself before the excitement began and work started. So much to do and so little time. He hoped Menaka had planned the meals.

Ajay brought the middle of his palm to his forehead. *Great*, he thought, *and she's still sleeping like a queen.* The kettle screeched loudly, as if in agreement.

With a pre-occupied mind, Ajay swirled some brown sugar into his tea before adding the cream. He prayed Gangga's wedding would go as planned and with little drama. Gangga was thirty years old. If she was back in India, she'd be equivalent to an old maid. He struggled and tried very hard to overlook the demands of his society, tried very hard to condone the gossips that crept through their lives until eventually forcing them to adhere. He looked around at his neighbors, Canadian neighbors, and colleagues and wished his life and his children's lives were as simple and as straight forward. But knew it would never be.

Living in Canada didn't change the fact that they were Indians. In fact, sometimes he thought they were more Indian than the Indians in India. They had to try harder to hold on to their values. Wasn't it easier to stray in a foreign land than in your own?

Ajay sat at the dining table, occasionally sipping his tea, enjoying the momentary solitude before the hullaballoo began. The sudden sound of soft footsteps approaching the kitchen annoyed him. He was further distressed when he saw the owner of the footsteps, his wife. She looked like she hadn't had any sleep. Her morning hair stuck out wildly around her face and her robe fell down her droopy shoulders, giving her no sense of fashion or elegance. Many times, his friends had commented on how much younger he looked compared to Menaka. Ajay took pride in looking after himself. The hours he'd put in the gym did pay off. He also knew he stood out in his group of friends as the better looking one, with no beer-belly or a drooping chin like most of them. He ran his finger through his hair and smoothened its morning unruliness. He watched his wife and wished she'd at least join the gym to get rid of her love handles.

Although Menaka was less than a feet away from him, she didn't acknowledge his presence.

Ajay watched as she scooped three tablespoons of instant Nescafe into her mug. Steam flew into the air as she added the still hot water. Menaka sat down at the far end of the table. She took a sip of the coffee before pushing her chair back. She stood on her toes and reached into one of the reddish-brown cherry kitchen cabinets above the stove. Ajay watched his wife over the rim of his glasses, not liking what he was seeing. As he expected, Menaka produced a large brown bottle from the cabinet, poured some of its content onto her mug of coffee and sat down again.

"Menaka, surely you're not drinking now?" Ajay's tone was a mix of disapproval and disappointment. "It's just past five in the morning."

"Please, Ajay, stay out of my business. I have a long day ahead of me and you woke me up so bloody early. I need this to steady my nerves."

"Steady your nerves? Hah, that's a good one."

"I said leave me be, okay?"

"I don't believe you, Menaka. Today is such an important day for our daughter and you've started drinking so early. Can't you for once put your desires aside and concentrate on your family?"

The chair screeched angrily against the wooden floor as Menaka stood up again. "Don't you talk to me about putting my desires aside. Ajay, if you know what's good, stay out of my business."

Ajay, taken aback by Menaka's remark, stood up as well. What exactly did she mean?

"What rubbish are you talking now?"

"Exactly that, rubbish."

"What is wrong with you? Can you not for one day have some self-control? Have you become that dependant on it?"

"Self-control? You're one to talk about self-control?"

Ajay's face burnt with the anger he was trying to contain. "I feel like I don't know you anymore."

"It's mutual."

Her nonchalant attitude toward him angered Ajay further. "What does that mean?"

"Drop it, Ajay."

"No, I'm not going to drop it. You started something, so let's finish it."

"You won't like it."

"Won't like what?"

"I said drop it."

"If you have something to say to me, say it. Stop playing games. We're not teenagers."

"I told you I don't want to talk about it, not today."

"Talk about what?" Ajay's voice quivered very lightly, just as his palms sweated, very lightly. Something in the way Menaka spoke worried him.

"Look," she paused as if waiting for some dramatic effect. "…I know."

"Know what?" Although he raised his voice, it sounded puny to his ears. Surely she couldn't be referring to – surely not? He grabbed to the side of the table to calm his shaky hands.

"About your…your…," She paused again. This time she looked as if she was searching for the appropriate word, her lips were pursed tightly. Ajay's heart rate increased with every intake of his breath. He waited and prayed his wife would not continue talking. Suddenly, he didn't want to hear it anymore, he didn't want to know.

"Indecent behavior," she said finally, her voice soft like a whisper. "I have known since it began, but I kept quiet, for the sake of this family. So, please, don't start lecturing me on desires and responsibilities."

He'd heard the devastating effect shock could sometimes render upon people, but this was the first time he was experiencing it. He felt the walls closing up on him. His lungs worked harder to gather enough oxygen into his body and into his brain to stop him from blacking out. He fell backwards into his chair with a sudden thump. Ajay clenched his clammy fingers together and closed his eyes that he didn't see when his youngest daughter dashed into the kitchen in her pajamas and stopped dead in front of them.

"Papa? Mama? What are you doing here so early?" He heard Jamuna's voice but it didn't quite register into his brain.

"Jamuna, why are you up at this hour?" Menaka's voice pulled Ajay back to the present. That was when he noticed Jamuna staring at them with her big brown eyes, terror written all over her pretty face.

Did she hear them arguing? Dear God, why did this have to happen now, today of all days?

"Jamuna, beta, go back to your room, we'll talk later," said Ajay gently. He expected her to defy, to confront them of what was in front of her; a big bottle of rum and of their conversation. But she did none of those. She nodded feebly and turned to exit the kitchen when Ajay saw her face slamming into Jason's chest. Where did Jason come from?

"Jason, did you spend the night here?" Ajay addressed his nephew's friend, trying his best to keep his voice steady.

"Mr. Sharma?" Jason gaped at him but quickly recovered. "Sorry, I didn't see you here. Yeah, I crashed here last night with…err…in… well…," Jason stumbled with his words. His blue eyes darted all over the room.

"Is Vikram still sleeping then?" Vikram was Ajay's nephew. Vikram had been living with Ajay and his family for a year now while completing his studies at a local college. His parents lived in Toronto where they owned and operated a grocery store.

"I came in for some water, but I see you are in the middle of something important. I'll get it later." Ajay noticed Jason turned back to leave but not before throwing a quick glance at the bottle on the dining table.

Ajay dropped his head into his hand, pushed his hair back and said, "Menaka…?" He looked up to see his wife gone.

The bottle of rum stood in front of him, lonely and abandoned. The dark liquid inside glittered like a brown jewel under the kitchen light. Ajay got up from his chair, picked the bottle up and stashed it quickly back into the cabinet, out of sight. Menaka's words throbbed his head, gripped his mind with painful claws. His head hurt. There was a wedding on. He needed to stay focused. But he couldn't divert his mind from Menaka's outburst. What did Menaka mean by his indecent behavior? Did she know? If Menaka knew, who else did?

Chapter two – Menaka

Menaka was back on her bed, taking cover under the comforter. She lay there listening to the steady rhythm of the rain outside. She, unlike Ajay, found the rain rather troublesome. She didn't like the wet puddles of water on the road, the sloppy wet grass, the gloominess, the lack of sunshine and the depressing dreariness that took her deeper into her own dejection. It had been raining recklessly for a week now and she could sense depression settling in within her like an uninvited guest. Conversation with Ajay that morning had only made it worse. Even the single shot of rum in her coffee didn't do its usual trick.

It hadn't been easy; finding out about the infidelity.

She didn't know when it had started. By the time the news reached her, it had spread through the veins of the grapevine like an inveterate disease. Just like Julia Roberts in the movie '*Something To Talk About*', she was the last to find out. Everyone in her circle of friends knew of it, she was sure of that. Menaka Sharma might not understand many things, including her husband, but she wasn't naïve. She could sense the mockery, the sympathy, the thank-god-it's-not-me look thrown her direction every time she was among her friends.

Menaka rolled over and stared at the ceiling – thirty three years, has it already been that long? She wasn't sure when the other woman had sneaked in and used her charm on her husband. It was hard to tell with Ajay. He had always been indifferent toward her. He'd always acted nonchalant about anything related to her or their marriage. How could it be her fault if she didn't notice any change in his behavior since the affair, how could she have known?

It had been an arranged marriage, like most marriages were those days in India. She had liked him for his gentle manners. She'd never seen him raise his voice at anyone. He was always calm, placid. Unlike her, who was the loud one in the family. If he was like the cool water, she was the burning fire. She had always been head-strong and adamant, and he'd known that about her. But he accepted her, didn't he? Did he not promise to honor and respect her as they made the seven rounds around the sacred fire on their wedding day? Did the vows mean nothing to him?

Still staring at the ceiling, Menaka's thought moved to her daughters. All of them, save Kaveri, favored him to her. She knew that, and with time came to accept it. Although Kaveri's resentment toward her father intrigued Menaka, she didn't discourage it. It was nice to be the favored one, albeit to only one of them.

Feeling restless, Menaka pushed her duvet off and walked to the window. Only in Vancouver it would rain like this, non-stop. Canada hadn't done them good, she thought suddenly. If they had stayed in India, she was sure Ajay wouldn't have strayed. If not anything else, the Indian values would've held him together, would've put some fear in him.

At first, when Menaka heard about it five years ago she wasn't shocked. No, she simply didn't believe it. Ajay was a busy man, with work and his family. How could he possibly find time to slot another woman into his life? So when Mrs. Bhaduri, her close friend, warned her about it one day at a friend's wedding, Menaka had laughed at her.

"My husband is not like any other man. He's very devoted to his family. Whoever's feeding you with this information?" she had asked, not angry but amused.

"I saw it with my two eyes, Menaka. I saw him with another woman just two days ago. Tell me this, where was Ajay Friday evening?"

Menaka had searched her brain. Friday…was he home for dinner? No, he wasn't. Menaka remembered because she didn't prepare any dinner that evening. None of her children, including Vikram, had been home. She had actually appreciated the time alone, which was rare in her house. But where was Ajay? Menaka had thought hard.

She knew Ajay mentioned something, but she couldn't remember. She remembered silently castigating herself for not having paid attention to what he was saying.

"I think he was out with a friend," Menaka's mouth formed the words while her mind questioned them. Where was he? Something resembling a big, hard lump had appeared and stayed in her throat, forcing her to swallow a few times in an attempt to get rid of it.

"I saw him, Menaka. I was with Mr. Bhaduri at *Silvercity*. Ajay was there, watching '*Khabi Alveda Na Kehna*' with a woman. We couldn't see her clearly. They were sitting a few rows in front of us and he had his hand over her shoulders. They were giggling like a couple of teenagers throughout the movie."

Every word that flew out of Mrs. Bhaduri's mouth had felt like sharp darts being thrown at her and none missed the spot – her heart. Standing by the window now, Menaka resisted the urge to clutch her bosom that still hurt from that night. Menaka had even defended Ajay that day to Mrs. Bhaduri.

"How did you know it was Ajay since you couldn't see them?" Menaka had forced the words out.

"Mr. Bhaduri saw him in the men's room during the interval. He came out of the bathroom and tried to call out to Ajay, but Ajay was walking with an unusual speed, so Mr. Bhaduri ended up following him into the theatre, only to see him walk to his chair in front of us..."

Menaka had wanted to say it was her they saw him with, but it was too late now. Mrs. Bhaduri already knew she didn't go out that evening and hadn't she just mentioned earlier how she wished she'd gone to watch '*Khabi Alveda Na Kehna*'?

She had waited for a week before saying anything to Ajay. She hadn't known how to approach him with the question. What would she ask? *Ajay, are you or are you not having an affair?* Or *Ajay, I know about your affair. I think you should leave.*

Menaka touched the cool surface of the window with her palm, she leaned forward and let her forehead touch the glass. She knew why she didn't ask Ajay directly about his affair. She couldn't. She had given it a lot of thought, of what would happen to her if the truth surfaced. She'd be known as a divorcee, as the woman who couldn't hold on to her husband. And what about the children?

Her head had swirled as she imagined being in the court, in front of a judge, being told whether she had the custody of her children or not. Her imagination stopped there. She couldn't go on, couldn't bring herself to even contemplate life on her own. She'd be known as the failed wife and a divorcee. She wouldn't be able to face her parents and her family back in India. What would they say? Her father would be disgraced more than heartbroken. She couldn't do it.

When she had decided to live with it, to overlook it and live with it, it had felt like the hardest thing to do. She had to go on living day by day with this man, knowing what was happening, pretending everything was fine just to safeguard her dignity. It was a lot, took a lot out of her but her self-respect was important. And in any case, Menaka had consoled herself, affairs didn't last long. Eventually he'd get tired of the other woman, he'd come back to her.

Still, she had wanted to hear it from Ajay, from his mouth, to believe the existence of the other woman in his life. If she was willing to tolerate, to allow the woman into their lives, the least Ajay could do was dignify her with some honesty.

Stepping back from the window now, Menaka approached her bed again. She was beginning to feel drowsy, but not drowsy enough not to remember that day, the day that she had confronted him.

It was late one evening that she had finally mustered the courage to approach Ajay. Menaka had made sure all the children were not around to eavesdrop, deliberately or otherwise.

"I was thinking, shall we go for a movie this evening since tomorrow is a weekend?" Menaka had begun, speaking with premeditated nonchalance while piling Ajay's plate with some rice and curry. If Ajay stiffened even ever so slightly by her suggestion, he didn't show it. He simply mixed the curry with his rice, allowing the yellow-carroty concoction to spread through the whites of the rice.

"Which one?" he had asked.

"*Khabi Alveda Na Kehna*? Shahrukh's latest movie and all my friends were saying how good it was. Apparently Karan Johar did wonders this time, attempting the forbidden so to say. You know, married couples involved in sordid affairs. Which Indian movie had done that so far? So bold of Karan Johar, don't you think?" Menaka had read about the movie in one of the Indian Movie magazines. When she learned the movie was about two married people falling in love, Menaka had let out a loud, bitter laugh.

"I don't quite enjoy movies like that. Why don't you go with one of your lady friends?"

It wasn't his lack of interest that had convinced her of his affair; it was his lack of appetite thereafter. Ajay had simply stood up and walked away without touching his dinner. Watching him, Menaka had felt all life draining out of her.

She closed her eyes now while lying on her bed and a vivid picture of their lives together flashed behind her lids. Their dreams, their children, their vacations, their property – when had the other woman been a part of everything that encompassed her life?

Menaka had struggled for months thereafter to come in terms with Ajay's affair. That was when she had found solace in her drinking. At first it was only in the evenings, to help her sleep better. Then something would trigger her nerves during the day; Ajay working late, a mysterious phone call, or some urgency at the office that required him to leave the house instantly that she'd started drinking in the daytime as well. It steadied her, she found. Alcohol provided relief that her life didn't.

And now, the man who drove her into the arms of alcohol was lecturing her about it. The nerve! But she knew she shouldn't have said anything to Ajay, not that morning. Now things were going to be awkward between them. And they had a wedding to worry about. How was she going to go through the day without facing Ajay? She just had to bite the bullet and be civil to him until after the wedding. There was nothing else to do. She'd rest a bit more now. The rum was taking its effect, and she was feeling drowsy. Might as well since she needed the rest…to face the day…to face Ajay…to face reality…to finally confront it…to…

Chapter three – Gangga

When at first she heard the shrilling sound, she was so deep in sleep that it seemed like a dream. But when the noise continued, pounding in her eardrums, she woke up with a jolt. At first, she felt disoriented. When she looked around her bedroom, Gangga realized she was at her parents' house, back in her old room – the one she shared with Jamuna now. She glanced over at Jamuna's bed; it hadn't been slept in. The loud trill was still persistent.

Gangga searched around her, throwing the duvet aside. She realized then that the sound was coming from under her pillow. She lifted the lavender covered pillow and saw her Motorola cell-phone's screen blinking in coordination with the beep.

This better be good, she muttered under her breath before answering the call.

"Hello?" her voice was rushed, somewhat impatient.

"Hi, sunshine. Good morning. What're you doing?" It was the deep, pleasantly hoarse male voice with a slight hint of Indian accent that she'd come to know so well.

"Subash?" she gasped. "Why do you have to wake me up so early? Have you any idea what time it is? Call me in another two hours. I need to sleep."

"How can you possibly think of sleeping when we have such an important day ahead of us?"

"Subash," the sound of her gentle laughter resonated against the walls of the room, "that's why I need to have my full eight hours of sleep. Do you want your bride to have bags under her eyes and red puffy cheeks? I need to look radiant to stand next to you."

"You'll look radiant even with no sleep at all, my love. Talk to me for a bit. I'm feeling nervous, excited, worried. Gosh, Gangga, I can't believe I'm actually getting married and that too, to you. The most gorgeous, lovely Indian girl I've ever met."

"Why are you nervous then?"

"Aren't you?" he asked her back.

"No, should I be? You're not going to stand me up or something are you?"

It was Subash's turn to laugh. "Not if you held a gun to my head!"

"So, why are you nervous?"

"I don't know. Maybe because you're so perfect in every way that I can't believe my luck, maybe because getting married is not something I do on a regular basis, maybe because I love you so much and don't want anything to jinx it."

"Nothing will jinx it. You worry too much. Just relax and let things fall into place."

Subash's apprehension amused her. Shouldn't she the one to be anxious like most brides? But for Gangga it was just another day, an important day nevertheless. She was getting married, it was a big deal but not completely life altering. Nothing was going to change in her life except for her living arrangements.

"You surprise me," she heard Subash say.

"Why?"

"You're not the least tense. You sound so calm."

"Is that a bad thing?"

"No. That's why you're so perfect for me. I'll always be on edge and you the opposite. Together we'll create the perfect equilibrium."

"Such a philosopher you are."

"That I am."

"Okay, now let me go back to sleep, please," begged Gangga. "And it's bad luck for the bride and groom to talk on the day of their wedding."

"No, I think it's bad luck if they see each other. No one said anything about talking. I'll let you go back to sleep for now since tonight you have to stay up."

"Aahh, yes, the wedding." Gangga knew the wedding would drag until late evening, but she was hoping by nine or ten the crowd would've dispersed.

"You're so naïve, so innocently sweet. My love, tonight is also our first night." Subash's voice wavered slightly when he said 'first night'. Gangga couldn't help smiling. Subash and she had decided that they'd wait until they were wed to have sex. It wasn't Gangga's decision, but Subash's. He didn't believe in sex before marriage and she didn't broach the subject further, respecting his decision. At least he wasn't like the men she'd dated who'd wanted only the sex. Subash was a breath of fresh air to her. She remembered him telling her one evening, while they were smooching passionately behind the wheels of his Mercedes, "You're like a tiger in a cat's costume – can't wait to unveil you."

But she didn't realize how much he was anticipating their wedding night, it was almost funny.

"Subash, you're incorrigible," she said now. "Do you expect me to come into your bedroom all dressed up with a tumbler of milk as well?"

"What's wrong with that?"

"Right. And I guess you'd want me to finish the milk that you deliberately leave in the glass for me?" asked Gangga, still amused. She'd seen enough Hindi movies to know what '*First Night*' meant to the Indian newlyweds. The bride, adorned beautifully in expensive sari and gold jewelries, would walk slowly with her head bowed into her husband's room, with a tumbler of milk – preferably a silver one. He'd drink half of the milk and she'd finish the rest. Then he'd gently hold her by her shoulders and sit her on the bed which was usually covered lavishly with red rose petals. Typically, that was how far they'd show in movies. What followed next always left to the audiences' imaginations.

"Well, if you don't want to drink the milk I leave for you, you don't have to."

Gangga chose to ignore Subash's tone, which sounded like a sulky five-year-old's. She eyed her pillow longingly. Why did Subash have to pick the morning before the wedding for this conversation? It annoyed Gangga.

"I seriously do hope you are joking," her voice was impatient. " You'd expect me to be a virgin next." As the words flowed out, Gangga's mind registered what they meant and she wanted to swallow each word back, but it was too late. A part of Gangga had always suspected that Subash thought her a virgin, although he never asked or said anything about it.

Subash went dead silent on the other end. She couldn't even hear him breathing. A sudden, unfathomable fear settled deep within her.

"Subash, are you there?" she asked after a while.

He remained silent.

"Subash, I'm sorry, I didn't mean that."

Silence pursued. Gangga probed, her voice sounding desperate, "Subash, sweetheart, please talk to me."

When he spoke, Subash sounded like someone else – his voice cold, indifferent, strange. "I *did* expect to marry a virgin…"

Gangga clutched the cell-phone as if clutching on to him. She felt cold, unusually cold.

"I'm sorry, that came out wrong."

"But it's the truth, isn't it?" he sounded like he was talking to himself.

"Subash, did you seriously think I was a virgin?" she asked despite knowing very well that he did. She wished she had broached this subject sooner, wished she'd been frank with him. But, the truth of the matter was, she didn't think it was a big deal. She certainly didn't expect Subash to be a virgin and desperately hoped he wasn't one.

"Why not?" Subash asked now. "Are you not an Indian girl? Did you not agree to an arranged marriage? What was I supposed to think? How was I supposed to know?" His voice cracked with emotion and he let out a lingering sigh…a sigh of disappointment, Gangga noted with fear.

"But, sweetheart, this is Canada. I was born here."

"So that makes you what? A slut?"

And he took it a little too far. Gangga, in all her remorse, couldn't contain the hurtful remark. "Subash! What gives you the right to insult me that way? How dare you?" Her voice quivered, her hand that was holding the phone shook, her heart beat violently against her chest.

"I dare because you lied to me, you led me on. I'm not so sure about this wedding anymore, Gangga. I need to think."

"I beg your pardon?" Was she hearing him right?

And he hung up, just like that.

Gangga stared at the phone in her hand, her heart pounding hard against her ribs, her breath rising and falling inconsistently, her mind swirled with confusion, with questions like someone was stirring hard at her brain with a stick. What just happened? Did her fiancé just call off their wedding? She sat motionless. Seconds trickled into minutes. When she finally decided to move, it was to dial his number. The phone rang on the other end until Subash's voicemail picked up, asking to leave a message. Gangga disconnected the phone but dialed it all over again.

She tried again and with the same result, and again – each time with less urgency but more confusion. She called him at least twenty times before throwing her cell-phone against the dark earthy brown wall of Jamuna's room. The phone hit the wall and fell onto the carpeted floor, with its battery spilling out. She sat gawping at it, mute. Her insides were shaking with rage and fear. What was happening? Did Subash just dump her on their wedding day? She asked that question over and over, playing their conversation in her head over and over, as if trying to decipher each word, as if trying to make sense of it all. The feelings that were void earlier hit her roughly like a bad wind. She sat holding to the side of the bed, afraid to let go, rocking to and fro to calm herself. For the first time since she embarked on this journey to becoming a wife, Gangga felt anxious, nervous, and terribly afraid.

When her father had first mentioned the notion of an arranged marriage six months ago, Gangga had been furious. How dare her parents interfere with her life? She'd been rebellious and defiant. Both Ajay and Menaka tried very hard to convince her. She refused point blank, standing adamantly on her decision, not altering.

"We're not asking you to get married to him, just meet him, get to know him, what do you have to lose?" Ajay had asked.

"A lot!" she had shouted with vehemence. "My pride, dignity, reputation. God, Papa, who does arranged marriages anymore? We are not living in the eighties here, Papa." Then with a calmer voice, "I'd like to find my own husband. But thanks for trying."

"You're going to be thirty in a few months, beta. When are you going to find a husband?" her mother had asked, sounding despondent.

"Kaveri Didi got married on her own. You didn't force any man down her throat. Why do it to me?"

"Kaveri's found Raj, a decent Indian boy. Now if you have anyone like that in mind, please let us know. Then we can stop all this nonsense."

Gangga didn't have an answer. She didn't know anyone; or more precisely, any Indian man who'd want to marry her.

Gangga hadn't been in a serious relationship for a very long time. The one long term relationship she had ended on a mutual basis. Dave and she had been dating for a year when Dave, a Punjabi guy, told her he was settling for a girl of his parents' choice. The girl was a Punjabi, unlike Gangga, and she was from India. Dave was sure she'd make a better daughter-in-law to his parents than Gangga would. After Dave, Gangga dated two other men, both non-Indians. Tom was an Italian and he was a waiter at the same restaurant where she was the hostess. After a few delicious sexual encounters, Gangga found Tom to be a little too young. And also very immature, especially when she found herself constantly advising him on his finances and lifestyle. She then met a Greek doctor, who not only swept her off her feet but promised a lifelong relationship with her…but not as his wife for he was already married to a Greek woman. No, he wanted Gangga as his mistress. That happened just over a year ago. After that heartbreaking incident, Gangga had stayed away from men. Not being aware of these episodes, her parents were forcing her to marry a total stranger.

But after that day, her parents didn't mention Subash to Gangga. And just when she thought her parents had given up trying to fix her with some unknown Indian man, Subash called, sounding cool and nonchalant.

She had been straight forward in telling him she wasn't interested in getting married. Subash surprised her by saying he wasn't either. That he was calling her only at his parents' insistence. That once they had spoken, they could each tell their respective parents of their disapprovals.

"Why can't you tell your parents you're not interested? Why do you have to call me first?" Gangga had asked, with mixed feelings. She had been relieved Subash wasn't interested in marrying her but disappointed at the same time. Which woman could withstand the hurt and bitterness of rejection? Gangga couldn't began to imagine how some women in some parts of the world go through the match making processes so casually and take rejections so well. Did it not hurt their pride and self esteem like it did hers?

"I could. I guess I was curious as well, you know...to know how you sounded," he had said.

"And, what do you think?"

"I think...well, I think..."

"Yes?"

"I think I like it...I like your voice very much."

And that was what did it. Gangga found herself falling in love with Subash just through their phone conversations. Subash's praises made her blush, his compliments made her heart flutter and when he smiled on the other end, she found herself smiling on her end. She'd not had a man who thought she was walking divinity. Subash could not find anything wrong with her. When they decided to meet, a week later, Gangga had been nervous. What if she wasn't all that Subash expected? What if she disappointed him, not Indian enough for him with her partially dyed hair with streaks of burgundy and light blond; the natural blackness of it hardly visible, and her triple pierced ears? She was thankful at least her belly-button ring was hidden under her clothes.

All it had taken was one look at her for Subash to fall head over heels in love with her. He mentioned repeatedly that to his eyes, she appeared absolutely flawless. The dyed hair or the extra ear rings didn't irk him a tiny bit. She had noticed his initial nervousness but once they started talking, he fell completely at ease. She had found him charming in his earthy brown khaki pants and casual burgundy polo shirt. His thick black hair was slicked back and glistened under the bright light of the restaurant's chandelier. He was clean shaven and he had the most marvelous eyes, brown with a speck of green right in the middle of the pupils. Gangga fell for him deeper after that evening.

Although they had ended the evening amicably, Subash dropping her off at her apartment with a slight bow, they saw each other every consecutive night thereafter. Five weeks later they were engaged. And now six months later they were getting married. Or, at least she had thought they were until that morning.

Chapter four – Jamuna

The rain was reckless with the drops getting bigger and heavier. It sounded louder, harsher, and almost threatening. Jamuna sat on the love seat in the basement of her father's house with legs curled up and her feet tucked under. She was facing the window; the dim glow of the table lamp gave her side profile an angelic look, with her dark brown hair flowing in curls down her shoulders, her skin shiny and smooth like butter. She had a polyester yellow and red Winnie the Pooh robe on. For as long as her memory took her, she'd liked that color – yellow. It was a color she associated herself with; bright and vibrant. Her friends said her eyes shone majestically every time she wore anything yellow, and that the color accentuated their deep golden brown. People always commented on her eyes, of their unusual brownness, which Jason often said drove him crazy.

Jamuna listened to the rain outside. It was unsettling. She felt scared, confused and deeply mortified. She hadn't meant to bump into her parents in the kitchen earlier, not having expected to see them up so early. She couldn't help wondering if they suspected anything. They did appear quite distressed. And damn Jason for barging in right after her, with no shirt on, on top of that. Surely her parents would've suspected something. Was that why her father suggested he'd talk to her later? God, what predicament had she brought upon herself now? And of all days, the day of the wedding!

Hugging her arms to her chest, allowing the soft polyester to comfort her, Jamuna thought of the first time she met Jason, a year ago. She didn't think much of him then. It was quite common to find Vikram's friends loitering in the basement after their classes. Vikram and Jason hung out in the house more than most youngsters she knew. Jamuna often wondered why they were not at a bar somewhere downing bottles of cheap beer or secretly puffing marijuana behind some bushes like most guys their ages did. She concluded they were either all geeks or they were smoking pot down in the basement.

Her parents had renovated their unfinished basement when Vikram decided to live with them temporarily while attending college. The basement had two bedrooms. One was occupied by Vikram and the other was a constantly occupied guest room. An old leather couch and a wooden work desk occupied the tiny living room. And a micro-mini kitchen adjacent to the living room concluded the rest of the suite. Vikram never really used the kitchen. It was meant more for their frequent guests. Right now Jamuna's aunt, Devika, and her husband Siva Bose who were there for the wedding occupied the room with their teenage daughter, Priya.

Jason constantly crashed in Vikram's room. As a result, Jamuna, the only daughter still living at home, often crossed path with him. At first, after the initial introduction, Jamuna was wary of Jason. She found him occupying too much of Vikram's time. Vikram and she had a bond, a close one. He was like the big brother she never had. Before Jason came into the picture, Jamuna did everything with Vikram, following him around like a loyal pet. Vikram enjoyed her company and attention. He gloated with pride every time she solicited his advice or when she asked his opinion about something. It swelled his ego to have someone look up to him. His younger twin brothers were still much younger than him and behaved like no one else existed in the whole world except for the two of them.

Jamuna couldn't help smiling now as she thought of the time when Vikram decided to get her and Jason acquainted. It had been Vikram's way to include Jamuna in his life, but, oh, how that small effort had changed her whole life.

Jamuna sank deeper into the couch and closed her eyes. She could hear the sound of heavy rain outside but her mind was full of Jason, of how fate in the shape of Vikram had brought them closer together.

At first there hadn't been any attraction between Jason and her, physical or emotional. He was her cousin's friend and she was his best friend's cousin. There was nothing more to it. For Jamuna, the idea of being attracted to a *white* guy was unheard of. For Jason, being attracted to an Indian girl was *unheard* of, although for different reasons.

Jason, with his complete Caucasian background, couldn't at all relate to Vikram and Jamuna's way of life. Although language wasn't a barrier, everything else was. He had often walked into the house only to be suffocated by the strong, heady smell of Indian spices. At first it had nauseated him. He had associated the smell with dirty socks. Although with time he became immune to the aroma of Indian cooking, he could never bring himself to taste any of the Indian food. Vikram and Jamuna had once tried to make him take a bite of their butter chicken, but he had refused, saying he'd gag to death. And the movies! He had often found Jamuna and Vikram huddled on the couch together, glued to the TV, watching Hindi movies. They became so absorbed in the movies that most of the time they didn't even realize he was in the room. The only thing that he found interesting about the movies was the gorgeous actress in her skimpy little outfits. According to him, it had been a new learning experience – which Jamuna highly doubted. He just enjoyed the sensual vibes emanating through the screen.

He told her later that in the beginning the idea of falling for her had seemed farcical, although he had liked her. He had liked her gentle mannerism, her quiet musical voice, her polite subtle sarcasms and her positive attitude toward almost just about everything. To which Jamuna had replied, "What's the point of being pessimistic when life is so short?"

A soft giggle escaped her now as she remembered one instant where Jason had chastised her polite sarcasm.

"Don't worry, my feelings are not easily hurt, your politeness is misplaced," he'd said bluntly when she'd graciously rebuked him for forgetting to take off his shoes inside the house.

Jamuna remember asking Jason, much later, when was it that he had found her attractive.

"As soon as I saw you," he had winked and she'd called him a liar.

But he did admit eventually. As he spent more and more time in Vikram's place, either to study or to watch the games or just to crash, he began to notice Jamuna more. He became aware of her elegant, gentle demeanor when she was in the same room. He became interested of her observations and intelligence. He became conscious of the piercing glance of her big, brown eyes, especially if he'd said something silly. A few times when his hand accidentally brushed hers, he'd felt the physical tremor all the way to his toes. Jamuna recalled laughing at his confession, thinking what a hopeless romantic he was, one that she loved to bits.

Sudden thunder boomed outside, startling Jamuna. She dragged herself to the window. Water was gathering in puddles along the driveway which sometimes extended into bigger ones. It had been on another rainy day, Jamuna reminisced, when Jason had finally confessed his love for her.

Soon, the main reason Jason visited Vikram had been to see Jamuna. He started calling her 'J', saying her name was too complicated to pronounce. Slowly he started dropping by when Vikram wasn't around. They'd end up discussing some literature paper which Jason was having trouble with or go through Byron together, Jamuna's idol.

The first few times Jason had pretended not to know Vikram was still in class. But Jamuna cornered him on one such visit. "I told you yesterday Vikram was going to be late today as well. What's going on Jason?"

"What do you mean?" Jason had stammered, looking around the basement suite in an attempt to avoid Jamuna's piercing gaze.

"What are you doing here? I know, as well as you do, you're not here to see Vikram."

"Of course I am. Why else would I be here, J?"

"Was that why you stayed all but five minutes yesterday when Vikram arrived?"

Jason had shot her a guilty look. Jamuna stared at him for a while before sitting down on the couch next to him.

"I think I know what you want?" she had said, her voice calmer.

"You do?" Jason's shock had been too obvious.

"It has something to do with me, right?"

Jason had dropped his gaze to the ground and nodded feebly. His aberrant shyness had puzzled her.

"All you had to do was ask, you know. I really don't mind."

"You don't?"

"Of course not, why would I? Granted, I need to find some time out of my busy schedule to focus on you, but I think I can manage. I mean, most of the time I'm home in the evenings anyways. If Vikram doesn't mind, I think we can do it."

"Vikram? What does Vikram got to do with anything?" Jason had shouted, baffling Jamuna. She was further surprised to find him glowering at her, his lips tightly pursed.

"Jason, why are you yelling? Here I am offering to help you and you're staring at me as if I'm puffing out blue smoke."

"Blue smoke?"

"Never mind."

"J, what do you mean help me? Is that what you think this is?"

"Isn't it? Jason, why is so hard to admit you need help in that department?"

"Because I don't," the boom in his voice had matched the roaring thunder outside.

"Yes, you do," Jamuna had insisted. "Stop being so egotistical. It doesn't hurt to admit. And Milton is a hard one too."

"I am not ego – what? Milton? What on earth are you talking about?"

"I saw your first assignment on 'Paradise Lost'. You left it with Vikram. Dude, you're not going to like this, but you've got the whole book wrong. And I've read Milton hundreds of times; I can help you with your paper. But please don't expect me to give out the answers. I will coach you, nothing more. Okay, deal?"

Later Jason had admitted that it had taken him a few staggering seconds to completely comprehend the blabber emanating from Jamuna's mouth. He'd stared at her, speechless, before taking a few steps closer to her. He'd cupped her face in his hands and kissed her hard on the mouth.

"You are so adorably stupid and I absolutely love you. I love you, J, so damn much!" he'd said after releasing her.

It had been such a defining moment that Jamuna could feel the traces of his kiss until now. Still gazing at the rain outside, Jamuna bit her bottom lip. It hadn't been easy, admitting she loved him but admit she did.

After that, despite herself and her reservations toward *white* men, or rather her parents' reservations, Jamuna fell so madly in love with Jason. At first, for a week both Jason and she stayed away from each other. Jason, much to her relief and disappointment, didn't show his face at her house for a week after he kissed her. Being relieved initially for not having to confront him or her feelings toward him, she'd been thankful. But a few days later, when there still was no news or sign of him, she'd become weary, afraid. If he loved her as he had claimed, where was he? She was tempted to ask Vikram but refrained, in case he became inquisitive. So she waited.

Jason showed up late one evening while she was still at work. She saw his old, 1989 3-series BMW parked by the curb when she got home. Her first impulse had been to go straight to the basement and confront him, but she didn't. Instead, she shut herself in the bedroom and buried her head into the pillow, willing herself not to cry.

Finally, not being able to stand the agony of not knowing, she'd dashed downstairs. She saw Vikram and Jason sitting on the old leather couch with a bottle of beer in their hands. Whatever conversation that was taking place between them was obviously funny since both their faces were crumpled in mirth. Jamuna's insides steamed like water left on the stove for too long. She'd been confused and miserable for the past week thinking about Jason and his confession, and here he was – all happy and cheerful!

"Hi Jamuna, want a drink?" she heard Vikram ask.

Jason turned to look at her, deadpan. Jamuna, ignoring her cousin's question, glowered at Jason.

"Where were you?" her tone accusatory.

"What?"

"Where were you this past week?"

"I…hmmm…I was away." Jason stammered. Vikram looked startled.

"Away where?" she'd demanded.

"Just away, why?"

"Why? The nerve, Jason. After what you did to me. You kissed me and took off for a week with no news whatsoever and now you're behaving as if nothing happened. You're a total, complete *jackass*, and to think I actually fell for you, for your words and to think I've been so bloody miserable just thinking about you…jerk!" Her eyes gleamed menacingly with unshed tears.

Vikram had graciously excused himself and exited the basement.

"Hah!" Jason had smiled. "So you *have* been thinking about me? Did you miss me?"

"No! Why would I miss a total jackass like you?" she'd snorted and turned her back toward him to hide her tears.

"Because you love me. Go on, admit it." There was humor in his voice. Jamuna's temper raised a notch higher. Was it all fun and games to him? She opened her mouth to lash at him when Jason intervened.

"Look, J, I had to go to Kelowna for a week. I wanted to visit my mum and dad. And I thought at the same time to give you some time to ponder about us."

Jamuna let out another snort but remained with her back to him.

Jason continued, "I understand the cultural barrier between us. I told you I love you because I do, but I don't want to influence your feelings for me."

Jamuna pursued her lips, feeling calmer. *He did love her.*

"So, do you?" Jason had asked.

Jamuna didn't answer; instead, she swung around and threw herself at him, hugging him fiercely.

What followed thereafter was only too natural and expected. Vikram was very accommodating. He allowed them to spend time in the basement. Sometimes when Jason stayed over, Jamuna would sneak into the basement in the middle of the night to be with him.

Things were going so smoothly between them, until now, Jamuna thought, gritting her teeth. She turned away from the window, walked to the couch and plunked on it. Why did he have to choose that day for a fight? Couldn't he have waited one more day?

Jason didn't digest the discovery of Gangga's wedding being an arranged one well. He'd been appalled. Early that morning, cuddled together on the bed, post-coital, content – Jason had casually asked Jamuna what she thought of arranged marriages.

"I don't know. Why do you ask?"

"Do you agree with the way things are done?"

"What is there to agree or disagree? That's how marriages are done in our society, have been for years, centuries. But it's not something I dwell upon. Why do you ask?"

"Will you settle for one?"

"What kind of a question is that?"

"If your dad found you a decent chap, like he did your sister, would you marry the chap or would you fight for me?"

"Gee…I don't know. Hmm, really depends on what kind of a guy he is. I mean, if he's some prince from some exotic country, I'd be stupid not to accept his hand in marriage, but if he's just some commoner, then I really have to weigh the pros and cons." Jamuna had laughed.

"You think this is funny, J? I really need to know. I don't want to be wasting my time here." That was when Jamuna noticed the frustration in his voice.

"What do you mean 'wasting your time'? I am a waste of your time?" Jamuna sat up on the bed, her shoulders straight, rigid as if she was getting ready for war.

"No, you are not! Why can't you be straight forward and tell me? Will you or will you not fight for me?"

"Jason, I'm not settling for any arranged marriage. And my parents haven't even suggested something like that. Will you relax? We have a long way to go anyway."

"But I need to know. Because if not…"

"If not what, Jason?"

"If not I need to move on."

His words stung. The ultimatum in his voice tore her heart. Jamuna had roughly pushed the comforters aside and marched out of the room. She passed Vikram who was sleeping on the couch and went upstairs. Blotches of red dots appeared on her cheeks as she tried to control her anger. The steps felt her anger as well as she stomped on them, her mind conjuring up hundreds of 'what ifs' and 'so-be-its'. Well if he really wanted to move on, without her, then he was welcome to do so, she'd finally decided. She wasn't going to sit around and subject herself to infantile accusations and how dare he give her an ultimatum?

That was when she had found herself in the kitchen, in front of her parents. The look Ajay gave her had been confusing. Her mother seemed upset. Jamuna didn't know what to think. Was she in trouble? Did they somehow know about Jason and her? And stupid Jason had to follow suit. Surely any human being in the right mind could've seen what was happening. And her father did say he'd talk to her later. Shit, was she in trouble?

When she left the kitchen, Jamuna had wanted to go back to her room, the one she was sharing with Gangga at the moment. But Jason took her by the elbow and led her back to the basement. She tried pushing him away, telling him she wanted to go back to her room. In the midst of their commotion, Vikram, who was snoring on the couch, woke up. He looked at Jamuna, then at Jason, then back at Jamuna before grabbing his comforter and pillow and moseying into his room.

"You should go home, Jason. It's a long day here today." Jamuna had hissed once Vikram was out of sight.

"No, J, I want to talk. Look I'm sorry about…" He didn't finish his sentence; Jamuna's palm was facing him.

"Save it!" she'd said. "There's a wedding on today and I really don't have the time or the mood to argue with you. We'll talk later." She dropped herself on the couch. Jason had gaped at her for a minute, then had gone into Vikram's room for his keys and shirt, and left without a goodbye. Jamuna had watched him walk up the stairs of the basement to the main door and felt utterly wretched. She had felt like running after him and telling him that of course she'd choose him. She'd felt like promising him a lifetime of happiness, but she didn't, she couldn't.

Curled up on the couch now, she contemplated her decision. Would she really choose Jason and break the hearts of all those who loved her? Would she dare cross the line her parents had drawn? She didn't know the answer to these questions. She felt close to tears again. Finally, Jamuna steadied herself and walked up the stairs to her room. There was a wedding on and she needed to remain composed to face Gangga's big day. Her problems just had to wait another day.

Chapter five – Devika

She could hear the whispers outside in the living room. The basement was small and the rooms were close together. She knew there was some dispute earlier that morning; she could hear the voices through the thin walls. At first she wasn't sure whose voices they were. She wasn't sure whether the male voice belonged to Vikram or that *'gora'* friend of his. Vikram sounded like a pure Canadian with his accent, there wasn't a trace of Indian slang in his lingo. Even Gangga and Jamuna spoke in the same manner. Not that it mattered to her. Her daughter was the same way, could hardly speak any Hindi. It had troubled her in the beginning. After all, one shouldn't lose touch with one's roots and cultural upbringing. But she knew there was nothing she could do, not now at least. She'd wait until Priya graduated, then she'd get her daughter married to a nice, decent Indian boy from India. Ajay would help her, he had to. Priya was his responsibility too. But Priya was still in college. And Ajay had Jamuna to worry about after Gangga's wedding before he could think of Priya.

Devika threw a quick glance at the clock by their bedside. It was five past six in the morning. Still early. She wondered who woke up so early. Was it Vikram? And the girl? Who was she? Sounded very much like Gangga. But what was Gangga doing down in the basement, in Vikram's room on top of that? What were they arguing about? Maybe she was stressed out about the wedding, thought Devika. Weddings are, after all, very stressful events. She remembered her own wedding, twenty years ago. She'd been so young. Hardly twenty years old. What a night that had been. She couldn't remember being so confused and angry at that time.

Every Indian woman lived for the day she got married, but not Devika. She had dreaded it. It was arranged. Her husband's family was one of the most reputable and respected families in their neighborhood at that time. Devika remembered her father being so proud that both his daughters married into some upper class, rich families. She didn't have any choice. She couldn't even refuse her husband. Not only was she young, naïve and spineless, she was also pregnant at the time, with another man's child.

Taking a deep breath in as the bitter truth coiled within her like a poisonous snake, Devika turned to look at Priya lying next to her. She was sound asleep, her lids closed tightly. Little dark tendrils covered part of her face, hiding it. Devika gently pushed the hair away from her daughter's face; such a lovely face, round like the moon with her sharp nose and big round eyes, and her mouth – a little pink petal of lusciousness. She was too pretty, not very unlike Ajay's daughters. They all had distinct facial similarities. In fact Jamuna and Priya looked like sisters more than cousins...well cousins to the eyes of the world.

Devika shut her eyes abruptly, as if to shut the truth out. Not that she wanted to. But she had to for everyone's sake. She didn't really care about her marriage –her dead marriage. She glanced over at the single bed in the corner of the room – the bed meant for Priya but occupied by Siva, her husband. She couldn't remember the last time she had shared her bed with her husband. How long ago was it? All she knew was throughout their marriage somehow Siva had sensed her lack of passion and love toward him. He'd noticed the vastness she'd created between them. He'd felt the absence of any sort of attraction and the emotional void between them. If Siva was not a shy, reserved man, he probably would've gotten to the root of their marital problems. But being the way he was, he left things as they were and Devika had been only too relieved. She was glad Siva hadn't been inquisitive or curious about her behavior. For, if he had been, she wouldn't have known what to tell him. How could she tell her husband that she was in love with her sister's husband? That she had been since Ajay came into their family, as Menaka's husband. And how could she tell Siva about Priya – about Ajay being Priya's father? As much as she didn't care about her marriage, she still cared about Ajay's marriage to her sister. Menaka would hate her and so would her three nieces. And what about Priya? No, Devika decided the truth would do more harm than good.

* * *

What happened between Ajay and her had been divine intrusion. When Ajay married Menaka, Devika was unknown to him. He saw her a few times at the wedding but she was a stranger to him as Menaka had been. Her father had insisted that the bride and groom spent a few days in his house before leaving permanently to Ajay's parents' house. As such, Ajay had stayed at Devika's parents' house for three days.

On the night of their wedding, Devika had assumed Ajay and Menaka would spend the entire evening in their bedroom. So she was quite surprised to see him loitering on the veranda late into the night. She was up doing her final thesis for the degree course she was taking at one of the local Universities. Curious, she went out to the veranda to talk to him. She found him standing by the wooden railing on the balcony staring out into the pitch blackness of the night. A whiff of spicy aftershave wafted toward her.

"Jijaji, is everything okay?" Ajay spun around; his eyes widening in shock.

"Yes…yes, sorry if I'd disturbed you. I didn't realize anyone was up. Did I wake you?" he looked fresh, and still in his traditional groom costume. Clearly he hadn't been to bed, thought Devika.

"No you didn't. I was up doing my thesis. The date-line is in two weeks and I have a lot to do. Where's my sister?" asked Devika, stepping out on the balcony.

"She's sleeping. I couldn't sleep and I didn't want to read or anything in case I woke her up so I came out here."

Devika watched Ajay and thought he looked lost. His deep, dark eyes looked distant, almost ambiguous, as if he was contemplating his fate. She felt a pang of sympathy toward him. She knew Menaka's sleeping habit. Menaka didn't have the capability to stay up late. She had to be in bed at ten o'clock every night, no matter where they were or what they were doing. She wouldn't even stay up with her family to watch a late night movie or play a card game of some sort. She claimed that lack of sleep made her grumpy and tired. She treasured her sleep like it was priceless. Devika often joked with her saying sleeping was

Menaka's favorite past time. But she could've at least tried to stay up on her wedding night. Poor Ajay, he had a lot to learn about her sister's habits. Devika hoped he had the patience and the tolerance to live with Menaka.

"Would you like some tea?" offered Devika. Ajay looked at her for a second before nodding his head.

And that was how it had begun. Ajay and Devika stayed up late into the night that day. They talked about her course, about Ajay's work, his future plan, about their hobbies, likes and dislikes. When they went to bed much later that day, Ajay lied down next to his new wife, who was by then snoring softly, and thought of her sister. And Devika was awake most of the night, her mind full of thoughts of her brother-in-law. The following evening, Devika's parents took them out for dinner. Devika saw Menaka and Ajay together and vowed she'd not harbor any inappropriate feelings for her brother- in- law. She liked him and she was happy her sister married someone as nice and good looking as Ajay.

After dinner, as expected, Ajay and Menaka went into their bedroom together. Devika watched them and involuntarily a little sigh escaped her. Unable to sleep that night, she sat in front of the TV watching an old black and white movie. Half way through the movie, Ajay came down from his room and joined her on the couch.

"Didi sleeping?" she asked, feeling slightly nervous.

"Yeap," he let the word out with some frustration.

Although curious, Devika kept her silence. They sat quietly watching the rest of the movie. The proximity between them was close enough that Devika could smell his after shave. Her skin tickled as goose bumps spread all over her mercilessly. She sat clutching her body, unsure of what to do or say. When the movie ended, Devika stood up to switch the TV off. But she felt Ajay's hand on hers, pulling her down. She plopped back on the couch next to him.

"Stay with me for a while longer," he said. His eyes were soft with yearning. It scared her. She shouldn't be sitting there, next to her sister's husband and holding his hand. It was so wrong but why didn't it feel wrong? Devika looked into Ajay's eyes and found herself drinking in the depth of emotion in them. She lost herself in his gaze. When he leant forward she didn't turn away. When he held her face gently between his hands she didn't push them away. When he brought his lips to meet hers she opened them in invitation. Their kiss lasted for a long time. When Devika went to bed that night she couldn't think of anything else, she couldn't weigh the situation she was in, she couldn't judge her behavior, she couldn't because all she could do was think of Ajay.

The following evening, their last evening in Devika's parents' house, Ajay didn't come down looking for her. She sat in front of the TV past midnight, feeling confused and unsure. She wanted Ajay to come down, at the same time she wished he wouldn't for she didn't have the will to turn him away. And that was exactly what she should be doing. As realization sank in, Devika quickly departed to her room and closed the door. When she switched on the table lamp by her bed she all but shrieked – for there was Ajay, sitting on her bed with a big smile on his face.

"Jijaji (*brother-in-law*)...what are you doing here?" Devika hissed.

"I'm visiting and please, don't call me that."

"You have to leave."

"I don't have to do anything of that sort."

"Yes you do. This is not right. What would Didi say if she finds out?"

"*If she finds out*. Honestly, I don't care. I married the wrong sister."

"Jijaji...?"

"I did. And don't call me that. Come and sit here, Devika."

That was the beginning of Ajay and Devika's lifelong affair.

Ajay and Menaka left in the morning to Ajay's parents' house. Devika, although felt her world crashing in front of her eyes, was thankful for their departure. She felt like a worm infested apple where from outside it looked fine, but once cut open the insides were black. Guilt gnawed at her conscience. How could she have slept with her sister's husband, how could she? As much as she liked him, was attracted to him she should've contained herself. She was shameless! And look at her now, she'd lost her virginity and she wasn't even married yet. What would her parents do if they found out? They'd chase her onto the streets. They'd disown her. To be rid herself of these terrifying, troubling thoughts, she devoted all her attention and time into her thesis.

Although she saw Ajay and Menaka periodically, she stayed away from them. Ajay would try on many occasions to get her alone, to talk to her but she'd distance herself from him. She was happy when Kaveri was born for she thought that meant Ajay and Menaka were happy. Then, Gangga was born. Devika dotted on her two nieces. And Ajay, after his few attempts to approach her turned futile, kept his distance from her as well. So much so that when Devika visited them, she would get a few greeting words from him and that was it. Although it hurt her she knew that was the right thing to do.

It was when Menaka became pregnant for the third time that Ajay and Devika found their ways into each other's heart and life again.

It had been an evening like any other –getting the two girls, four-year-old Kaveri and Gangga who was two, into their bedtime rituals. Which consisted of quick baths, forcing them into their pajamas before settling down with a book. Devika was visiting her nieces and had offered to help the girls with their routine. She was reading them *The Cat in the Hat* when she heard a faint noise emanating from the kitchen. At first it sounded like someone was whispering. Thinking her sister was having a conversation with Ajay; Devika resumed her reading and then went into the kitchen to fetch the girls' milk bottles. That was when she found Menaka leaning over the sink. Her back was heaving as if she was crying. Ajay stood a few meters away with his hands across his chest. His face was contorted as if he was in physical pain, his brow furrowed closer together.

"Didi, what's wrong?" Devika reached out to Menaka but staggered backward when Menaka swatted her hand away violently.

"Stay out of this, Devika!"

"Sorry." Devika shrunk away from Menaka too quickly. She wasn't alien to Menaka's temper. Menaka was relentless when she became angry. Her words were venomous. Devika didn't want to be the victim of her sister's wrath. Poor Ajay had to live with it now. Ajay took a step closer to Devika.

"Don't take you anger out on your sister. She was only concerned." Devika looked at Ajay and wished he would stop talking. It wasn't a good idea to defy her sister when fire flared out of her nose.

"She is my sister, I will yell at her if I wanted to. You stay out of this," Menaka bellowed.

"Enough, Menaka. We have a guest in the house; the kids are waiting to go to bed. Control yourself, calm down. Go send the kids to bed," ordered Ajay and ducked just on time to avoid a plate flying right at his face. The plate hit the wall behind Ajay and fell onto the carpeted floor which saved it from scattering into bits of glasses. Devika inched closer to the living room. She froze when Ajay walked past her and went to see the two girls who by then have crept into their rooms.

Later that evening, Devika decided to pack her belongings. She knew she had overstayed her welcome. Maybe that was what Menaka and Ajay were arguing about. She wasn't sure but she wasn't going to stick around to find out. She was furiously shoving clothes into her suitcase when she heard a soft knock on her door. Before she could respond to it, it opened and Ajay walked in.

"Jijaji?" she whispered. Was something wrong? She looked past him to see if Menaka was standing there as well, and sighed with relief when she didn't see her sister. Ajay closed the door at the back of him.

"Why are you packing?" he asked.

"I'm leaving in the morning. Maybe you and Didi need some time alone. I don't want to be an intruder." She shrugged.

"Don't leave, Devika. You have no idea how much you have helped us by being here...the kids and I. You're like the little break of sunlight on a very dark cloud. You have no idea how living with your sister has been." Ajay stared at her with tired, hollow eyes. Devika wanted to tell him she did know how it was living with her sister, but her novelty toward Menaka stopped her. She would not bad mouth her sister behind her back.

"I have to get back to work," she said feebly.

"You're off for another two weeks. I know. Please stay, for the kids at least. You bring so much joy to their lives...," he paused before adding, "...and mine."

Devika, startled by the sudden revelation, gaped at Ajay. And it all came back to her. Powerful emotion flooded and shook her. His gaze was fixed on her sternly and she saw the same desperation and yearning that had been there the first time they were together. Only this time there was something else as well, could it be love? Devika didn't dare hope.

That night when they made love it was better than the first time. And also that night Devika realized that no matter how much she denied it, she was totally and hopelessly in love with her brother- in-law.

They continued to see each other even after Devika had left to her parents' house. And when Menaka gave birth to Jamuna, Devika was back at their house, helping her with babysitting the two older children. In the midst of this, Devika learned her parents' had found her a nice boy to get married to.

Grief stricken, she had run to Ajay for comfort. Ajay had been petrified. The thought of loosing Devika was inconceivable. He couldn't imagine going through a life where Devika would belong to someone else, where she couldn't be a part of his life, where her priorities would be different and her love… would she stop loving him? Ajay tried talking her out of it.

"No, Devika, don't do it," he had pleaded.

"Ajay, I don't want to, I really don't. But what else is there to do. There's no place in your life for me. My parents are worried, they say my age is catching up and you know how it is here. If I don't marry now, I probably never will." Ajay had stared at her. He knew she was speaking the truth. She was almost twenty- five and that was considered an old age for an unmarried girl in India. But Devika was so vital to his being that he couldn't bring himself to let go of her.

"Can you not somehow buy time? A couple more years?" he asked.

"Then what?"

"I have a plan, Devika, and that involves divorcing Menaka and marrying you. But I need some time. I can't marry you and continue living here. I'm arranging for business overseas. But all these take time."

Devika gawked at him like a confused child. She didn't realize he had a plan, a plan that involved her. For the first time, she was convinced of Ajay's love for her. He had never professed it and she'd assumed it wasn't there. But he was planning on marrying her. She felt her heart lift up and soar into the sky. Her love hadn't been misplaced.

A few days later, she called and told him that the wedding was on, was taking place. As much as his offer was tempting, as much as she wanted to spend the rest of her life with him, as much as she wanted to be the central being of his life, she couldn't betray Menaka; she'd done enough betrayal by sleeping with Ajay.

The day after her wedding, Ajay migrated to Canada with his family. Devika buried all her emotions deep inside her and locked them there permanently. She devoted her life to making her marriage work and to her daughter, born eight months after her marriage. Ajay didn't know Priya was his for a very long time. He didn't know that was what prompted Devika to marry Siva.

It was during a holiday back in India, that he suspected Priya was his. One look at her round face was all it took. One couldn't deny Priya's resemblance to him even if they wanted to. Upon confronting Devika, his suspicion was confirmed. That was when he made arrangements for Siva to work for his company in Vancouver. Siva had been too overwhelmed to turn the offer down. Devika, knowing the reason behind Ajay's offer, had not been too keen.

"I'm not doing this for you, if that's what you're thinking. I am doing this for Priya. I want to give her the best education, the best kind of life and I want her to be close to me. So, Devika, please put your arrogance and pride aside for your daughter's sake." And he had walked out of the room, leaving Devika gaping after him.

But once in Vancouver, the affair started all over again, from where they'd left off. Living just miles away from Menaka's house, Devika constantly found herself and Priya at her sister's place. Some days, they stayed overnight after a heavy dinner and a game of cards. That was how they became constant occupants of the guest room in the basement. The affair re-started when one evening Ajay knocked on the guest room where Devika was spending the night alone. Priya was sleeping in Jamuna's room and Menaka as usual was in bed. Siva was away on business. Ajay couldn't contain himself knowing Devika was within his reach, under his roof. And when he knocked on her door, she didn't even wait for him to enter before throwing herself into his arms. So the affair had resumed...yet again and this time it didn't end.

* * *

Devika slowly eased herself off the bed, so as not to wake Priya. She draped herself in a thick robe. It was a cold morning and this rain seemed so ruthless on such an eventful day. Devika hoped for everything to go smoothly. She hoped Gangga would find happiness in her marriage, unlike herself or Menaka for that matter. And from what she'd been hearing, Kaveri's marriage was on the rocks. That was what Ajay had been telling her. Although he didn't approve of Kaveri marrying Raj, he didn't want to see the marriage end either.

Maybe they were all jinxed, Devika thought suddenly. Maybe everyone related to the Sharmas was jinxed, starting with Menaka for marrying a Sharma, then Devika for falling in love with a Sharma, and now Kaveri for being born a Sharma. She prayed Priya would not be victim of the same faith, or Jamuna and Gangga for that matter. Devika was fond of all her nieces. She did, after all, spend a lot of precious time with them. And she knew all Ajay's daughters looked up to her and loved her unconditionally. She was their cool aunt, one not at all like their mother. Devika was gentle, kind, warm and caring. She was more maternal toward them than Menaka could ever be.

Devika strolled into the little living room of the basement quietly when she found Jamuna sitting on the couch staring at the wall. Was it Jamuna she had heard earlier? What was she doing down in the basement and why was she arguing with Vikram? It had sounded very much like a lover's dispute. Devika froze momentarily. Reckless thoughts swam in her mind. Was Jamuna involved with Vikram in some way? Surely not. How could they? They were cousins for heaven's sake. She should warn Ajay and fast, today if possible, even if there was a wedding on.

Chapter six – Kaveri

By the time Kaveri reached her parents' house, the clock struck eight half an hour ago. Her gaze swept across the yard as she got out of the cab. Two tent *wallahs* were working in the midst of the rain, raincoats stuck to their bodies, their hair plastered to their heads like a toupee. The roof of the tent bulged inward like a pregnant woman, bearing the weight of the overnight rain water. Her father's adamant obsession of wanting a tent in the yard for every wedding was ludicrous to Kaveri. Why couldn't he see this wasn't India? People in Canada didn't have tents on their front yards like colorful sheds. Incongruity aside, it told people they were different and Kaveri despised that.

All her life she tried to blend in, to be like the rest, to be known as one of them but unsuccessfully. Even if language wasn't a problem, her skin color was. It set her apart from the rest. And being born in the Sharma family didn't help matters. Her father, although had lived in the country for nearly thirty years, still held on to his outdated beliefs, to his obsolete values. She found it unbearably hypocritical. Kaveri was only too happy not to be living under the same roof any longer. Marriage to Raj, although lacking in every aspect, gave her the freedom she needed.

When Kaveri first met Raj, she hadn't been interested in him. She knew him since their fathers were acquaintances. She'd met him a few times during social functions. He stood out in the crowd with his long wavy hair, lengthy figure and a smile to lure the devil. Although she was charmed by his good looks and his quaint mannerism, she kept herself at a distance. Indian men didn't attract Kaveri, and by choice. She wanted to get married to a white man, for two reasons: one, she found their clear milky skin, curls of blond locks and sea-blue eyes deadly attractive and two, because to her father, the whites were like a bad word, a taboo. She craved for a taste of the forbidden. And to be able to see the torment on her father's face would be satisfying enough.

Kaveri didn't share her sisters' devotion to Ajay. She wasn't sure when she started developing distaste toward Ajay, but she had an inkling it was sometime after Jamuna's birth. She was six years old when Jamuna was born, too little to understand human affection. But she knew when she saw Ajay in Devika's room one evening, holding her hand and sitting very close, his face almost touching hers, that he was doing something wrong.

Devika was Kaveri's pillar of strength, she had been since young. She had always been there for Kaveri, especially when Menaka's attention waned; first with the birth of Gangga, then with Jamuna. Seeing Devika that day with her father didn't sprout any dislike or hatred toward her aunt. It was her father she held grudges against. As she grew older, human affections and passions became clearer, Kaveri realized what it took to make babies. The hatred for her father grew. Not enough that she had to share everything with Gangga, he had to make her mother pop Jamuna out too. Growing up with Gangga had been unchallenging; Gangga followed her around like an obedient puppy. Kaveri remembered Gangga trailing her to every nook and corner of their house. It had been a blissful feeling, she had felt wanted. But Jamuna's presence had ruined everything.

Kaveri had hated Jamuna at first sight. Jamuna was a picture perfect baby with her creamy white skin, her flower pink lips and two big, brown marbles for eyes. She had looked like a doll, with soft brown curls falling to her forehead. And Gangga, who had so far doted on Kaveri, diverted her attention toward Jamuna. Gangga no longer was her compliant follower. And her mother was too caught up with the new baby to pay much attention to Kaveri. Devika had been the one who had paid any attention to her. She could have drowned herself in the frog swamp at the back of their house and no one would've noticed. Her hatred for Ajay blossomed like a well fertilized plant in her heart, its leaves wrapping around the cells of her core, not leaving any vacant space.

Gangga and Jamuna looked up to Ajay like he was God personified. They worshipped the ground he walked, in every sense of the word. To their eyes, Ajay was impeccable, perfect. And their affection wasn't one sided. Gangga and Jamuna never failed to impress him academically and socially.

Kaveri was the black sheep among them. Being born darker than the rest, she was never her father's pride. She knew that. Every time he praised Jamuna's grades, or her excellent Tae Kwon Do patterns or her ability to play the piano flawlessly, Kaveri's heart tightened as jealousy constricted it.

Somehow, it wasn't the same with Gangga. Kaveri found she was able to tolerate Gangga. Gangga, although fairer than her and did well in her career, wasn't a beauty. People didn't turn their heads when she walked by. Truck drivers didn't whistle at her when she went jogging around the block. But they did Jamuna. Anytime the three of them were out together, everyone's eyes would be on Jamuna, luring or marveling at her beauty. She hadn't seen one male cashier who didn't flirt with Jamuna. It was unfair, Kaveri thought, for God to grant upon one person such qualities, such gift. Why should one sister shine of all three? Why couldn't they have been equals or why couldn't she have been the beauty? It had angered Kaveri in the beginning and slowly the anger transformed itself into unquenchable jealousy. It infuriated her more to see Ajay's love and affection for Jamuna, it deepened her disaffection toward her sister and the hatred for her father. It was that hatred toward Ajay which caused Kaveri to retaliate in every way she deemed possible.

But her desire to induce eternal torment on her father by marrying a white man didn't materialize. There wasn't any white men or Indian men for that matter who showed any interest in her. Thus she settled by marrying Raj – which, much to her mirth, brought plenty of torment to her father.

Kaveri wasn't in love with Raj. And she knew the only reason he even spoke to her was to be close to Jamuna. Oh, she could see it, Raj's obvious attraction for Jamuna. He spent hours in her parents' house in the pretext of visiting her when Kaveri knew all along he was there to get a glimpse of her sister, to just be near her, within the same vicinity.

Everyone knew of Raj's flamboyant nature. He was a playboy, hence Ajay's resentment toward him. Kaveri had entertained Raj simply to defy her father. It pleased her to see Ajay's face cringe with distaste at the sight of Raj. And Raj brazenly flirted with Kaveri in everyone's presence, hoping to get some kind of reaction from Jamuna, who save for words of greetings, ignored him like he was an insignificant specimen.

Kaveri and Raj's wedding had been a pure stroke of coincidence, or luck if one might call it. Raj's parents – the Dhillons, were visiting Ajay and Menaka one evening when they caught a glimpse of their son with Kaveri. The two were seated closely on the couch, with Raj's arms around Kaveri and laughing at something on TV. That was what prompted the Dhillons to approach Ajay and Menaka with view of marriage. They saw Kaveri as Raj's salvation. They believed once he married someone like Kaveri – a girl from a respected Hindu Indian family, he'd change. He'd become a better person. He'd stop with his night clubs and long nights away from home. They knew their son well; they just chose to play ignorant.

Ajay had been against it, saying their children were simply friends, nothing more. But Menaka had been elated. Kaveri was her favorite and it had pleased her immensely to know The Dhillons were interested in her as their daughter-in-law. Of course, Raj had protested, saying he never viewed Kaveri in that sense, that he was only interested in her as a friend. Kaveri had kept quiet throughout the whole marriage talk until Ajay sounded his opinion, saying Raj wasn't the right husband for Kaveri. That was all she needed to go all out in making sure she married Raj, just to spite her father. It had been easy with her mother's support. Her father in the end was rendered speechless and gave in feebly. As for Raj's consent, it didn't take much. All he needed was a threat from his father saying he'd erase Raj's name from his will if he refused to marry Kaveri. Thus, the much unsuitable marriage took place.

Now, as Kaveri stood at the front porch of her parents' house reliving her wedding days, she couldn't help wonder if it had all been worth it. She'd married Raj, but look at her now. Their marriage was devoid of any form of love or affection. There were two strangers living under the same roof. Kaveri doubted Raj even cared about her. And sex, well she was only too glad he didn't demand it of her. There were the rare occasions when he came back drunk or when they'd been on their honeymoon that they'd tolerated it. It had been more out of formality than desire. There wasn't any aspiration from either party. Now, after two years, sex had become a distant, once-upon-a-time thing.

But the freedom this marriage offered was what Kaveri cherished. She needed to be married to Raj to stay away from her father. Now that she was a married woman, she was a forbidden territory to Ajay. He couldn't hurt her with his disaffection any longer. She didn't have to pretend like it didn't matter as he praised Jamuna endlessly. She didn't have to suffer in jealousy when he showed Jamuna off to his friends at gatherings. No, Kaveri had her own identity now, one that could not be tainted by Ajay Sharma even if he tried. That was good enough reason for her to stay in a loveless marriage.

"Kaveri?" the front door opened and Devika stuck her head out. "Why are you standing outside?"

"Devika Aunty," Kaveri's voice didn't betray her affection for Devika. "When did you come? Where is Siva Uncle?" Kaveri threw her arms around Devika and hugged her tightly.

"Still sleeping, they are all still sleeping. The house looks and feels like normal. No one seems to be in a hurry to get things going. And look at Gangga. Shouldn't she be up, getting herself ready? And look at that tent guy. What on earth is he doing poking the tent like that? He's going to tear it and all that water is going to splash right on his head. Serves him right too. And this *barish*, Kaveri, what is up with that? Haven't seen rain this bad all the years I've been here."

Kaveri laughed, her voice mingled with the sound of the rain and vanished into the ground. She looked around her, at the rain, at the workers, at her father's house…there was no sense of belonging. She turned back and embraced Devika's gaze on her. Kaveri knew her aunt's overzealous manner in everything. She was a perfectionist. The rain obviously was a hindrance in her aunt's mind on a wedding day. Kaveri couldn't care less. She wasn't thrilled about Gangga's wedding or for Gangga, for that matter. Gangga was of no threat to her. It made no difference in her life whether Gangga was married or not. The only thing she envied Gangga was the fact that she was able to move out of their parents' house and live in her own apartment. Her income, unlike Kaveri's measly cashier pittance, provided enough funds to purchase an apartment, although a single bedroom one. Now that Gangga was marrying Subash, the rich dude, she was set for life. She could even sell her apartment and move in with Subash, which Kaveri presumed would be the ideal thing to do.

Still, one thing puzzled her – Gangga's decision to go for an arranged marriage. Maybe Gangga was having problem finding the suitable boy too, smiled Kaveri. She wasn't the only loser in the family after all. Now, if she could only taint Jamuna's image that would be perfect.

"So, no one is up yet, huh?" Kaveri asked Devika. They were in the house now and headed for the basement.

"I think so, beta, although Jamuna was up earlier. I saw her down in the basement."

"What was she doing down in the basement so early in the morning?"

"I don't know. Kaveri, I'm worried about Jamuna. Can I tell you something? Promise not to tell anyone?"

Kaveri paused on her steps. She watched Devika walk into the diminutive kitchen and put the kettle on.

"What is it, Aunty?" Kaveri prompted, hoping her voice didn't sound impatient.

"It's just that…," Devika paused and Kaveri fidgeted, urging her aunt to continue with her gaze. "Earlier, I heard some voices, coming from Vikram's room. Sounded like someone was arguing. At first I thought it was Gangga and Vikram."

"Why would Gangga be in Vikram's room?"

"I don't know, but it wasn't her at all, it was Jamuna. She was in Vikram's room so early in the morning. I don't know what they were fighting about. I don't know what to think…I mean, is something going on between them? They're cousins, *baghvan*. I shouldn't be thinking this way, but I have seen how close those two are. They even sometimes eat out of the same plate. And that kind of closeness is never good. Don't know whether I should tell your father or not. And today is the wedding day, should I tell him?"

Kaveri's antennas shot up. Jamuna and Vikram? But that was great news, exactly what she needed to scorch Jamuna's reputation. Ah, and to be able to see Ajay's face when she revealed the truth about his gem of a daughter. A cold shiver ran down her spine. Revenge was sweet. But she must be careful, Kaveri reminded herself. And Devika musn't get involved, not at all.

"No, Aunty," she responded quickly. "I will find out what's going on. I'm sure it's nothing. And there's a wedding on today. Let's not create any havoc," she said, silently adding 'not yet' under her breath. Devika nodded and turned around to attend to the whistling kettle.

After she drank her tea, Kaveri went up to the main floor. It was quiet. Devika was right, thought Kaveri, where was the hustle and bustle of the wedding? There was no one around. She walked over to Jamuna's room and knocked on the door. Without waiting for any response, she walked in. Gangga was sitting cross-legged on her bed, her hair disheveled and her eyes were wide, looking bewildered. Jamuna was sitting on her bed, with the same expression only prettier. Swallowing the urge to make a hurtful remark, Kaveri flashed a wide artificial grin, one that didn't reach her eyes.

"Hello sisters, did someone die?" she joked. "Why the forlorn faces? There's a wedding on people."

Only, no one responded. Gangga didn't even turn to look at her and Jamuna kept staring at the wall in front of her.

"Hey, you two, what's going on?" she asked again.

The girls kept their silence. Kaveri was about to open her mouth again when Menaka barged into the room, her hair bundled in a messy bun, her nightdress wrinkled and her eyes sunken.

"What are you still doing in your pajamas?" she shrieked at the sight of Gangga. "Get up and get changed. Breakfast is going to start soon, as soon as your Chandni Aunty shows up with her clan. Mrs. Mehra is coming around noon to do your make up and you have to get all your trays ready before then. And have you packed your bag? Isn't Subash planning on taking you right away after the wedding to the Fairmount? And Jamuna, shouldn't you be getting ready as well? I expect you to help your sister. Do I have to do everything around here? As if this is *my shaadi*!"

Menaka turned away from her daughters when her gaze fell on Kaveri. Her subdued face brightened immediately and her voice softened, "When did you come, beta? Come, let's go into the kitchen."

"Just now, Mama. You go first, I'll be there in a second," said Kaveri.

When Menaka left, Kaveri turned back toward Gangga, "What is the matter, Gangga? Is something wrong?"

"Everything is so wrong, didi," Gangga finally spoke, her voice heavy. "I don't know how to face Papa and Mama. I don't know what to do."

"What is the matter for heaven's sake? You are getting married today and look at your condition. You look like there's a funeral on instead of a wedding," Kaveri sounded impatient.

"Just as well. I don't know whether there will be a wedding," announced Gangga and broke into loud sobs.

"No wedding?" Kaveri lowered herself on the bed. She tried to keep the sudden fluttering in her heart under control. "Gangga, what's going on?"

But Gangga wasn't speaking. Her head shook as she sobbed into her hands. Kaveri rolled her eyes up to the ceiling. "Oh for God's sake. Jamuna, what is going on?" she asked Jamuna instead.

Jamuna, clearly startled at being addressed by her older sister, looked shocked. Her brown eyes gazed at Kaveri and her mouth gaped opened, but there was no sound.

"What? Are you going to keep quiet as well?" asked Kaveri.

"No, didi," she finally stammered. "I think Subash –he hung up on Gangga didi and is refusing to answer her phone calls."

"Okay, maybe he's busy. No use being paranoid over something so small."

"It's not small. I don't think it is. He wanted, well he wanted to marry – he thought that – " Jamuna paused.

"What?"

"Subash thought I was a virgin," Gangga spoke in between her sobs.

Kaveri felt like she was trying to solve an impossible puzzle. Her sisters were not making any sense. "So, what is the problem?"

"I am not a bloody virgin," Gangga's sob had subsided; her voice came out like an angry growl. "Which damn century is he living in? Who expects to marry a virgin? So bloody out-dated. Now that he found out I am not one, he's not sure about marrying me."

"I know," supported Jamuna in a small voice. "I mean, how many girls are virgins on their wedding nights?"

Silence ensued. The sisters didn't meet each others' eyes. The room felt cold, as if the outside coldness had seeped in. The only sound was the distant rumbling of thunder intertwined with the loud drip of rain.

"I was," Kaveri's voice shook the silence, sliced through it and brought her sisters' heads up. "I was a virgin on my wedding night," Kaveri added. Her eyes swept over the confused, bewildered looks of her sisters. A smug smile settled on her face. "At the end of the day, we are still Indians. There are etiquettes and morals instilled in us by our parents. Just because we live in this modern world, doesn't mean we degrade ourselves by losing our self- respects. Jamuna, you too?"

Kaveri watched as Jamuna cringed, as her hands twisted and untwisted the end of a blanket, as her cheeks turned crimson.

"I see." Kaveri stood up, standing tall over her sisters. "Well, Gangga, you have a lot of explaining to do. Frankly I don't care if there's a wedding on or not, especially with the weather so rotten. Don't worry, I won't say anything to Mama and Papa. You can do that yourself."

She left Jamuna's room feeling on top of the world. So far Gangga's wedding had been immaterial to her. But now that there might not be a wedding, Kaveri was silently overjoyed. Not only would Ajay lose face in front of all his friends and relatives, he'd be shattered to tiny bits of unrecognizable pieces when he finds out about Jamuna's relationship with Vikram. Ah, this was getting better by the minute, Kaveri allowed herself a silent, satisfactory smirk.

Once Kaveri left the room:

"Why did she say something like that? Why was she so horrid to us?" asked Jamuna, her eyes were fixed on the door which still vibrated the banging sound after Kaveri had slammed it on her way out.

"Because she is a wretched witch!" said Gangga. She wiped her eyes with a crunched up Kleenex.

"Didi, no, don't say that."

"Jamuna, you are naive. You don't know the real Kaveri like I do. I have seen her true colors. It's time you realized too. She's not nice Jamuna, never has been." Gangga looked at her swollen face in the mirror.

"But she's our sister."

"I know, and that's the sad part."

"What are we going to do?" asked Jamuna, referring to the wedding.

Gangga sat back down on the bed. She looked exhausted with rings under her eyes and red, puffy cheeks – not at all how a bride should look in the morning of her wedding. Jamuna's heart went to her sister.

"I don't know," she whispered. Then, with a more vibrant voice, "Jamuna, tell me something. Have you slept with someone?"

Jamuna jerked back, shocked at the abrupt change in topic.

"It's okay to tell me. You know I've always kept all your secrets. And if it makes you feel any better, I've slept with more than one man."

"You have?"

"Yeap. And if Subash doesn't like it, he can shove it! Maybe this whole thing is a blessing in disguise. I mean, imagine him finding out on our wedding night I wasn't a virgin, what then? This is so much better. And what was I thinking? How was I going to spend the rest of my life married to someone like him? No, I'm glad this happened – well, not glad but I guess it's better now than later. My only worry now is to break the news to Papa before all the guests start showing up at the wedding hall."

Even as she spoke, she knew she was lying, to herself and to Jamuna. This was her wedding day. She was prepared to marry Subash, had even convinced herself she was in love with him, and she was. And she was dying inside not knowing what Subash wanted. Was he going to marry her? But for now she needed a distraction and focusing on Jamuna and her love life seemed like a wise thing to do.

"Didi, you are so brave. How are we going to tell Papa?"

Gangga's eyes softened as she regarded her sister. Jamuna had taken this to be her problem as well, unlike Kaveri who'd left them to fend for themselves.

"I'll worry about that. Now tell me, who did you sleep with? Come on, humor me will you. Trust me; I need all the wit I can afford to get right now to keep me sane for later."

"Well – I, it's…, it's Jason"

"Which Jason?"

"How many Jason do you know?" Jamuna managed a slow smile.

"Vikram's friend? That Jason?" Gangga shrieked.

"Yes, that Jason. I'm in love with him, we both are. Didi please don't tell anyone," begged Jamuna.

"Oh. My. God! How on earth did that happen?"

Jamuna told Gangga her story from the beginning. Gangga sat

listening to her, not quite believing what she was hearing. It sounded like a lovely fairy-tale.

"Holy crap!" Was all she said when Jamuna had finished talking.

"Please don't tell anyone, please."

"Of course I won't. Let's just make sure Kaveri doesn't get a sniff of this. She'd fry you dry if she did!"

"Oh, didi!" Jamuna let out a breath of exasperation, "This is your day. Let's try and see how we can help you get over today, okay?"

"Okay…" Gangga's voice lacked confidence.

How was she going to salvage the day, if not the marriage? By now she was positive Subash had dumped her on their wedding day. She sat solemnly on her bed, thinking. It was past eight in the morning, one more hour before the big family breakfast began and four more hours before Mrs. Mehra showed up to adorn her. Should she look for Ajay and tell him the truth, before it was too late?

"Should we tell Papa, you think?" asked Jamuna, as if reading Gangga's mind.

"I was thinking of the same thing. We should tell him before Mrs. Mehra comes. God, this is going to give Kaveri so much to gloat about."

Part Two – Mid-Morning

Chapter seven – Ajay & Devika

This rain is making everything impossible, Ajay fumed silently. How was he going to get everything ready on time for the reception if it continued to rain like this? The tent was a disaster. Ajay couldn't remember the number of times the tent *wallah* had emptied the water that accumulated on the roof of the tent. It filled up so fast. One would think it was the monsoon season in Vancouver with the rain that reckless.

He'd managed to avoid Menaka the whole morning. For once he was glad to see Kaveri at home. She'd keep Menaka occupied and out of his face. He saw them that morning, huddled together in a corner of the kitchen, whispering like a pair of gossipers. Kaveri didn't even lift her head to look at him. It didn't bother Ajay. He was used to her hostility. At first he'd wondered what drew her away from him. But as he saw her grow up into an insolent, arrogant, jealous young woman, he'd given up. He'd seen her ill treatment toward Jamuna and Ajay knew the reason behind it. It only made him pity her. He wished one day she'd see that he didn't view his three daughters differently. To Ajay, they were his three princesses – with their own individual uniqueness.

But he was glad for one thing, for the closeness Kaveri shared with Menaka. At least she had Menaka to turn to in case she needed to. He dismissed Kaveri from his mind brusquely; a bigger issue was troubling him.

His earlier dispute with Menaka distressed him. What would

Menaka want to do? But the more he thought about it, dwelled upon it, the more relieved he became. He actually had one less thing to worry about. Suddenly he knew – he'd wait until Gangga's wedding was over. Then he'd pack his bags and move out. Maybe at last, after all these miserable years of being Menaka's husband, he'd be happy. And maybe he could spend the rest of what's left of his life with his true love – Devika. Of course he had to think of Jamuna. She could move in with him since he knew for sure she'd not live with Menaka. Vikram could rent a room on his own somewhere close by. And he'd move into the two-bedroom rental apartment he owned out in Langley. It'd be good to move out of the busy city.

"God lord, what has gotten into me?" Ajay said loudly, hitting his forehead with the palm of his hand. Divorce or separation wasn't even mentioned by Menáka and here he was, counting his eggs. If Menaka had known of his relationship with Devika long ago, why did she remain his wife? Why did she not leave him? Ajay knew his wife didn't love him, so why then? For the sake of the family? Or for her own selfish reason?

Whatever it was, it had to wait until after the wedding, Ajay finally decided. He walked over to the tent *wallah* and told him to leave it be. There was no use even contemplating having the tent any longer. The rain was making it impossible. As much as he would like to have a tent on his front yard, he didn't want to look stupid either. He'd just have to move the reception indoors.

He was turning back to go back into the house when he spotted Devika, walking toward him with an umbrella. The sight of her always took his breath away. Her hips swayed gently with each easy glide in her elegant light burgundy *salwar- kameez* and her high heels. The locks on her shoulder length hair moved seductively following the rhythm of the gentle morning cold breeze. Her brown eyes glimmered under her long lashes. Age had done Devika good, smiled Ajay. She stood in front of him and held the umbrella over his head.

"You're going to catch a cold standing under the rain this long, Ajay. Why is the tent being removed?" she asked.

Ajay turned to look at the tent and sighed, "It keeps filling up with rain water. There's no point."

"What about the reception tonight?"

"We'll have to have it indoors. Why are you out here?"

"Just came to see you. Where's Menaka didi?"

"Don't know and don't care!"

"Ajay, don't be like that."

"No Devika, please don't tell me not to be like that. I'm tired of this, of being in this marriage. I don't love her, have never loved her and I'm tired of putting up with her crap. Enough is enough, Devika. It's time we put an end to this and save us all our miseries, you and me."

"Ajay, what has gotten into you? Why are you talking like this?"

"Because I am tired. Very tired. I don't want to live with her anymore. I can't tolerate it. There's no love, no respect, no tolerance or patience left in this marriage. It's devoid of everything, everything that spells marriage. I have to end it."

"You can't," gasped Devika. Her hand flew to her mouth.

"Don't be shocked. Do you know what's worse than being divorced? Being in a loveless marriage. I'm getting older. The kids are all grown up. It's time I started thinking of myself, of my life and I don't want to spend what's left of it being married to your sister." Ajay looked like he'd just come out of a battle – drained, sapped.

"What will happen to Didi if you left her? Where would she go? Ajay, she'd be torn into pieces if she found out about us..."

"She already knows. She'd known for years and she only told me today."

"Didi knows?" Devika's voice trembled.

"Yes, she does. And the strange thing is she's still married to me. She knows I'm in love with her sister and she's still civil to you. What does that tell you about her? Any decent person would've not only left the husband but banished the sister from her life. But Menaka remained married to me. Don't ask me why, I don't have the answer to it. Look Devika, once this wedding is over, I'm leaving Menaka. I want you to pack your bags and come with me. We're going to be together if it means renouncing everyone else. I've had it, had enough with this life we've created for ourselves! Had enough of this hypocrisy and of this theatrical play! It's time the truth came out. I love you and thanks for bringing me the umbrella." Ajay paused and fixed his eyes on Devika. He gently removed a strand of wet hair from her face and traced the contour of her cheek with a finger and allowed the finger to linger on her face longer than necessary. "Now if you'll excuse me, I have to go plan the day." Ajay walked away quickly without glancing back at Devika.

Devika stood rooted on her spot. She didn't dare move. The rain fell onto her opened umbrella and the drops fell around her slowly. She watched the drops and Ajay's words came flooding into her brain. Suddenly, fear overtook her. How long had Menaka known? Had she known when Ajay visited her? Had she known when they had sex in the basement below? Had she known all along? God, how was she going to face her sister? She felt humiliated, wretched. But why hadn't Menaka said anything to her? It wasn't like Menaka not to confront people. If anything she lived for it. God, what was going on? Devika brought her hand to her heaving chest.

Her mind swirled with questions, "And this Ajay, he wants me to pack my bags and move in with him, just like that? What is he thinking? I have a family, a husband to think of. I can't just leave everything, leave Siva just like that – can I?"

By the time Ajay reached the kitchen, he was soaking wet. He saw Menaka bustling around, looking important and busy. Kaveri was sitting at the island, slowly sipping her tea. Ajay grabbed a kitchen towel and attempted to dry his hair. He didn't feel like talking to Menaka or Kaveri, but there was a wedding on in fewer than ten hours and he needed to make sure all preparations were taking place. His sister and her husband (Vikram's parents) would be arriving any minute and so would Kaveri's in-laws – The Dhillons. He didn't know whether that useless son-in-law of his would be there, and he didn't care either.

"What have you planned for breakfast?" he asked Menaka casually.

"You don't worry about it," came the brusque reply.

"Chandni and her husband will be here soon. Is everything ready?"

"I'm sure they wouldn't die of starvation if we're a few minutes late."

"Fine, I guess the Dhillons wouldn't die of starvation either then!" said Ajay smugly and exited the kitchen. He knew how Menaka doted on Kaveri's in-laws and he knew he'd struck a chord, albeit a minor one. It still gave him a small satisfaction. In his bedroom, Ajay quickly changed into some dry clothes and threw himself onto the bed.

Exhaustion settled on him heavily, and to think the day hadn't even begun. So much to do and he was already feeling so tired, emotionally drained. He recapped his earlier conversation with Devika in the rain. He had meant every word he said to her. He'd had enough of these lies and hypocrisy that he called life. But was leaving Menaka the right thing to do? And would Devika leave her husband for him? What about the children? And Priya? How would she feel if she found out he was her biological father? What if the truth did that girl more harm than good?

Ajay closed his eyes and found himself thinking of Devika. From the first time he saw her, at his wedding, he'd been enthralled by her beauty, her gentle manner, and her sense of humor. He wished he could say it wasn't about sex, but he couldn't. Sex with Devika was different; it made him feel like a man. With Menaka, it was always monotonous, mundane, and almost mechanical like a routine. He'd sometimes have to force himself to want to want her. She never showed any enthusiasm toward him or toward love-making. Ajay remembered the first time he had sex with Menaka on their honeymoon more than thirty years ago. It had been one of the worst experiences. She'd lain on the bed and had allowed him to caress her and make-love to her, but she didn't respond much. Her hands lay motionless on her side; her body remained still, didn't arch and curve toward him. When he kissed her on the lips, it had been like kissing a mannequin – lifeless. And when he rolled off her, he had no idea he'd be forcing himself for the rest of his life with her.

Many times, on many occasions, he'd contemplated leaving her. He didn't think she'd even mind, for that was how she was with him – there was no passion, no love, and no eagerness toward him. The first time he wanted to leave her, she became pregnant with Kaveri. He'd been excited by the news. Maybe that was what they needed to give their marriage a boost. But with the arrival of Kaveri, Menaka had behaved like Ajay didn't exist in her life. All that had mattered to her then was Kaveri. That was when he decided to leave her for the second time. So when Menaka became pregnant with Gangga, he was heartbroken. He cursed himself for getting her pregnant. It had been on a late evening after they'd come back from a get-together with their friends and he'd been a little tipsy, as had she. They'd both had wanted it that night, the only night.

But Gangga changed his life. She was so unlike Kaveri. She adored him and loved him like he was the greatest father on the planet. She doted on him and still did to that day. The third time he decided to leave Menaka was when she threw a tantrum at him while pregnant with Jamuna and while Devika was staying with them. But Devika convinced him not to and by then, he'd found Devika again. He'd been so happy to have Devika in his life that living with Menaka had been bearable. The fourth time he'd wanted to leave Menaka had been when Devika announced she was pregnant. But, that didn't materialize when Devika married Siva and he migrated to Canada.

And, now, here he was – contemplating leaving Menaka for the fifth time. Could he blame himself for doubting it this time? All he knew was, time was running out and if he didn't do something, life would pass by him without Devika in it permanently. He still wanted her like he did the first time, if not more. She completed him in more ways than one, but would she leave her husband for him? He wasn't sure.

Ajay didn't know much of Devika's relationship with Siva, he chose not to know. From what he could see, they were happy. They still slept in the same room every time they came over for a visit. She still cooked for him and served him his meals like a good wife. She still ironed his clothes and brought him a glass of water when he asked for it. If she was happy, was it right of him to want to tarnish it? Would he take away her happiness, her family just to have her to himself, just to make him happy? He wouldn't. Devika's happiness mattered to him more than his own. If she was happy, he'd not take that away from her. But that didn't mean he wasn't leaving Menaka. He still planned on it, after the wedding.

Devika managed to drag herself back to the guest-room in the basement-suite. Siva was not on his bed and Priya was still sleeping. She shook her daughter gently to wake her.

"What time is it?" Priya rubbed her eyes.

"It's past eight. Everyone will be here for breakfast soon. Why don't you go and have a shower?"

"Where's Gangga didi?"

"Upstairs, I think. Come on, get up." Devika nudged at her daughter gently.

Priya sat on the bed and buried her face into her mother's bosom. Devika caressed her daughter's curls and planted a kiss on her head. Priya was her true reason for living. She was the symbol of her love. She was a constant reminder of Ajay and of their love and Devika cherished her daughter like the precious gem that she was. Suddenly her hands stopped caressing Priya's hair. What would happen to Priya if she found out the truth? What if Priya started hating her and distanced herself from her? What would Devika do if Priya wasn't in her life? No, she couldn't do it, decided Devika; she couldn't leave Siva. Ajay had to understand and appreciate her decision. She'd tell him, after the wedding, that she wouldn't under any circumstances cause any pain to Priya. Her daughter's happiness was what mattered to Devika. Ajay just had to accept it.

Just then Siva walked into the room. His hair was wet from his shower. Devika gently pushed Priya away from her and told her to get ready.

"What time is breakfast?" asked Siva as soon as Priya left the room.

"Nine o'clock." Devika couldn't remember the last time Siva and she had had a proper conversation. They were civil to each other, although in a monotone way. Sometimes a whole day could pass by without them having said anything to each other. If it bothered Siva, he didn't show it and it suited Devika since she really didn't have anything much to say to her husband. Her only complaint was did he have to be the same way with Priya? It'd be nice to see him making some effort to get close to Priya.

"Should I go upstairs first?" Siva's voice broke into her thoughts. She contemplated his suggestion before deciding against it.

"I'll come with you."

Maybe if Ajay saw her being close to her husband, he wouldn't pursue her or ask her to pack her bags, thought Devika as she followed her husband. She had to do this for Priya. There was nothing more to it.

Chapter eight – Gangga

Gangga walked out of her bathroom and saw Jamuna struggling with her bra stripes, adjusting and re-adjusting them with a frown. Her long hair pulled back from her face in a ponytail that it made her look like a high-school girl.

"What's up with you?" she asked.

"This stupid bra is suddenly so tight on me. I think it shrunk or something."

"Try a different one."

"I did, I tried four of them so far, and they're all so tight. Didi, have I put on weight?"

Gangga studied Jamuna. Her breasts looked slightly swollen; the nipples were darker, which made her skin look fairer. But, Gangga noticed her sister's face looked pudgy as if she hadn't been sleeping.

"I don't know, are you pms-ing?"

"Maybe. God, this is so bloody frustrating. How am I going to fit into the sari-blouse tonight if I don't fit into my bras?" Jamuna threw the bra on the bed and pulled a large t-shirt on.

"Are you forgetting something?"

"What?"

"We don't know whether there's going to be a wedding!"

Gangga joined Jamuna on her bed and dropped her face into her hands, with her back hunched forward. Jamuna rubbed her sister's back and clicked her tongue, making soothing sounds as if Gangga were a whiny baby refusing to fall asleep.

"What am I going to do, Jamuna?" Gangga faced her sister. "Everyone's going to show up for breakfast any minute now. Should I tell Papa?" Gangga's voice shook, how was she going to face the day?

"Actually…I've been thinking," Jamuna said softly.

"What?"

"What if we went ahead with the wedding, let everything take place, and you go sit at the *mandap* (altar), let the priest do his thing, and when they call the groom in he wouldn't be there…we'd have made it look like he stood you up."

Gangga stared at her sister for a long time before saying, "Only problem is, the groom will have to sit at the *mandap* before the bride. They'd call me in, not him."

"Shit!"

"Not quite."

"Huh?"

"Jamuna, we might have something here," Gangga paused and thought for a bit. "I like that."

"I don't get it."

"We'll go with the flow and when the time comes, he won't show up. I'll pretend like I didn't know anything or that we even spoke this morning. We'd all assume he got cold feet and chickened out. And tomorrow, we can deal with the truth."

"There's one problem," Jamuna pointed out.

"What?"

"Kaveri Didi knows."

"Shit!"

"Double that… I feel sick," Jamuna got up quickly and ran to the bathroom. Gangga watched her sister and was touched at how much Jamuna was affected by everything. She'd always been a gentle soul, mused Gangga. Then, there was Kaveri. God, why did she have to open her big mouth in front of Kaveri? The smug look on Kaveri's face when she'd said 'I was a virgin' had been too obvious. Of course Kaveri had been a virgin on her wedding night, which man in his right mind would want to sleep with her? As soon as she thought it, Gangga wished she didn't. Kaveri was one person who held strong to her principals.

Although, Gangga had no idea how Kaveri remained a virgin until in her thirties. Wasn't she at least curious to find out how sex felt like?

But this wasn't the time to ponder about Kaveri and her lack of interest in sex, or her principles in life, Gangga reminded herself firmly. She looked at her cell phone on Jamuna's vanity table. Should she call Subash again? What would she say? *Hi, I' m sorry I'm not a virgin, but will you still marry me?*

Just as she was staring at her phone, it started to ring as if she had willed it. Gangga let out a shriek when she saw the caller ID – it was Subash.

"Hello?" she said cautiously after a long inhale of breath.

"Hi, sorry I didn't answer you calls earlier," he didn't sound at all apologetic.

"No, that's fine. So, what's up?" Shit, did she just say that? What's up? Like he was making a casual call? But she couldn't think, her brain felt frozen.

"I've been thinking about our earlier conversation…and…well."

Gangga clutched her phone, her heart pounding, "And?"

"After much thought, I forgive you."

Gangga jerked back from the phone, her frozen brain thawing at an unusual speed. "What?"

"I forgive you. And the wedding will go on as planned." There was not a slight hint of care or concern for her in any manner. He was brusque.

"You forgive me?" *Jackass.*

"You think what you've done is acceptable?" Now he sounded disgusted.

"What I've done is done, Subash and that was before you? I didn't cheat on you."

"The time of occurrence is not the point here. Regardless of when it was, the deed is done. I'm the one at the losing end. Surely you can see that."

Her insides turned, she was repulsed at herself. She *was* an Indian woman after all, brought up with good Indian values…one of which was to remain a virgin until the night of her wedding. And Subash was an Indian man, expecting to marry a woman true to her roots and values. He was right, she was a disgrace.

"Are you still there?" She heard him ask.

"Yes…I am. I do have a question though."

"Yes?"

"Since you insist on my being a virgin, are you telling me you're one?"

Silence pursued.

Then, "If you must know – yes, I am."

"Oh." How did she respond to that? Gangga searched her brain and finally decided to stick to the issue at hand. "So, the wedding?"

"We came this far, didn't we? And think of all the hearts we'd have to break if I called the wedding off, and then there's your reputation to safeguard. It's never a good thing for a woman to be dumped on her wedding day, so yes, it's on."

After she ended her call, Gangga's cell phone found its way to the wall once again, and out came the batteries, spilling onto the floor. What was it he had said? Safeguard her reputation? He made it look like he was doing her a favor by marrying her. *And he was a virgin*? Shit! She should call him back and tell him this had all been a big, gargantuan mistake and they should call the wedding off…she should call him back, shouldn't she? So what if her father lost his face among their relatives, so what if all the wedding preparations went to waste and so what if everyone sniggered at them with their backs turned toward them…so what!

Only, she couldn't do it. Gangga couldn't see her father humiliated just because she couldn't safeguard her virginity. Then there was the other fear, the more prominent one, who would marry her? No Indian man would want to marry a thirty- something old woman who'd not only been dumped on her wedding day by her fiancé, but who also wasn't a virgin. And, the hardest thing of all, she loved Subash and wanted to marry him.

"Who was that?" Gangga heard Jamuna's disembodied voice emanating from the bathroom.

"That was Subash. Are you okay in there?"

Jamuna walked out looking scruffy and disoriented, her hair, no longer in a ponytail, thrown around her pretty face like a wild net, her face pastel with shallow dark rings around her eyes.

"God, I don't know why I feel so sick. I just feel awful. Don't think I have the energy for today's breakfast-crowd." Jamuna slumped on the bed next to Gangga. "What did he say?"

"Who? Subash? Whole bunch of crap that made me feel like crap. But at least the wedding is back on. You can relax now," said Gangga rubbing her sister on the back. Jamuna was really taking this too hard, poor girl.

"What did he say, didi?"

"Nothing, really. Only that he forgives me and that the wedding is on."

"Forgives you? Is he insane?"

"I know what you mean, but it is my fault after all."

"How is it your fault?"

"I shouldn't have lost my virginity, I guess."

"For heaven's sake, didi! You can't possibly mean that. This is the twenty-first century. I mean, when women are not expected to drape themselves in white saris and shave their heads bald once their husbands die, why are we expected to remain virgins until we're married? So bloody clichéd and hypocritical, don't you think? Did you ask him whether he's still a virgin?"

"I did and he is."

"You've got to be joking! God, I feel sick again!"

"Jamuna, maybe you need to eat something," said Gangga, concerned for Jamuna and relieved at the same time for the digression.

"No, I can't think of food right now. I don't know how to sit at the breakfast table and listen to all the gibberish that's going to flow in like new garbage with old smell. Oh, and just wait, the attention is going to be on me now? *Next will be your turn, Jamuna. We found your two sisters such charming husbands, we will for you too…don't you worry, beta*," Jamuna mimicked their father's sister's voice. "I remember how it was at Kaveri didi's wedding. All eyes and mouths and ears were on you…you were the next target, remember?"

"How can I not? But what would you do, Jamuna? Are you serious about Jason?"

Jamuna sighed and shook her head. "I don't know, didi. All I know is I love him so much, but love alone isn't enough, is it?"

"Apparently not," Gangga snorted. "There seem to be many other requirements to find your happily ever after, and virginity is one of them!"

"I'm a failure in that department."

" Let's hope you don't end up with a 'Subash'…" Gangga stopped abruptly in midsentence and turned to look at Jamuna with a new concern.

"What's wrong?" asked Jamuna.

"Jamuna, when did you last get your period?"

"Oh…I don't know…few months back. Don't worry, I'm not pms-ing, just nerves I guess," shrugged Jamuna.

"I'd rather if you were pms-ing."

"What do you mean?"

"Can you call Jason?"

"Why?"

"Ask him to get his ass back here ASAP."

"Why?" Jamuna whined.

"And tell him to stop at Shoppers on the way here and grab a 'First-Response' kit."

Chapter nine – Jamuna & Jason

Jason walked into Vikram's room to find Jamuna sitting hugging her knees on the top of the bed, Vikram sprawled by her feet and Gangga facing the small mirror on the wall, inspecting something on her face with extra scrutiny. But as soon as they heard the door, all eyes fell on him – accusatory glances. Jason walked over to Jamuna without conviction, unsure of her feelings and moods. Hadn't there been cases where men were brutally injured by women they'd impregnated?

"Hi…," he cleared his throat.

"Did you bring it?" Gangga asked instead with hands extended toward him. She grabbed the thin, rectangular box from his hand and tossed it at Jamuna.

While Jamuna disappeared into the bathroom, the other three sat on Vikram's bed as nervous as fathers-to-be.

"God, I hate all this waiting," Vikram blurted out suddenly. Gangga shot him an angry look.

"What're you complaining about? You're the safe one." She then darted her eyes toward Jason, who visibly cringed under her look.

"I still hate waiting," whined Vikram. "Dude, what were you thinking? Have you not heard of safe sex?" he asked Jason.

"Or abstinence?" Gangga butted in.

"Look, you guys are over-reacting. I'm sure she's not pregnant. I mean, she can't be…can she?" If there was an empty pail underneath Jason, it'd be full with his sweat.

In the bathroom, Jamuna fiddled with the rectangular shaped box unsuccessfully, and the un-sturdiness of her fingers wasn't helping matters either. Finally, after many shaky attempts, she managed to open the top flap of the box and spilled its content into the sink. Jamuna stood staring at the pink pregnancy-kit for what seemed like an eternity. Why did they have to make it pink? Why couldn't it be blue or black or brown? Pink was like an affirmation, an avowal… that only women screwed up! When in truth, it was men who screwed up and women ended up the victims. If only Jason had been more careful, this wouldn't have happened, Jamuna cringed. She wouldn't be standing in the bathroom, on Gangga's wedding day, staring at a pink pregnancy-test kit!

If Subash was contemplating not marrying Gangga just because she was not a virgin, wait till her turn comes, Jamuna mused. Who would marry a single mother? She had royally screwed things up. How was she going to face her parents? And how was she going to support a baby on her own? She knew she'd shame her family if the pregnancy test turned out positive. Why go that far, Jamuna thought grimly, she'd already shamed her family by sleeping with Jason.

Jamuna sat on the toilet bowl and brought her head to her knees. Her stomach hurt, her head pounded as did her heart. There was a sudden tap on the door followed by Gangga's voice.

"Jamuna, it only takes two minutes for the result, you've been in there for more than ten…what's going on?"

"I can't do it!"

"What? Why not?"

Jamuna started crying. Was it supposed to be easy? She didn't go around taking pregnancy tests whenever she felt like it. This could change her life forever and she wasn't sure she was prepared to face that kind of an ultimatum.

"J, open the door." This time it was Jason.

Jamuna sat rooted on the toilet bowl as if it were her sanctuary. Jason kept on knocking, insisting she opened the door. Then she heard Gangga's panicky voice in the background, telling Jason to move aside so she could hammer the door down. That did it. Knowing Gangga, she would not only bring the door down, she'd bring the whole house down.

When Jamuna opened the bathroom door, Gangga *was* holding a hammer.

"Didi, please put the hammer down."

"So, what's the verdict?" asked Gangga, with the two boys standing behind her, as if hiding.

"I told you, I haven't done it yet. I couldn't do it. I'm scared to find out," Jamuna started crying again. Jason quickly walked toward her and wrapped his arms around her before she pushed him away.

"This is all your fault, you brute!" she spat angrily.

"Hey…I don't remember you ever complaining, but when it comes to the reality of it, it's my fault? How is that fair?"

"It's fair because you're not the one who's pregnant!"

"We don't know that yet."

"What if I am, Jason? What then?"

Virkam interfered at this junction. "Gangga, I think we should leave these two alone. Is it time for breakfast yet?"

"I don't hear any loud voices up there," said Gangga.

"It's past nine, should we go and check?" asked Vikram.

"I'll go and check, you stay here and watch some TV. I don't want anyone up there to suspect anything. Make sure no one comes into your room, okay?"

Once Gangga went upstairs and Vikram retreated to the couch, Jason faced Jamuna with new verve.

"J, if you are pregnant, then we'll get married. There're no ifs, ands or buts about it," he told her.

"Huh?" Jamuna sat on Vikram's bed, or rather fell into it with a thump. Jason sat next to her and held her hand.

How could this be happening to her? No one would agree to her marrying Jason, especially her father. For Ajay, marriage was a matter of karmic destiny that needed to be arranged accordingly and based on astrological harmony. A lot was involved in weddings as far as her father and family were concerned. There was never such thing as love being the main component of marriages that happened in the Sharma family. Even when Kaveri had insisted on marrying Raj, although their mother gave full consent, she had still ran to the *panditji* (priest) first, with both Kaveri's and Raj's astrology charts. The wedding only took place after the p*anditji* gave his consent.

Ajay, who had been against it in the beginning, gave in once the astrological numbers matched. Even he wouldn't tempt or argue with fate. Such being the case, how would anyone allow Jamuna to marry Jason? Did he even have an astrology chart? And she also didn't think *Panditji* would be able to determine anything based on the name 'Jason'. Every Indian name had a meaning attached to it which played a role in determining their fate. Jamuna, Gangga and Kaveri were named after famous holy rivers in India. Jamuna, although she didn't believe in all this karmic, *kismet* bullshit, knew it mattered to her in the end, because it mattered to her father and to her family.

And, if they did get married, what then? How would their lives unfold? Which direction would it take? What faith would they follow and what names would their children carry? And the wedding itself; where would it take place, temple or church?

She wanted her wedding to be witnessed by her God, and she wanted to make the seven rounds around the fire with her husband, promising a new pledge with each circle. All these mattered to Jamuna. All her life, albeit in Canada, she'd only really known and been exposed to traditional Hindu weddings. Every single, small aspect of the weddings had its symbolic meaning and that mattered to Jamuna. Marriage was sacred to her eyes and a lifetime commitment, not only to the two people getting married, but their families as well. Jamuna couldn't begin to imagine what kind of relationship her family would have with Jason's family if they were married.

"J, we need to talk about this," Jason said now and Jamuna felt the little squeeze he gave her hand.

"I don't know what to say, what to think or what to feel. I'm so confused."

"That's why we need to talk, we're in this together, J, you and me, we're a team."

"What do you think we should do?"

"I told you what I thought, we should get married."

"Get real, will you? I can't possibly marry you."

A ghastly gloom settled on Jason's face. He had to visibly compose himself before speaking again.

"Why not? Do you not love me?"

"You know I do, but marriage is such a big thing, Jason, especially for my family. They'd never accept you and I can't go against my father's wishes."

"I don't believe this…I don't fucking believe this!"Jason stood up.

His hands trembled, he swallowed a few times. "What are you doing with me, J? If you never planned on marrying me, why are you with me?"

Jamuna brushed a fresh drop of tear from her cheek. These past two years with Jason, she did not once contemplate marriage. All she knew was she loved him and wanted to be with him. She didn't think about their future together. Marriage was never on the agenda. She wanted to concentrate on her career, get a house and become more settled before she thought of marriage. It seemed so far away into the unknown future that she never pondered about it or worried about it. But all that had changed now.

Jamuna buried her face in her hands. Her sobs came out muffled. She did love Jason and did want a life with him, forever and ever but how could she ignore her family and their expectations?

She felt Jason's hands on her shoulders all of a sudden and he shook her feverishly.

"Were you screwing with me, J? I need to know. Was I just some sort of an experiment to you? Were you just fooling around?" he was trembling, his voice shook.

Jamuna watched him through blurry eyes and whispered, "No."

"Are you sure, J? Because by the sound of it, you're not at all sure about us."

"I *am* sure about us, Jason. I just don't know about marriage."

"That's just fucking great." Jason stood up and walked to the door where he stopped to look at her briefly. "I hope the test is negative, I'm not sure I want you to have my baby."

Jamuna watched him go and wiped her eyes with the end of her double XL t-shirt. She was on the verge of a breakdown, she felt like going upstairs and throwing the truth out at everyone, her family, her relatives. She didn't care if they sniggered at her, if they called her futile and a disgrace. She didn't care. She was hurting, her heart felt like it was split opened into two.

Jason's words echoed in her ears. He didn't mean them…did he?

Was she really not worthy to be the mother of his child? She saw him walking away and she didn't even have the decency to stop him and convince him that she loved him and wanted to have his baby and yes, she'll marry him and spend the rest of her life with him, even if it meant disowning her family, or being disowned – for that was what it'd be. But she couldn't do it, not to her father. She didn't care about her relatives. Her aunts and uncles were not or never had been important, except maybe Devika. But Devika would never shun her; she'd always stand by her side.

Jamuna didn't know when Vikram materialized next to her. As his arms came around her, Jamuna leaned against him, allowing him to douse her with sympathy.

"What am I going to do, Vikram?"

Vikram let out a sigh, "Did you take the test?"

Jamuna shook her head.

"Why don't you take the test, then we'll think about what to do next. There's no point thinking about it now and wallowing in self pity, is there? What did Jason say?"

Jamuna refused to talk about Jason, she remained silent.

"We should go up." Vikram was easing Jamuna away from him when he saw a figure perched at the opened door of his room. It was Kaveri, eyeing them like they were a pair of crooks indulged in some corny affair.

"Kaveri? When did you come?" he asked. He got up and gave his oldest cousin an awkward hug. Kaveri and Vikram never quite saw eye to eye. This time it was the other way around, Vikram couldn't stand Kaveri and her malicious, vindictive heart. He'd seen her forbidding callousness toward Jamuna.

"Just this morning," she replied sweetly. "What're you two doing here? Is everything all right?" She threw a suspicious look at Jamuna.

"Of course, why do you ask?"

"Because it doesn't look like everything's fine. Jamuna, Mama wants you upstairs, pronto! There're things to do, you know. After all, there is a wedding on," Kaveri spoke with a voice reserved for beggars – curt and cold. She then turned toward Vikram and flashed him a lovely smile, "Come on up, Vikram, come have some tea while waiting for breakfast." Kaveri hooked an arm around Vikram's, who followed her with a quick glance over at Jamuna.

"Why isn't breakfast served yet?" he asked on the way up.

"Chandi Aunty and her family are a little delayed. God, the place is already getting crowded. I can't stand it."

"There's a lot you can't stand, Kaveri."

"Oh, but you're not one of them."

"Lucky me."

Jamuna waited until Kaveri's voice had disappeared before burying her face in a pillow and crying to her heart's content. She wondered whether Jason was already on his way home. Would he even be at the wedding tonight? She'd ruined everything between them. She wouldn't be surprised if he refused to ever look at her again. God, what was she going to do?

But Jason couldn't go back to his house. Not that he didn't want to; there was nothing more he wanted to do but he wasn't allowed, by Ajay. Jason was walking to his car after the row with Jamuna when Ajay spotted him and stopped him. Ajay had just finished with the tent *wallah*, paying him for taking down the tent when the flower van arrived. He directed the flower lady into the house to meet Menaka when he saw Jason, drenched to his toe, fiddling with his car key.

"Jason?" he called. "Are you leaving?"

"Yes, Mr. Sharma. I have to catch up on some school work," Jason replied gauchely. He prayed Ajay wouldn't start questioning him about this morning, when Jason had barged into Menaka and him in the midst of something that involved a bottle of scotch.

"But you must have breakfast with us. Come, there's a big meal planned for this morning, although I don't know what it is…but, come." Ajay draped his arm over Jason's wet shoulders. "And we'll get Vikram to loan you some clean clothes."

"No, Mr. Sharma, thanks. But I must really get home."

"No such thing, young man. You're my guest and Vikram's best friend. You must eat with us, I insist. Come along."

Jason sighed and followed quietly like an obedient pet. At least he was thankful Ajay didn't mention anything about that morning's incident. Maybe he didn't suspect anything. Might as well, since there was nothing to suspect anymore.

Chapter ten – Kaveri

Kaveri walked into the kitchen with Vikram in tow at the same time Ajay walked in with Jason. Ajay instructed Vikram to get some dry clothes for Jason. Relieved at the request and diversion, Vikram and Jason reverted back to their domain. Kaveri, frustrated at having lost Vikram – the only person she really cared to talk to, became even more frustrated when she saw Jason tailgating Vikram. She found Jason deadly attractive; smart, handsome with a distant brooding look, tall but not lanky, muscles in the right places – not too overwhelming instead fiercely sexy…and best of all, white skinned. How she'd love to have him all to herself. If only she wasn't married to boring, old Raj, she'd be all over Jason like a starved dog that'd been thrown a bone. And starved she was!

"Kaveri," she heard Menaka call from behind the island that separated the kitchen from the dining room. "Set the table for me. Apparently Chandni's five minutes away. She's always late for everything. Why couldn't she have planned to arrive yesterday instead of the morning before the wedding? She could at least be helping me with the arrangements. Look at me now…stuck with such a big chore, all by myself, and I don't even know where Jamuna is. It's not like her to disappear somewhere for so many hours, and Gangga? Where is she? Shouldn't she be here, waiting for everyone to show up? It is her wedding after all! And what happened to your in-laws? Are they coming?"

"Who knows, Mama."

Kaveri noticed Devika dropping some triangular shaped samosas into the sizzling oil over the stove. Her mother was filling individual bowls with a thick, yellow concoction which Kaveri knew was 'dhal'. She also saw a serving plate piled high with chapattis. She sighed; not that she was expecting pancakes and bacon but a little bit of variety would be nice. As it was, they only really ate chapattis at her house, since that was all her-mother-in-law ever made. (Kaveri's in-laws lived with them in the same house, or rather, she lived with her in-laws in their house. Raj seemed comfortable living with his parents, that even the idea of moving out seemed incongruous to him. Kaveri knew because when she suggested the possibility of moving out to him once, he'd looked at her like she was an out-of-tune opera singer.)

Kaveri gathered some plain white Chinas and started arranging them on the table, ignoring the look her mother was giving her. She knew what her mother thought, that she was a disrespectful daughter-in-law. But she couldn't tolerate her in-laws much more than she could tolerate her husband. She found her father-in-law highly opinionated about everything on the planet. He had something to say about everything and he was a loyal contributor to the 'opinion' section in the local paper. If the garbage truck missed its regular day due to bad road conditions, he'd write about it, or if a customer service clerk at the local produce store was insolent, he'd write about it. Once he wrote about his dismay at seeing little girls being dressed like models by their parents, he said they were attracting unnecessary attention to their girls. What irked Kaveri the most was when he wrote about how the modern women were disrespectful toward their in-laws and he left the paper, opened to the 'opinion' section, on the dining room table. That struck a chord. Kaveri, although didn't feel badly, wondered whether he was expecting some form of an apology from her. Of course, he never received any.

Priya walked into the kitchen as Kaveri was setting the table and asked if she could help. Kaveri dismissed her with an arrogant shrug and continued with the plates as if Priya's presence disrupted the worldly task she was involved in. Unsurprisingly, Priya wasn't her favorite either. She watched Priya at the corner of her eyes, as her cousin made her way to the island to ask her mother if she could help with anything, and was consumed with envy. How could a bright pink like that look nice on anyone? But it blended so well with Priya's skin color and brightened her already rosy cheeks. And all those curls fell around her face so effortlessly it made Kaveri sick. Kaveri could never wear pink of any shade, she found it too gaudy against her dark skin and as for her hair, it was too straight and frizzy that if she didn't blow dry it after every shower, she'd look like she's just woken up, with unruly, wiry hair. Kaveri took in a deep breath and calmed herself lest the envy turned her green.

She diverted her mind and eyes from Priya and focused her thoughts on something else...something comforting, something soothing... something nasty...Jamuna in Vikram's arms...what was all that about? And she had clearly been crying? Aunty Devika had been right all along, something was definitely going on between Vikram and Jamuna, decided Kaveri. Now, if only she could gather some evidence of those two love birds. What lovely scene it would be to see Jamuna crumple in shame in front of all their relatives and Ajay when Kaveri revealed the truth. Should she do it before the wedding or after? Oh, but didn't Gangga say they might not even be a wedding? That almost skipped her mind in all her excitement about Jamuna and Vikram. Where was Gangga anyway?

The door bell rang.

"Kaveri, beta, do you mind getting the door? I don't know where everyone is," mumbled Menaka as she instructed Priya at the same time to put the kettle on for the morning '*chai*'. "I think we'd need to make two batches. I hope your mother taught you how to make good '*chai*'." Menaka spoke as if Devika wasn't in the kitchen.

Kaveri was only too glad to leave the kitchen. The crowd was not even there yet and she was already starting to feel claustrophobic. But, Kaveri was a little late, for Jamuna was already at the door, changed and dressed in a yellow salwar-kameez. Kaveri, instead of retreating to the kitchen, stood by the wall dividing the kitchen and the dining room, and watched. She knew it was her husband and his parents from his too-friendly voice. Kaveri watched as her husband greeted Jamuna charmingly and demanding a hug from her.

"What? No hug for your Jija?"

Jamuna smiled and leaned forward slightly for a brief, casual hug, but Kaveri was not to know that. What she did know was her husband's hands tightly clutching her sister's body and his one hand making its way lower down her back until it finally rested at the bump just above her buttocks. Kaveri could see very well the way his hands deliberately lingered on that spot. If his parents hadn't interrupted from behind, with their nonchalant greetings toward Jamuna, Kaveri suspected his hands would permanently have remained on her sister's buttocks! And Jamuna was all over her husband too, hugging him in that indecent manner. What would people say? What disgrace? Well, not for long because Kaveri intended to fix her, once and for all. She was just waiting for the right time.

"So, where is everyone? And where's the bride?" asked her mother-in-law, while her father-in-law let himself into the living room and grabbed the newspaper that was on one of the coffee tables.

That was when everyone, including Kaveri, noticed Devika's husband. He was sitting quietly on one of the corner chairs hidden behind a newspaper. But when he saw Kaveri's father-in-law, he stood up to shake his hand. After which, both of them sat amicably next to each other with newspapers. That pretty much concluded his visit, thought Kaveri of her father-in-law. Now, if only her husband would acquire the same motion, but that would be like asking Casanova to practice celibacy! Sucking in her breath, Kaveri made her way to her mother-in-law and touched her feet. (A form of respect toward the elders).

"Get me a cup of *chai*, Kaveri," instructed her mother-in-law, heading toward the kitchen herself. *Why can't she get her own bloody tea!* Kaveri kept her thoughts to herself and smiled sweetly. Then her eyes fell on Raj, her husband, and she winched as if the sight of him pricked her.

"Hello, wife," he said casually. "Couldn't have waited for us this morning, huh?" Why did he always have to talk down to her, especially among the throng?

"I came early to help," her reply was curt, to match his tone.

"Whatever. Get me some tea." And he walked past her, as if she was insignificant and her excuse had been insignificant. Kaveri walked into the kitchen after her mother-in-law and her husband with a sense of foreboding; her initial excitement and vigor replaced with dread. She poured the tea Priya had prepared in her mother's elegant little china cups with matching saucers. Typical Indian brood, she thought. Couldn't they at least try and have coffee instead, just for a change?

Kaveri was serving her father-in-law in the living room when Ajay joined the men, he shook hands with her father-in-law and patted Devika's husband on the shoulders before settling himself on the chair next to them. *Bloody hypocrite*, thought Kaveri as she handed him a cup of tea. Ajay took it without glancing at her. Did he even know she was there? Did he even care? As it was, he never bothered about her, now that she was married, Kaveri felt like her father sometimes behaved as if she didn't exist. Not that she cared, but a little 'thanks' would have been nice.

But Kaveri knew better then to expect anything from the men in her life, including her husband. It was common knowledge and general acceptance that men were of higher prominence than women in their society and living in Canada did little, if nothing at all, to change that fact. And her one hope to break-free from that decree by marrying a white guy was permanently annihilated now that she was forever conjugally tied to Raj; a tie, according to the Hindu custom, shouldn't be broken in this life and in their next seven lives. Kaveri wished the rituals and the axioms did not matter to her, but they did. The only way her marriage to Raj would dissolve was if one of them died. Till death do us part, sniggered Kaveri sullenly – not gaining any comfort in the security of her marriage, while many women would yearn for such safe haven.

Suddenly the living room was filled with an unusually loud, shrieking female voice that seemed to vibrate throughout the whole house and Kaveri was sure, shook the house a little. Kaveri saw Menaka shake her head and exclaim softly, "The *moon* is apparently here… finally." Chandni in Hindi meant 'moon.' Ajay's sister – Chandni and her husband had arrived. After the commotion in the living room, Chandni and her husband Mahesh, entered the kitchen, with their twins, two nine-year-old boys who looked nothing like their elder brother, Vikram.

The twins – Johan and Karan, took their positions at the dining table, brought out their Nintendo games and blanked the surroundings out. It was as if no one existed in their worlds, only them and the games. Youngsters nowadays, grumbled Kaveri. She saw Chandni walking in circles, kissing and hugging everyone, exclaiming loudly of how wonderful and grown up everyone looked, marveling at Priya's beauty and complimenting Jamuna at her wonderful lusciousness. Then she saw Kaveri and sailed toward her like a legless witch. Kaveri shrunk inwardly, wishing desperately she had the power to become invisible, but it was too late. Chandni smothered her with kisses and said how glorious she looked.

"Looks like married life is doing you good, Kaveri. Look at that glow…"

Was she implying that Kaveri hadn't looked good before?

Then, as an answer to her prayer, her mother called.

"Kaveri, go and find Vikram downstairs, tell him his parents are here. And where is Gangga?"

Kaveri excused herself and all but ran down the stairs to the basement.

Vikram and Jason were talking in hushed tones as she walked into Vikram's room, after a brief knock. They stopped talking abruptly as soon as they saw her. Something was definitely wrong, noted Kaveri, it was written all over their faces. They looked like a pair of criminals – sindicating something. Kaveri smelt trouble and her mood lightened at the mere thought of it. Trouble was always fun.

"Your parents are here," she said to Vikram.

"Okay, thanks," Vikram sounded uninterested. She didn't blame him, she'd be uninterested if Chandni was her mother.

"Oh, can I use your bathroom. It's just so crowded up there, I'd have to line up for the loo," she laughed nervously.

"Sure." And he was gone, with Jason.

Good, now some privacy and indulgence. Before she could push the bathroom door open, someone opened it from inside.

"Gangga?"

"Kaveri Didi? Why are you here?" Gangga sounded shocked and quickly placed her left hand to her back. Kaveri raised her eyebrows.

"Same reason you are," Kaveri said haughtily, "Everyone's waiting for you upstairs and you are here? Shouldn't you be entertaining the crowd that has showed up for your *non-wedding*?" Kaveri cynicism didn't get to Gangga; instead she stretched her cheeks in an artificial smile.

"Oh, right, the wedding," said Gangga before rushing off.

Kaveri watched Gangga walk away and felt a rush of adrenalin. Something was very fishy and Kaveri loved the stinky stench of fish… it exhilarated her. What was Gangga hiding at the back of her?

Kaveri entered the bathroom and closed the door behind her. She made sure the lock was secured before sitting on the toilet bowl with its lid down. She then produced a cigarette and a lighter from her small vanity bag. She lit the cigarette with slightly shaky fingers – more out of excitement and yearning than nerves. With every breath she took in she felt calmer. She closed her eyes and let the nicotine smoke fill her lungs. God, how she hated family gatherings. Everything was a big deal for everyone. Just watch, soon everyone would be asking about her baby. *Why wasn't there a baby yet?* But she had a plan this time. A devious plan so all the relatives' attentions would not be on her and her failing marriage. No, instead they'd be on Jamuna and her incestuous relationship with their cousin.

Shit! She almost burnt her lips. Kaveri threw the end of her cigarette into the toilet bowl and flushed it. And it was then that she saw it. The end of the rectangular box that was sticking out in between used tissues in the bin. Curious, she reached for the box and lifted it up and saw the words 'First Response' written on top of it. It took her a few seconds to realize what it actually was. But it was empty, the pregnancy kit wasn't there. Feeling giddy with excitement, Kaveri leaned heavily against the sink.

So that was what Gangga was hiding behind her. Good God!

Gangga is pregnant! Sweet…

This was getting juicier by the hour. Kaveri placed the empty box into her vanity bag and sprayed a little 'Happy' perfume around her before waltzing out of the bathroom. Now, all attentions would definitely not be on her!

Chapter twelve – Family Breakfast

Breakfast was an elaborate affair in the Sharma residence that morning. There was chaos, noise, racket and laughter at the elongated breakfast table. It was as if everyone spoke at once and tried to get each other's voice and demands heard above the clamor. Although Gangga, the star of the day, was to sit at the dining room table with the rest of the married people, she chose to sit at the island with the unmarried ones.

At the dining table, Ajay and Menaka sat opposite each other at each end. Kaveri's in-laws, The Dhillons, sat on Ajay's right, followed by Raj and Kaveri who sat next to them. On Ajay's left sat Mahesh and Chandni followed by Siva and Devika. So, Menaka had Kaveri on one side and Devika on the other.

"Why don't you pour everyone some tea?" Menaka asked, or rather instructed Kaveri. As Kaveri walked around with a tea-pot, filling empty tea-cups – occasional pushing the shawl that kept sliding off her shoulders, Devika passed around the chapattis and samosas. Chandni's voice was the loudest among the throng. She was regaling everyone of her tiresome journey.

"What happened to the day when you could just walk to your neighbors or relatives?" she asked, waving a piece of chapatti around. "Remember, Ajay, back in our village? We'd hop on a bull-cart if we wanted to go anywhere. Hadn't that been so much easier and fun? All this modern vehicles and technology are just too confusing and complicated. I mean, we were practically stripped at the airport…I almost lost it. If not for Mahesh, I would've used indecent words with that officer or whoever he was, such rudeness. Do I look like a terrorist in sari?"

A fleeting silence followed before Ajay and Mahesh ruptured into uncontrollable laughter. Meanwhile Siva and Mr. Dhillon exchanged uncomfortable looks.

"What?" Chandni looked at them, irate.

"Nothing. Here, have some samosa," said Ajay, handing her a samosa. Menaka observed her sister-in-law with sheer distaste. It was just like Chandni to be so dramatic, thought Menaka. And so bloody loud. *Did she have to talk like we are miles away?* Menaka stuck a piece of samosa in her mouth before she gave in and said something.

While Kaveri, who'd seated herself patiently down next to her husband, scorned at Chandni's endless and every bit irritating whine which sounded like the drone of a fly. She glanced over at the island by the kitchen and saw her sisters clumped together intimately with Vikram and Jason and Priya. Vikram's brothers, the twins – decided to eat in the living room, with the TV on. *Such anti-socials!* Kaveri bit into her chapatti unenthusiastically. She was dying inside with boredom. And she couldn't even hear herself think above the din. She had a lot to think and time was running out. She needed to come up with a master plan. When should she open the cans of worms? And where should she begin? Should she start with Jamuna and Vikram, or Gangga's wedding that was not going to take place or above all, the reason it was not taking place or best of all…Gangga's pregnancy. She almost wished it was Jamuna who was pregnant. That would be the perfect revenge for her – an illegitimate child through an incestuous relationship! Oh, imagine poor Ajay's face, where would he put it? And who knew, the shock might even trigger a heart attack. Kaveri put a hand at a heart to calm herself. No point counting the chicks before the eggs were hatched.

Ajay, although was joking and laughing with his family, felt unsettled. He'd managed to evade any form of confrontation with Menaka. And at the looks of it, Menaka was deliberately avoiding him as well. They were seated across from each other yet they refused to meet each other's eyes. Ajay wasn't looking forward to the next day. But he knew he had to come clean and decide his future, a future that would not involve Menaka. Then his gaze traveled over to Devika. But would it involve Devika? She was sitting next to her husband and Ajay noticed how she served him like an obedient wife. Could he take that away from her and Siva? He couldn't break a good marriage, he wouldn't do it. But he also needed to hear the words from Devika's mouth; he needed her to convince him she was happy with Siva and that she wouldn't contemplate life with Ajay. Until then, there was still hope.

"So, Kaveri," suddenly Chandni's loud voice shattered his thoughts. "When are we going to hold a little baby?"

Ajay noticed Kaveri's face clouding. And Raj started coughing on his food.

"We haven't talked about a baby yet," said Kaveri. She wasn't looking at anyone, only her plate.

"Hah? What's this new thing about 'talking' first before having a baby? Things like that don't have to be talked about, beta, they just happen. Huh, Raj?" Chandni had her eyes on Raj now.

"We have to plan things, Aunty," said Kaveri "This is not like the olden days where people reproduce like rabbits and let the babies run around wild. We have to be a bit more organized than that." She looked over at Raj for support but his eyes were glued to his plate. Kaveri wanted to take that plate and empty its contents on his head.

A few snorts materialized from the crowd. Everyone felt Kaveri's sharp words. Ajay wished she wouldn't be so harsh with her words, especially with the elders.

Mr. Dhillon, Kaveri's father-in-law looked up from his plate."That's an interesting analogy, Kaveri. So, we reproduce like rabbits?"

Kaveri felt outnumbered, she felt cornered and her husband wasn't doing anything to defend her.

"That's not what I meant. It's just different now, things have changed, so have people and priorities," Kaveri tried to explain.

"Are you saying babies are not part of your so-called priorities?" Chandni asked, clearly insulted.

"Really Chandni Aunty, you always know how to twist your words."

"Kaveri!" Ajay interjected – butting in before Kaveri went on a verbal rampage. Was that how she spoke to the elders and their guests? "*Mehman baghvan hotahe*!" Guests are like God.

Silence loomed over the dining room. Everyone, including those sitting at the island, paused half way through munching and swallowing and watched inaudibly.

"You apologize to you Aunty right this minute. You don't talk to your elders that way and certainly not in my house," said Ajay with angry eyes fixed on Kaveri.

"Ajay, don't create a scene, please," Menaka butted in.

"I *am* creating a scene? Why don't you say that to your impudent daughter? Is that how she talks to our guests? Such impertinence!" Ajay stood up.

"What did she say that was so wrong? And why is everyone attacking her at the breakfast table?" Menaka asked. This was her chance to get back at Ajay, her opportunity to oust her frustrations which had been bottling deep within her like aged pickles.

"Attacking her? Do you listen to yourself? Instead of advising her, you're supporting her rude behavior. You've spoilt her, Menaka."

Kaveri stood up as well and met her father eye to eye."I know I'm spoilt and rude but at least I'm not a disgrace, like your other daughters."

"Kaveri, enough!" warned Ajay. He could smell danger. Kaveri was up to something – he could see it in her dark eyes.

"Don't tell me when it's enough; I'm not a little kid anymore. Here, why don't you ask your beloved daughters what this was doing in the basement's bathroom?" All eyes watched as Kaveri took the 'First Response' box from her vanity bag and threw it onto the middle of the table. The rectangular box flew from Kaveri's hand, did a half summersault and landed with a bounce in the middle of the table, in between the bowl of dhal and the teapot. The words 'First Response' visibly glared at everyone.

Dead silence followed except for a few gasps from the women. The men were at first confused, glancing at each other unsurely. Especially Mr. Dhillon and Siva, who'd not seen a First Response before or any other pregnancy test kit.

Mr. Dhillon craned his neck to look at the box, his mouth chewing on something, "What's that?"

Siva shrugged and looked uninterested. Mahesh turned toward his wife, "First Response? Is that some sort of a thermometer?"

"No, it's a pregnancy test kit."

The words flew out of Kaveri's mouth and hovered above the

table – like an evil black smoke. The men squirmed, and were visibly embarrassed, especially Mr. Dhillon and Siva. Ajay looked perplexed. Chandni and Mahesh looked almost frightened. Menaka stood up and grabbed the box, her eyes flaming like that of an angry lioness's. Kaveri crossed her hands across her chest and snorted smugly, as if in triumph. From the island, Jamuna let out a small cry and grasped on to Gangga's hand. Little drops of water formed on Jason's pale forehead, which he quickly wiped with the back of his hand. Vikram felt a piece of samosa getting stuck in his throat and coughed a few times to either force it down or out, while Priya observed her cousins and Jason with new curiosity.

But the one who salvaged the moment was Devika. She stood up gingerly, took the box from Menaka's hand and gave everyone a sheepish smile. The white *dupatta* around her neck giving her an angelic look.

"Err…that's actually mine."

The moment was further salvaged by the door bell. The twins announced someone by the name of Mrs. Mehra was there. It was time for Gangga's adornment.

Part Three – Afternoon Before the Wedding

Chapter Thirteen – Ajay

Ajay excused himself and headed toward the door. Mrs. Mehra was standing there holding an umbrella and flashed him a big smile. Water was dripping from the end of her sari and her sandals were wet. Ajay felt instantly remorseful.

"Mrs.Mehra, come on in," he invited her. "We could've dropped Gangga over at your place; at least you wouldn't have gotten so wet. Come in, come in."

"You're kind, Mr. Sharma. I don't mind the rain, but this time, it's quite a long one, isn't it? Reminds me of the Indian rain." Mrs. Mehra stepped into the house and a puddle formed around her. Ajay shouted at Jamuna to grab Mrs. Mehra a clean, dry towel.

"We're just finishing breakfast. Come eat with us," he invited.

"No, no, thank you. I've already eaten. I don't mind a cup of *chai* though. So, where's everyone and our bride?"

"In the kitchen, come."

Ajay walked Mrs. Mehra into the kitchen and Menaka welcomed her. They grabbed an extra chair from the study and Mrs. Mehra sat with them. Although everyone tried to get back to being normal, the air was still heavy with Kaveri's earlier outburst and Devika's confession. Even Chandni was unusually quiet. Ajay noticed the unmarried crowd at the island had dispersed and disappeared, except for Vikram's twin brothers who were glued to the TV in the living room. He tried to concentrate on his breakfast but couldn't. He was too distracted. Why did Devika take a pregnancy test? Surely she wasn't pregnant. Did she suspect she was? Did that mean Siva and her were sexually...he couldn't think any further. It was hard enough to see her married to someone else, but to think she was still having sex was unimaginable. He'd assumed Devika wasn't romantically attracted to her husband, and wasn't having sex with him. He'd somehow presumed, or maybe hoped, that her marriage was dead like his was and that they were married only for the children's sake. Had he been too presumptuous? Was Devika truly happy with Siva? If that was the case, then he shouldn't even insinuate the idea of Devika moving in with him. He couldn't ruin Devika's happiness for his sake. She was someone else's wife and she was happy and was respected by her friends and family. If she left Siva, she'd be tainted, her reputation would be charred, and she'd be labeled indecent. And Priya would pay the price too. Which nice boy would marry a daughter of an indecent woman who left her husband to live with her sister's husband? No, he must stop.

He looked up from his plate and came eye to eye with Devika. She looked flustered, as if embarrassed. She quickly lowered her lids. Why wouldn't she be? Imagine admitting in front of everyone present that the pregnancy test kit had been hers. Ajay's anger toward Kaveri broadened. Daft girl! Why couldn't she for once keep her stupid mouth shut and let people be. Look at the consequences now?

Ajay realized he had to take some drastic measures. He must find some time to talk to Devika alone. He must tell her not to even contemplate what he'd suggested in the rain earlier, about her packing her bags and moving out with him. He must act fast before she decided to do something; worst of all before she came clean in front of Siva. But how? It was going to be a busy day. It was already almost noon. Six hours before the wedding. And there was still a lot to do. The cars needed to be ready. The trays had to be prepared. The caterers needed to be checked with and someone had to go to the wedding-hall with the caterers to help them set up. Someone had to pick up the *panditji*. Ajay also needed to assign transportations to take the family to the hall. And since reception was going to be indoors, someone had to be back early after the wedding to take care of the arrangements.

Suddenly everyone started moving around him concurrently. He looked up to see the women clearing breakfast dishes and the men making their escape to the living room. He was about to push his chair back and stand up when Devika's hand reached for his plate. He paused and managed a low whisper, "Can you meet me on the deck outside in half an hour?"

He glanced at her face and saw her nodding brusquely before turning away with his plate. Ajay quickly noted the time on the wall.

Half an hour to go…why did it feel like a lifetime of waiting?

Ajay walked into the living room and sat with the men. Kaveri's husband, Raj, was not among them. Just as well, thought Ajay to himself.

"Is your wife expecting?" Mr. Dhillon suddenly asked Siva. Ajay watched as Siva stumbled for words.

"Err…no, I mean, I'm not sure…maybe she thought she was expecting," Siva's face acquired some color, he looked embarrassed.

"Well, it's never too late to have a child and you have only one daughter. Although, I can't imagine my wife getting pregnant at this age or me getting her pregnant for that matter. You're a real stud!" Mr. Dhillon started laughing loudly.

Ajay felt his face burn with envy. He watched Siva shrink in mortification, his face by now had turned crimson like an over-ripe tomato. Mr. Dhillon was waiting for some kind of a come-back and Siva looked like he'd swollen glue.

"I'm sorry for the commotion earlier, on behalf of my daughter. I think she over-reacted under pressure," Ajay said to the men in an attempt to digress from the topic.

"You know how kids nowadays are, Ajay?" said Mr. Dhillon. "They are quick to speak their mind and don't wait to weigh the consequences of their actions. And Kaveri, now she's a high-strung one. Raj and her bicker like a pair of school kids every time they're at home. Sometimes, Ajay, I don't know how well they get along. I do wonder about their union. But '*Jo hogaya so hogaya,*' it's a done deal. They have to live with it and with each other, that's how it goes." Mr. Dhillon shrugged resignedly and that bothered Ajay.

Wasn't Mr.Dhillon the one who'd approached him with the idea of a marriage between Kaveri and Raj? Now, he was talking as if he'd washed his hands off those two. Shouldn't he try to help them if they were having issues instead of saying, what's done is done? Ajay wanted to say something. He wanted to say that that was not how it went, that they always had choices, that if the marriage was not working they should end it. But he refrained himself. Kaveri wasn't like his other daughters. She'd do the opposite just to spite him. If he suggested Kaveri wasn't happy with Raj, she'd bend backwards just to show she was happy. And knowing Kaveri, she'd probably insinuate Ajay was casting a *bad-eye* on her marriage. It was best if he kept his mouth shut. And what did it matter anyway; she was a grown woman and should be capable enough to look after herself. He had other things to worry about. He glanced at his watch and half an hour had passed. He excused himself from the men politely and walked to the back door.

In the eagerness to exit the house without being noticed, he'd forgotten to put his rain-jacket on. Although the deck had an awning, the rain drops still managed to wet the whole deck. And as he stood there, waiting for Devika, he was getting drenched.

"Ajay?' He swung around to see Devika standing at the back of him with an umbrella.

"You're going to get sick if you keep on doing this. Why couldn't you have brought an umbrella or put a raincoat on?" Devika complained.

She stepped closer to him and let the roof of the umbrella cover him partially. Ajay felt her closeness, a tranquil rose scent wafted toward him and he had to muster all his will-power not to touch her. He wanted to throw his arms around her and hold her tight. Why did she have to care so much? Why couldn't she be more like her sister – vile and uncaring? Wouldn't that have made life so much easier for him?

"Do you want to tell me what's going on?" he finally asked. He knew they were short for time. There was still a lot to do and standing out on the deck wasn't exactly the safest thing to do. Anyone could come out through the back door and see them together. His only consolation was the rain, which he hoped would prevent anyone from coming out.

"What do you mean?" Devika asked.

"Are you pregnant?"

"Oh, that…no, I'm not."

"Did you think you were?"

"No, well, it's just that…you know, yes, I thought I was," Devika was stammering.

"Right. Sorry you're not."

"No, I don't want to be. Look, Ajay, it's not what you think. I wish

I could explain to you better." Ajay glimpsed at Devika but she was staring at the rain, not at him. What was going on?

"You don't have to, Devika."

An awkward stillness ensued.

"You know, about this morning…I want you to forget what I said," Ajay broke the silence. Devika looked up at him, eyes crinkled in puzzlement.

"I don't want you to pack your bags and come with me. That was wrong of me. I shouldn't have assumed your life was miserable like mine. Siva is a good man and clearly you two are happy. I want you to be happy, Devika. And coming with me is not the right thing for you to do. Sorry if I'd put you in a bad spot," Ajay said. He threw his eyes at the rain drops that hadn't changed in size or quantum.

"Are you still leaving Didi?" Devika asked.

"Yes, I am. Tomorrow. I will talk to the kids tomorrow as well."

"Will you not think this through?"

"I have thought it through many times, Devika. Many times. I'm tired of trying to make things work."

"How about the children?"

"Kaveri and Gangga are taken care off. I'll find a good boy for Jamuna soon. In fact, Mrs.Mehra was telling me earlier she knew of a friend's son who might be a good choice. Meanwhile, she can come live with me. And Vikram can either remain in the basement suite or I'll help him find a rental suite somewhere close. Menaka can have the house."

"You've got everything planned."

"I have to. This time it's for real."

"There's nothing I can do to change your mind?"

"No."

"I see. Anything I can do to help?"

Ajay turned his eyes back on Devika. Her eyes glistened, she blinked and a drop of tear fell to her cheek. He reached out and stroked her cheek. She covered his fingers with hers. Then, on an impulse, Ajay bent down and brushed his lips over hers. Devika faltered and in the process, dropped the umbrella. But he felt her kissing him back, her lips opened, inviting. He grunted and leaned forward, probing her mouth open expertly – like he'd done many times before. He knew exactly how she responded to his kisses, to his touches. Ajay wanted to stay like that forever. But he couldn't. With a sigh, he withdrew from Devika brusquely. His heart felt like it was a soccer ball and someone had been kicking it repeatedly.

"Tell me one thing, and be truthful," he said, looking into her eyes.

Devika nodded.

"Are you happy?" he asked. It took a while but finally she nodded again.

"Promise?" he probed, searching her eyes for any hint of lies.

"Yes." But she didn't meet his gaze.

"Then I'll be happy knowing you are," said Ajay before turning away from her and walking back into the house.

Chapter Fourteen – Devika

Since Ajay went back into the house through the back door, Devika walked all the way to the front of the house, holding the umbrella in one hand and wiping her tears with the other. She had wanted to tell him the truth, both about the pregnancy test-kit and about Siva, but she couldn't. The pregnancy test-kit had actually worked to her advantage. At least she didn't have to explain anything to Ajay about her reason for not going with him. If she had told him Priya was her only reason for staying married to Siva, he'd have tried his best to persuade her to go with him. And he wouldn't have had to try that hard. She'd go with him right that minute if she had it her way. But life wasn't that simple. She was tied down, and Priya was only part of her reason.

At least Ajay hadn't probed her about the pregnancy test like the women had. As soon as the men left the kitchen, Menaka and Chandni had cornered her and demanded an explanation. Although Menaka and Chandni didn't get along that well, somehow at that moment they worked as a team. Kaveri was also present, looking not at all pleased.

"Are you pregnant, Devika?" Chandni had asked. When Devika didn't say anything, Menaka had shouted.

"Really, Devika! At your age? Are you not ashamed?"

Devika had remained calm and all the while trying to find the right believable thing to say. The truth was she didn't know who the pregnancy-test-kit belonged to. All she knew was one of the girls sitting at the island had used it. When Kaveri had thrown the box onto the middle of the dining table, all eyes had been on the box except for Devika's. She'd looked over at the island and got a glimpse of Gangga's shock and Jamuna's fear. Even the boys had behaved rather strangely – fidgeting on their seats as if their bottoms were on fire. Only Priya had looked like she had no idea what was going on. But the rest four knew something about the pregnancy test-kit. Devika realized then that if she didn't resuscitate the moment, things would turn nasty. So, she'd said it was hers. And Menaka was right, she had been embarrassed. But it was her mortification versus the girls' demise – she chose the former.

"I thought I was, but I was wrong," she'd let out a nervous laugh, avoiding the piercing gazes.

"So, you're not pregnant?" Chandni had asked.

"Of course not. It was silly of me, really."

"What made you think you were?" asked Chandni again.

"Oh…I…well, I sort of missed my period…and, well, I…," she'd spluttered like a little kid learning to say the alphabet.

"You silly, silly woman!" Chandni had laughed. Everyone turned to look at her. "At this age, if you missed your period it's called menopause, not pregnancy! Although, you're a little young to be experiencing menopausal symptoms, but one can never tell. One of my friends, she was only thirty-nine when she started hot-flushes."

"But, Devika, why did you have to take the test here? And during a wedding too? Couldn't you have timed it better?" asked Menaka, bitter as usual.

"And Devika Aunty," Kaveri suddenly spoke, "Where is the actual kit? Why wasn't it in the bin?"

"That's because I didn't take the test here. I took it two weeks ago, and for some reason, I'd put the empty box in my purse. And this morning, while I was looking for something, I found the box and just chucked in into the bin. Careless of me, sorry." She had no idea how she could come up with such believable lie, but it had worked. Although Kaveri had eyed her rather oddly before leaving the kitchen.

"Stupid, if you asked me," Menaka had said. "What if Vikram had found it? Or one of the twins? You're lucky it was only Kaveri."

Devika didn't think it was at all lucky that Kaveri was the one who found the box. For the first time in her life, Devika was having qualms about Kaveri and her intentions toward her sisters. What she didn't understand was, number one: what was Kaveri doing going through the bin in the basement-bathroom, and number two: why did she have to announce her findings so brutally in front of the whole clan? What were her motives?

Thinking back now, she regretted telling Kaveri about Vikram and Jamuna. What if Kaveri misused the information? Devika was already inside the house when it occurred to her that Vikram and Jamuna had been arguing that morning. Dear God, was Jamuna pregnant? With Vikram's child? Devika felt faint suddenly. If something was going on between those two, then Ajay must be warned.

Feeling drained after a hectic morning, what with the breakfast chaos and Ajay's decision, Devika didn't feel like going upstairs and facing Menaka. She wasn't sure how to behave in front of Menaka. She found it strange and very unlike Menaka to not have confronted her about her relationship with Ajay. If Menaka had known for a long time, like Ajay had claimed, why wasn't she showing any animosity toward Devika? She was her normal self, and that intrigued Devika. Had Ajay got the wrong information? And then there was Chandni, as much as she didn't mind Ajay's sister, Devika didn't have the strength for Chandni's non-stop chatters. She decided to go back to the guest-room and take a breather. She needed time to think.

But when she opened the guest-room's door, she saw Priya sitting on the bed and staring outside the window, at the rain.

"Priya? What are you doing here?" Devika crossed the room and sat next to her daughter.

"Just wanted some time to myself." Priya turned toward her mother. "What're you doing here?"

"Came for some peace time myself," smiled Devika. She reached out and pushed a strand of hair away from Priya's face. "Priya, I want you to know something. The pregnancy test…"

"I know Mama, it wasn't yours."

"How did you know?"

"You would've told me if you took a pregnancy test. And besides, I saw the looks on Gangga's and Jamuna's face – something is not quite right."

"I know. I saw the looks too. I'm afraid to find out."

"You should tell Ajay Uncle."

"No, let me talk to the girls first. I just wish Kaveri hadn't been so reckless, so tactless. What was she thinking? Poor Ajay looked so devastated." Devika glanced out of the window.

"Sometimes I feel like Kaveri didi is not Ajay Uncle's daughter, she's so different from Gangga and Jamuna didi, don't you think?"

"She's just set in her ways; she's a lot like your Menaka Aunty. She's just different, that's all."

"And ruthless."

"Don't say that, honey."

"But she is. Ajay Uncle is so nice but she treats him so poorly. I feel sorry for Ajay Uncle. Do you know I often wish he was my father? I'd love to have a father like him…instead…"

Devika's body went cold. She shuddered. "Instead of what?"

"Sorry, I shouldn't have said anything," Priya looked away from her mother.

"Shouldn't have said what? Honey, is there something you're not telling me?" Devika's voice was masked with fear. Devika was not blind; she knew Siva and Priya didn't share a special bond. They rarely communicated and Siva often behaved like Priya didn't exist. Devika tried rectifying the problem, and it had been easier when Priya was younger. She didn't know any better. But as she grew up, she noticed how other fathers behaved with their daughters and she realized her relationship with her father was odd. But Devika consoled herself thinking she made up for it and convinced herself that Priya was happy, that she didn't really need a father figure in her life. But had she been wrong all along?

"Nothing, Mama. It's just that, well sometimes I wonder why my own father is so different with me. I can't remember the last time he said more than two words to me. I don't really care, but I often wondered how it'd feel to have a loving father…that's all."

Devika gathered Priya in her arms and held her close. She was tempted to tell Priya the truth, maybe this was her cue. Maybe she should spill it out now. But she knew Priya wouldn't be able to deal with the truth. No child would be happy knowing the father she'd known all her life was not her biological father. And how would all that reflect upon Devika as a mother and as a woman? But sometimes she felt tired, tired of the deceit and lies. And how long did she continue lying? As long as it took? And how long was that?

"You father is a good man," she heard herself saying. "He means well. Your Papa loves you. He's just a very quiet man and doesn't display his emotions well."

"Mama, do you trust him?" Priya's words hit her so hard that she had to lower herself slowly down onto the bed. What had possessed her daughter to come up such accusation?

"Honey, why do you say that?" she choked on the words. She almost regretted getting into this conversation with her daughter. Especially when Siva was not the unfaithful one.

"I just wondered that's all.

"Wondered?"

"And, I've caught him on the phone with someone a few times, in an intimate conversation…"

"He's always on the phone, his work is such, and you know that. It doesn't mean anything."

"Yeah, but why did he have to always end the conversation abruptly every time I walked into the room?"

"He did it with me too; he's a very private man, that's all."

"It doesn't make you suspicious?"

Devika allowed the idea of Siva having an affair to pool around her head but she couldn't bring herself to believe it. It was a ridiculous notion, almost made Devika want to laugh. He was so emotionally detached and there was not an ounce of romance in his soul. How could he cheat on her? And with whom? He wasn't even good in bed. In fact, sex was dreadful with him. It was almost as if he had to compel himself to have sex with her and when they eventually stopped having sex a year into their marriage, he'd looked more relaxed and at ease. As if having sex with her had been a chore. How could he be capable of cheating on her?

And intimate conversations? Siva had never once said 'I love you' to her in all the years they'd been married. Siva did spend a lot of time on the phone. If there was one thing Siva was passionate about, it was his work. But, oh, how a part of Devika wished Priya was not wrong.

Chapter fourteen – Gangga

Gangga sat in Jamuna's room and waited for Mrs. Mehra. She was not looking forward to be transformed into a demure Indian bride. And she wasn't alien to the discomfort of being clad in a sari. She'd worn a sari before, on a number of occasions and no matter how many times she tried, she could never master the art of tying a sari. The long piece of cloth seemed to go to eternity as she wrapped it around her like one would a gauze roll to wrap a wound, snug but not too tight. Although everyone had marveled at how gorgeous she'd looked in a sari at Kaveri's wedding, she still found it hard to acquire the elegance that came with wearing one. How could she focus on elegance when each step she took required her full attention? She remembered walking with extra caution in case she tripped or in case the sari came loose around her. Since, really, all that was involved in securing a sari to the waist was a mere tuck into the petticoat – that was it! No pins or clips were used to make sure it stayed there. But women had been clad in saris for centuries, so obviously the tucking method proved efficient. Still, she needed assurance. For her wedding, she was going to insist that Mrs. Mehra used a safety pin or two or however many it took to go around her waist to attach the sari to her petticoat.

The door suddenly opened and Gangga glanced over expecting to see Mrs. Mehra, instead Jamuna walked in and handed her a cold face-cloth.

"Here," Jamuna said. "Mrs. Mehra asked me to give you this. She said to pad your face with the cloth, don't ask me why."

"Where is she?"

"Should be here shortly, I think she's helping Mama with the trays."

"Good, Jamuna, have you decided what you plan on doing?"

"No, didi, I haven't. And Jason's being so aloof; I don't know how to talk to him. And, didi, even if I did talk to him, what should I say?"

"What do you want to say?" Gangga put the cloth on her face and gave out a little yelp. "Shit, talk about rude-awakening! This thing is damn cold."

"It was in the freezer. Do you think Devika Aunty suspects something?" Gangga noticed Jamuna's divergence. She clearly wasn't keen on talking about Jason and their future together – if there was one. But Gangga was concerned for her sister.

"Not sure," Gangga said. "But what she did for us was priceless. We should talk to her. But for now I think we need to focus on you and what you plan on doing."

"No, didi. For now we should focus on you and your wedding. I'm sorry to have caused all these worries. This is your day, your big day. I want you to enjoy every bit of it and please, don't worry about me. I'm a big girl." Jamuna looked flustered and sickly. Gangga reached out and took Jamuna's hand in hers.

"I do worry about you, so don't tell me not to. You must talk to Jason and decide what you guys want to do. And, Jamuna, this is your life. Don't let our parents decide your future for you."

"You're one to talk, didi. Sorry, but isn't that what you're doing?"

Gangga became quiet. The truth stung but it was the truth nonetheless.

"It's not your fault or mine or Kaveri didi's," said Jamuna. "We're brought up to respect our elders and our tradition. The thing with us is we don't know how to behave otherwise, didi. Even if we wanted to we wouldn't because we don't know how to. Look at me, I love Jason and I know I can never love any other man as much as I love him but when it comes to marrying him, I can't do it. I can't defy our parents."

Just then the door opened and Mrs. Mehra walked in with what looked like a bamboo-basket. It was her vanity case. She smiled at the girls and placed the basket on the bed. Jamuna excused herself and left Gangga alone with Mrs. Mehra. Gangga watched her sister leave and wondered whether Jamuna had been right. Whether tradition had molded them such that even if they tried, they wouldn't be able to break it. Were they victims of culture and society that created such tradition? What about the generation after them? Would their children pay the same price? When it came to her daughter's time to get married, would she and Subash arrange her marriage? Gangga shivered at the thought of Subash. After the last call, she hadn't heard from him. His earlier words still echoed in her ears once in a while, reminding her over and over what a disgrace she was.

The hours passed by so fast and brusquely that Gangga was getting more nervous with each ticking second.

"*Arre*, Gangga, relax," Mrs. Mehra's sing-song voice shook her back to the present. "Every bride is nervous on her wedding day. Look at you, you're shaking and beta, why are you so pale? Are you feeling okay?"

Gangga winched as Mrs. Mehra pinched her cheeks to get blood flowing into her vain.

"I'm fine, Mrs. Mehra."

"Okay, let's do your nails first since they need time to dry. Then you can relax and we can do your make-up."

"Sure. How long will the make-up take?" asked Gangga. She wanted to talk to Jamuna and Devika before the wedding. She was going off with Subash after the reception and would not be back for a week from their honeymoon. If she didn't talk to Jamuna and Devika now, she might have to wait for a whole week and who knew what would happen during that period.

"About three hours," Mrs. Mehra said.

Three hours! That was ridiculously long.

Mrs. Mehra brought out some nail polishes from her basket and set to work on Gangga's nails. As she applied the blood-red nail polish, Mrs. Mehra started humming some old Hindi song tune. Gangga grimaced at her nail-color. Why couldn't Mrs. Mehra use some fancy, retro color? But she knew red was an auspicious color for a bride and the nail-polish had to match her red bridal sari. Gangga observed Mrs. Mehra as the older lady meticulously applied her nail polish and wondered how long she had been married and whether hers had been an arranged marriage as well.

Probably. And she probably had been a virgin too. Gangga sighed.

"Such a deep sigh can only mean one thing," Mrs. Mehra said.

Gangga lifted her eye brow.

"Anxiety," said Mrs. Mehra again. "It's never easy for girls, you know. Getting married is a big deal. It's a new beginning to a new life. A lot of adjustment to do, not only to the husband but his parents. But you know what they say, love conquers all."

"Was yours an arranged marriage?" Gangga clamped her mouth shut immediately for suddenly asking such a personal question. But Mrs. Mehra threw her head back and laughed heartily.

"No, it wasn't."

Gangga cocked her head. "No way!"

"I know it's shocking. But I fell in love with *him* before he became my husband. Love at first sight, and it truly was."

"Where did you meet him?"

"My father was a teacher in India. And my husband used to take arithmetic lessons from him. He was a few years older than me. I remember hiding behind the walls of my father's living room and admiring my husband. I admired him for a long time until he finally noticed me." Mrs. Mehra paused on her task and glanced out at the window with a distant look in her pale eyes.

"How did you get married?" asked Gangga, feeling excited and hopeful. If Mrs. Mehra had a love-marriage, then surely there was some hope. Surely tradition could be meddled with.

"Oh, one evening he came to my house and asked my parents for my hand in marriage."

Gangga's shoulders slumped as disappointment hit her. It had been an arranged marriage after all. She felt subjugated.

"But it hadn't been easy," Mrs. Mehra said. She diverted her eyes back to Gangga's fingers and started working on her nails.

"What hadn't been easy?"

"Getting my parents' approval. There had been a lot of uncertainty and my father wasn't convinced my husband would make me happy. He was very young at that time, still in college and so was I."

"So what made them agree?"

"Oh...I shouldn't go there. It's embarrassing. And also I shouldn't corrupt you with my stories," she said, waving a hand around wearily.

"You're not corrupting me," laughed Gangga. Really, how old did

Mrs. Mehra think she was, twelve? "Tell me, please. Whatever you did must've been the right thing to do, look at you now? Aren't you happily married?"

It was Mrs.Mehra's turn to laugh. And laugh she did. "Yes, I am very happy. And you're right; it must've been the right thing to do."

"Definitely. So, what was it?"

Mrs. Mehra looked at Gangga unsurely. Then she shrugged her shoulders.

"What the hell. You're getting married and this happened twenty years ago. It's not like this is going to affect you or your wedding in any manner."

"You're absolutely right. So, what did you do?"

"Well, I slept with him."

Gangga gasped.

"Yes, I did and my parents caught us together one day and that was it. It was either marriage or family reputation going down the drain."

"Wow. You were not a virgin bride then?"

"No, love, I wasn't. And I have no regrets. And besides, who cares if a girl is a virgin or not anymore, this is the twenty-first century."

"If only you knew. But, I salute you. What would've happened if your parents had objected?"

"Oh, we had a plan. We were going to elope."

Gangga stared at Mrs. Mehra with newfound respect. At least she had more guts than both Gangga and Jamuna combined. And this was twenty years ago.

"See, Gangga, it all comes down to love. If you believe in your love for each other, nothing else really counts."

"Not even tradition? Culture? Society? Because, Mrs.Mehra, after all is said and done, we still have to face the bigger crowd, don't we?"

"True, but what are tradition, culture and society and how crucial are they to your life? If you're thinking of a life that's confined to these elements then yes, you have to worry about it. But, in this day and age, your life is your own. If I had sat around, worrying about my society and tradition back in those days, I would've married one of my second cousins and given birth to unhealthy children. I wouldn't have married Mr. Mehra and found my happiness. I'm surprised you're talking about all these, Gangga. Are you not happy with this marriage?"

Gangga looked down at her nails. Mrs. Mehra's revelation had jolted her senses. She was beginning to doubt her decision to marry Subash. She loved him but did she love him enough to go ahead with a ceremony that, according to Hinduism, tied them together for the next seven lives? Was she right in taking such a big leap with someone who thought she was a disgrace for not having safeguarded her virginity? And what happened if Subash used this power over her for the rest of their lives together? What if she was rendered inferior and secondary in this union called marriage?

"Gangga?" Mrs. Mehra's voice nudged her again. "You're in very deep thought. What're you thinking?"

"Nothing. They look pretty," Gangga looked at her finished polished fingers. The red actually complemented the golden henna designs on her hands.

"You have beautiful fingers. And whoever did your henna did a wonderful job. Such intricate designs, very beautiful."

"Oh, it was one of Mama's friends who did it yesterday," said Gangga looking at reddish brown flowery patterns that adorned her hands.

"Very nice. Now, just relax for a few minutes. I'll come back in half an hour and work on your hair. Should I get some tea for you?"

"No, thanks. But if you see Jamuna can you ask her to come and keep me company?"

"Sure, beta." Mrs. Mehra was at the door when she turned back to look at Gangga. "And, Gangga, everyone finds their soul-mate in different ways. Don't take what I've said to heart and don't base that to judge your relationship. We all have our own stories, and you have yours. Remember, in the end, it's all about love."

Gangga watched the door close behind Mrs. Mehra and thought she was going to be sick. Her head swirled with questions. Was she right in marrying Subash? Should she be marrying Subash?

The door opened and Jamuna walked in with a glass of juice.

"How's the bride doing?"

"Miserable." Gangga gulped down the juice and felt even more wretched. If only she knew what the right thing to do was.

"What's wrong, didi?"

Gangga threw Jamuna an exasperated look. That was when Gangga decided, if she couldn't revive her life by not marrying Subash, she could at least salvage Jamuna's life. It wasn't too late for Jamuna. She turned to face Jamuna.

"Jamuna, you can control your own destiny, I know you can." Gangga peered hard at Jamuna.

"Didi, what're you talking about?"

"If Mrs. Mehra could change *kismet*, so can you!"

"Okay, you were here only for half an hour with Mrs. Mehra, did she hypnotize you?"

"Jamuna, Mrs. Mehra defied her family and slept with her husband before they were married and as a result, they got married. Don't you see? She interfered with fate and she found her happily-ever-after."

"But..."

"And you know what else? She said in the end it's all about love. If she could do it twenty years ago, in India, don't you think twenty years later, you can do it, in Canada?"

"Didi, she married a Mr. Mehra."

"So?"

"He's an Indian, a Brahmin on top of that. Do you think her family would've agreed if she had slept with a white guy or a non-Brahmin for that matter?"

"Well, I asked her what she'd have done if the family hadn't agreed and you know what she said?"

Gangga didn't wait for an answer, "That they were prepared to elope!"

"Are you suggesting I eloped?" Jamuna gasped.

"No, well not exactly. All I'm asking you is to give Jason a chance, give your life with him a chance and the life within you a chance."

"Even if it meant I have to defy Papa and Mama?"

"You don't know that yet. They may not disapprove of Jason."

"Didi, are you kidding me? Do you honestly think Papa would be okay with me marrying Jason?"

Gangga slowly shook her head after a moment of silence.

"And, didi, why don't you alter your destiny? Why *are* you marrying Subash? Don't you think you deserve someone better, someone who respects you for who you are?"

"Because I don't think there's anyone out there who'd marry me for who or what I am. I mean, I'm thirty years old, not a virgin, I work in a restaurant – which Indian man in his right mind would marry me?"

"Confusing, since you don't care if I married a non-Indian."

"But I want you to be happy and I know Jason makes you happy. And I don't have a non-Indian guy crazy about me like Jason is about you."

"What if there was? Would you marry him?"

Gangga couldn't answer, for she didn't know. She'd dated non-Indian men, but had never once contemplated marriage.

"Now didi, I need to ask you for a favor," Jamuna said.

"I don't like the sound of this."

"I want you to promise me that you'd stop worrying about me and concentrate on enjoying your day. Promise me."

"I promise."

"Good. I'm going to go and help Chandni Aunty with the flower garlands. Now relax and think of your wedding." Jamuna kissed her on both cheeks and left the room.

Gangga closed her eyes and sighed. As soon as she thought of Subash, his earlier words rang in her ears brutally. She forced her eyelids open and groaned.

"What the fuck is the right thing to do?" She looked around the room she was in and was overcome with sudden claustrophobia.

"I need to get out of here and think." Gangga stood up and headed for the living room.

Chapter fifteen – Jamuna

Jamuna entered the living room and almost gagged on the strong smell of jasmine that wafted toward her. Chandni was sitting on the couch making long, endless garlands with the white jasmine buds. Reluctantly, and praying for her gag reflex to remain under control, Jamuna joined her aunt. She took a piece of cut-up string and grabbed a handful of the white buds. She brought them to her lap and resisted the urge to throw them back on the table. Usually Jamuna loved the smell of jasmine, but not that day. It nauseated her. She brushed at her nose with the end of her sleeve.

"What's the matter?" asked Chandni. "Too strong?"

"Yeah," Jamuna looked away quickly. This was unbearable. How was she going to survive the rest of the day without feeling sick? And how was she going to survive the next nine months?

Jamuna had finally taken the pregnancy test – with Gangga's assurance and Vikram's patience. Gangga had gone into the basement's bathroom and brought the pregnancy test-kit for Jamuna. That was when Gangga had bumped into Kaveri. How Jamuna wished Gangga had taken the box the kit came in as well. Too late now, Kaveri already found it.

Jamuna had gone into her bathroom and had taken the test. She'd stood calmly and watched as the red lines formed on the kit. First her heart had flipped as she saw only one horizontal line forming across the tiny window. Then her heart double-flipped as another line formed vertically across the horizontal line. She stood staring at it for a long time before breaking down into loud sobs, in between which she'd been violently sick again – more due to anxiety than morning sickness. But she'd braced herself, taken a bath, and put on something vibrant like her yellow salwar-kameez and had gone to answer the door, just to see Kaveri's husband and in-laws. But she hadn't minded. The more people in the house, the easier it'd be to cope with her misery. At least she'd be distracted enough not to think about her predicament.

But Gangga had cornered her just before breakfast and led her back down to the basement, to be far away from everyone. Vikram and Jason were already there waiting for them.

"Tell us," Gangga had demanded.

Jamuna remember glancing up at Jason but his eyes were not on her. He was engrossed with the rain outside as if it were raining gold.

"Jamuna?" Gangga had sounded impatient.

"I'm pregnant," she was looking at Jason as she said it, but he didn't flicker a muscle nor did he turn to look at her. He kept staring at the rain through the window.

Vikram groaned before hitting a fist on the couch. "Fuck!"

"I know," said Jamuna.

"What now?" asked Vikram.

"I don't know," replied Jamuna, looking at her hands. Gangga threw her arms around her sister and had hugged her tight. Jamuna had wondered why Jason wasn't doing the same. Why wasn't he by her side, convincing her that everything would be all right?

That was when Priya had walked in and announced breakfast was served. And during breakfast, of course Kaveri had done the unthinkable by producing the evidence. If not for Devika Aunty taking the blame, or rather, the responsibility, Jamuna was sure she'd be dragging her suitcases down the road out in the rain.

Jamuna sighed deeply thinking of what awaited her the next day, after the wedding. Was she doomed? Would her father disown her? And Jason? He hadn't said a word to her all day. Why would he when he thought she wasn't worthy to be the mother of his child. Jamuna wished she knew what Jason thought now that he knew she was definitely pregnant. But she didn't know where Jason was. Or Vikram for that matter. Maybe they were in the basement. How she wished she could have some time alone with Jason. All she really wanted was someone to tell her everything would be all right.

"Jamuna, can you finish the rest?" suddenly Chandni's voice rang in her ears. "I have to go help with the laddoos."

Jamuna gave her aunt a meek nod and continued making little loops in the thread and inserting a bulb of jasmine into each loop before pulling it tight around the flower. She wasn't sure what the garlands were for, but it kept her busy. She was deep in her thoughts and task at hand when someone tugged at her arm. She looked up to see Kaveri's husband, Raj, standing next to her, looking smug and rather handsome in a grey sweater and a pair of worn-out jeans. He smiled down at her with dark, bold eyes. Jamuna noticed his straight hair combed back perfectly with not a single strand out of place. Raj was immaculate, in every way possible.

"Need some help?" Raj lowered himself on the couch next to Jamuna.

"I don't know, do you know how to make a garland?" Jamuna smiled. She'd always liked Raj. She knew he flirted with everyone that walked in a skirt, but he was always sweet with her. And he *was* her brother-in-law. She respected him.

"Do I know how to make a garland?" Raj mused.

Jamuna looked at him sideways.

"Do I know how to make a garland??" he repeated rather dramatically, his dark pupils danced with mirth.

Jamuna started laughing, "Yes, do you?"

"Err…Nope!"

"I thought so. Now, watch and learn." Jamuna slowed her pace and showed Raj how to make a loop with the thread and insert the flower into it before pulling it tight.

"That's so easy, here let me try." Raj got hold of a thread and started doing the loop. But his large, unfeminine fingers were too clumsy that he wasn't succeeding. Jamuna watched him and started giggling.

"You have to be gentle and patient," she explained as she demonstrated again.

"Right, in other word, like how I'd treat a woman."

"Okay, sure. Are you watching?"

"I am. But I don't think I can do it, sorry." Raj threw the thread on the table and sat back. Jamuna grumbled that he gave up too easily.

"That's me, I have little patience."

"I see that."

"But I have a lot of patience when it comes to beautiful women."

"Very obvious. You're lucky Kaveri didi married you. At the rate you're going, you'd be an old Don Juan – wifeless!"

"Not sure whether I call it luck," sighed Raj.

"Jijaji, can I ask you something?" Jamuna sounded serious all of a sudden. She wanted to talk to someone and Raj seemed like that someone.

"What? Pyar ka issue?" *Love issue?*

"Sort of, I'm confused," Jamuna fiddled with the half-finished garland in her hands. "When you married Kaveri didi, how did you know she was the one? I mean, if our parents didn't approach each other and discuss marriage, would you still have married Kaveri didi?"

Raj grunted and stretched his long legs out in front of him. Jamuna immediately regretted asking him anything. Maybe he wasn't at ease talking about his personal life.

"Sorry, jijaji, I didn't..."

"Don't be. Jamuna, there's something you should know about my marriage to your sister," Raj paused as if trying to find the right words. Jamuna felt something tight forming in her stomach. She didn't like how Raj sounded.

"I don't love your sister, never will. It's not her, it's me. I'm just not in love with her."

Taken aback by such brusque revelation, Jamuna asked, "Then why did you marry her?"

"Because if I didn't, my father wasn't going to make me his heir."

His answer had been simple, straight forward and it frightened her. She scooted farther from Raj.

"Look, Jamuna. I'm not sure why you're confused and who you're in love with. But, as someone with more experience than you, my advice is – don't bother falling in love because it's a waste of time."

Jamuna looked at Raj, seeing him differently for the first time.

"I fell in love with someone, in fact am still in love with her. And I was going to marry her. Hell, I've even proposed. And she said yes. But, I forgot, we don't have the right to live our lives as we want. Our parents use their wealth as ammunition against us."

"And their wealth is important because?"

"Because in the end I'm nothing without it. Everything I am now, everything that I own is courtesy of Mr. Dhillon. Sr. I work for him. I mean, look at me, all I really am in my company is a puppet. I may be the Managing Director of a multimillion dollar company, but who really comes to me for anything? Dad runs the company and my life."

"How much did you love this other person?"

"I loved… I love her very much and she will always be in my life. Look, it's a little more than that; she's a white-girl."

Jamuna gasped before lowering her gaze to the flowers in her hand – the white jasmine that was no longer the only reason for her nausea. Raj flashed her a quick look and his eyes widened with understanding.

"Don't do it, Jamuna. End it now. You won't ever find happiness otherwise. At least if you end it now, when the time comes for you to finally get married, you'd be over him. And that way you wouldn't despise the person you're married to. Every minute with him wouldn't be a torture. Every word that comes out of his mouth wouldn't be a nag. Every breath you take with him in your life wouldn't feel suffocating…" Raj looked at the flowers in Jamuna's hand and reached out to touch them. Jamuna pulled her hands back. She wasn't sure she respected Raj any longer.

"Jijaji, is the other person still in your life?" her voice quivered. Was her brother-in-law cheating on her sister?

"Susan will always be in my life." Then, "Shit!"

But it was too late. He'd already mentioned her name and Jamuna stared at him in horror.

"Susan Thomas?" her voice was softer than a whisper.

"Look, Jamuna, I…" Raj reached out and held her hands in his. Jamuna didn't pull her hands back this time, she wasn't thinking clearly. She didn't know what to think or how to feel. The shock had rendered her brain-dead.

Susan Thomas was Kaveri's best friend. She was someone Kaveri hung out with all the time before she got married and even after she got married. Jamuna couldn't think the number of times Susan had spent the evenings in their house while Kaveri still lived there. They were like sisters, Kaveri and Susan. Kaveri always made it clear to her and Gangga that she had Susan who was better than the two of them combined. Jamuna didn't really know Susan all that well. Susan never really bothered with her or acknowledged her. In short, Susan treated her just like Kaveri did. Kaveri was very proud of Susan that she flaunted her in front of everyone. And Susan had the most responsibilities during Kaveri's wedding. She behaved like she was family. She even wore a sari for the wedding. How long had she been sleeping with her best friend's husband? Jamuna shuddered. She was feeling sick again. She was about the get up when she realized her hands very clasped tightly within Raj's. But before she could shrug her hands from Raj's grasp, a loud, deafening scream loomed over them like a vicious thunder.

"JAMUNA!!!!!"

The voice shook both Jamuna and Raj so fiercely they jolted in their seats and turned around. Kaveri was standing behind them with eyes as wide as an owl's and flaring nose.

"Kaveri didi?" Jamuna stood up.

"Why, you conniving little slut! What the hell do you think you're doing with my husband?"

"She wasn't doing anything," Raj said. He stood up and approached his wife with a look of distaste on his handsome face. "We were just talking. Don't make a big deal out of this."

"Don't make a big deal? Do you think I'm some sort of a school girl who doesn't know anything? Do you think I can't tell? You were sitting there flirting with her, go on, admit it!"

"Grow up, Kaveri. We were just talking and I was trying to help Jamuna with the garlands."

"And I'm supposed to believe that?"

"Frankly, I don't care if you do," said Raj and walked past Kaveri when he was blocked by others who'd appeared from out of nowhere.

Everyone stood around gaping like chimpanzees on the highway – clueless and awestruck. Devika and Menaka had arrived at the scene in haste, with bewildered eyes. Chandni was looking more amused than anything. Gangga had also materialized in the scene, as had Mrs. Mehra. Jamuna noticed the men were not there, blessedly enough.

"What's going on?" Menaka demanded in a rushed, impatient voice. Jamuna glanced from Raj to Kaveri to Menaka and fell mute.

"Why don't you ask that daughter of yours?" Kaveri pointed a malicious finger at Jamuna. All eyes fell on her and Jamuna wished at that point that the earth would open up and swallow her whole. She felt her cheeks flaming. Why was Kaveri creating such a scene? Did her sister really believe she was after her husband?

"Jamuna?" Menaka's voice boomed again. "Do you want to tell me what's going on?"

Jamuna looked at her mother and couldn't find her voice. She felt choked. Tears were starting to form at the brim of her eyes. Jamuna suddenly felt Gangga's arm around her and buried her face into her sister's chest.

"For fuck's sake," Kaveri swore. "Stop being such a drama-queen. She was flirting with my husband, that's what she was doing."

The room went still. Then Jamuna heard the sharp sound of someone being slapped followed by Kaveri's painful moan. Thinking Raj had slapped his wife; Jamuna looked up from Gangga's bosom only to see Menaka standing in front of Kaveri, with a stern expression.

"Have you no manners, Kaveri? And no respect for others?"

"Mama, should you not be saying that to that slut?"

"Kaveri! Watch your mouth. I will not allow such indecent words in my house," Menaka said.

"But you'll allow indecent behaviors? This is a bloody joke! What's the matter, Mama? Don't you believe me? Do you think I'd make something like that up? I saw them together, sitting here, in an intimate position…"

"Enough Kaveri," Raj interrupted. "We were making some garlands and Jamuna was showing me how to do them, that was all. Get a grip, Kaveri. You've created enough hullabaloos for one day!" Raj looked at his wife disgustedly as if she was an annoying insect waiting to be crushed and walked out of the living room.

"Yeah, sure, walk away. Why don't you be a man and own up?" shouted Kaveri but Raj was gone.

"Kaveri didi, I think you need to calm down," Gangga said.

"I don't need to take any advice from you, Gangga. Oh, just so that you all know, there really isn't going to be any wedding today. Subash had called it off when he found out our Gangga here wasn't a virgin!" Kaveri said snootily. She crossed her hands over her chest as if she'd achieved the impossible. Jamuna watched her elder sister and for the first time in her entire life, felt a deep hatred building inside of her. Kaveri was, without a doubt, a vile person.

"What are you talking about?" demanded Menaka. The room once again had become cold. The rain splashed against the window, creating whimsical sounds. Jamuna wished the rain had some kind of a magical power, where once someone stood under it; it could strip them of their worries and problems and sluice them clean. Now, if only.

"Rubbish!" said Gangga. "That's what she's talking, pure rubbish. Did Subash call you and cancel the wedding? He sure didn't say anything to me."

"Liar!" yelled Kaveri. "What are you going to tell everyone when he doesn't show up at the wedding hall?"

"Nothing, because he will show up."

"Besharam!" *Shameless*. Menaka shook her head. "I always knew you were not fond of your sisters, but this is going too far, Kaveri. It's your sister's wedding today. Can you not be happy for her instead of creating such dramas? And why would you accuse Jamuna of going after your husband? Are you and Raj having problems?"

Kaveri, for once, was speechless.

"Are you, Kaveri? Or do you just enjoy seeing your sisters get humiliated? First, you did it at breakfast. Now, here. Where are you going to cause a scene next, at the wedding?" asked Menaka. Although her voice was calmer, her eyes still bore the same hard expression.

"Mama, I expected at least you to be on my side," Kaveri's voice had gone small.

"I'm not on anyone's side. If you're having problems with your husband you shouldn't be taking it out on others, Kaveri. Talk about it."

"What? With you?"

"Why not?"

"Hah! That's a good one, Mama. But you know what, at least I'm cautious. I'm not going to make the same mistake you did."

"Mistake?"

"Is that how you talk to your mother?" Chandni butted in only to be told to mind her own business.

"This has got nothing to do with you, Chandni Aunty," Kaveri gave her aunt a depraved look. Chandni shook her head and exited the room. Mrs. Mehra followed her silently. Devika who'd been quiet all these while turned around to go as well. Jamuna saw her mother's gaunt face and felt a pang of pity for her. Why would Kaveri talk down to their mother? But at the same time she couldn't help being curious.

Kaveri started moving toward the door when Menaka stopped her.

"What did you mean, Kaveri?"

Jamuna watched as Kaveri slowly turned to look at their mother and with a chilling voice said, "I'm not going to lose my husband to my sister."

Everyone, except for Chandni, heard the comment and watched Menaka's face turn pastel like a corpse's. But only Jamuna saw someone else's face that went through the same transformation – Devika's. And, for the third time that morning, she ran to the bathroom to be sick all over again.

Chapter sixteen – Menaka

She walked into the kitchen to find Chandni arranging some trays. Menaka quickly retraced her steps back and away from the kitchen. She didn't know how much Chandni heard but it was enough to make her sister-in-law prod her with questions. Menaka just wanted to be alone for a few minutes; to calm her nerves. What had gotten into Kaveri that day? Why such outburst and accusations? And what did she mean when she said she didn't want to lose her husband to her sister? Was she deluded to think Jamuna and Raj were in a relationship? Menaka didn't know what caused her eldest daughter to walk around with such bitterness in her. *It's all this Ajay's fault,* she carped. If only he'd been a bit more loving toward Kaveri, like he was with Gangga and Jamuna, she wouldn't have turned out this way – bitter and suspicious.

The only place Menaka could think of to be alone was her bedroom. She walked to the room and prayed Ajay wouldn't be there. She passed Gangga, Jamuna and Devika in the living room. They were whispering something, with their heads touching. She stopped and observed. Jamuna looked pale and sickly. Why had she run off to the bathroom in such manner? And why did she look so withdrawn, like life was sucked out of her? Then her eyes fell on Gangga. It was her big day and so much had happened to taint it. Menaka hoped it wasn't some sort of bad omen. What had Kaveri meant by there not being a wedding? Where did she even come up with such crap? And what was this new thing about Gangga not being a virgin? Menaka suddenly clutched her chest. What was happening? Why did she have this foreboding feeling that she didn't know her children at all? Had she not been a good mother to them? Even now, look at them; clutching on to Devika like she was their savior. Just as her eyes settled on Devika, her sister turned around and their eyes locked for the briefest second. Devika quickly darted her eyes away, as it the sight of Menaka had stung her.

Feeling absolutely wretched, Menaka hurried to her room. Ajay wasn't there. She locked her door behind her and fell against it. She felt drained and humiliated. How on earth did Kaveri know about Ajay's affair? And why did she have to bring it up in front of everyone? Damn this Ajay. He'd ruined everything for her, everything. Now that Kaveri knew, Menaka was sure Raj knew as well. And how long would it be before The Dhillons heard about it? And Chandni and Mahesh? Then there was Devika and Siva! Oh, Mrs. Mehra had been there too. How long was it before everyone knew about it and laughed at her on her back? How long?

"*God, I really need to steady my nerves.*"

After checking to make sure the door was properly secured, Menaka reached over to her side-table. She opened the bottom drawer and withdrew a bottle of scotch. She then went into the bathroom and searched for a cup. There wasn't any.

"*Oh, what the hell.*"

Menaka unscrewed the lid of the bottle and took a long swig of the drink. Then she took another one. She sat on her bed and took one last gulp before putting the bottle away. Then she fell flat on her bed and closed her eyes.

She didn't know how long she was asleep. She woke up to a loud pounding on the door. At first she was confused. Why was someone pounding on her door so bloody loudly? It was adding to her headache. Where was she? Then she heard Ajay's voice asking her to open the door.

Slowly she eased herself off the bed, feeling disoriented. She was reaching for the door handle, wondering why it was locked in the first place, when it all came back to her.

She opened the door and saw Ajay's face – the usual calmness was replaced with a deep fury. He walked into the room and slammed the door.

"What were you doing?" he hissed. "And why was the door locked?"

"Please, Ajay. I've got a headache. What time is it?"

"Were you sleeping? God, Menaka, there's a wedding on in less than four hours and you were sleeping? What is wrong with you?"

Menaka snapped. It was real easy for Ajay to waltz in there and accuse her of what…what did he accuse her of? She couldn't think. Menaka plopped onto the bed and cradled her head in her hand.

"Menaka…"

"Look, Ajay, I know there's a wedding on, so please save the lecture. Can you leave me alone? I need to be alone."

"We all need to be alone. Can you please, for this one day, I beg you – please, please don't drink and create a scene?"

The anger that hit Menaka was hideous and strong. She stood up and brought her hands to her hips.

"I create a scene? *I*? Where were you just now when your daughter was going around accusing everyone of infidelity and treachery? Where were you when your daughter told me, to my face, in front of everyone and Mrs. Mehra, that she was not going to make the same mistake I did? Where were you when she told everyone that she isn't going to let her husband be seduced by her sister like mine did…" Menaka paused. She plopped back onto the bed.

She looked up at Ajay and saw all colors draining from his face.

"That was what she meant, I get it now," she said slowly as realization dawned on her.

"Menaka, you're tired. Maybe you do need a rest," Ajay said quickly. But it was the wrong thing to say. It set Menaka thinking.

"Ajay…tell me something," she paused as if trying to compose herself. "Is it Devika you're sleeping with?"

"Menaka, now you've really lost it…"

"Please don't patronize me. For once, Ajay, for once – be honest with me."

Menaka watched as Ajay stood in front of her. She couldn't read his expression. But dread was creeping up on her slow and steady.

"Ajay? Are you sleeping with my sister?" her voice was rougher, heavier as if it carried the weight of her chest.

Then, "No, Menaka, I'm not." He said it with such straight face that she almost believed him…almost. But he darted his eyes from her face too quickly that she doubted him. She wanted so badly to believe him, but how could she when throughout their lives together he'd been cheating on her?

"I have to go get the cars organized. Are you coming?" He still wasn't looking at her.

She didn't answer him. She got up and walked into the bathroom. Menaka held on to the sink to help balance herself. Her headache had worsened and she felt dizzy. She looked up and saw her reflection in the mirror above the sink. Her hair which was in a bun had come loosed around her face. Her mascara was smudged, as was her lipstick. Menaka grimaced. She didn't like the face that was staring back at her. The face of a loser. She'd failed to be a good wife and a good mother. Menaka flashed some cold water over her face. But it did nothing to recover her mood. She felt defeated. And, as much as she'd like to hold Ajay responsible for her condition, she couldn't. Deep down she knew the fault had never been his. It had always been hers. She'd been bitter about her marriage and the man she'd married to since the day she got married.

Marrying Ajay had been her duty. She did it for her parents' sake. She owed them that much, and was constantly reminded of, for bringing her up and giving her a good education. She hadn't wanted to marry Ajay or anyone else, not at that time. She'd been young and vigorous and life awaited her with open arms. She'd just finished college and was eager to experience life as a career woman. She'd wanted to know how it felt to be working in an office, to get paid, to manage her own finances. She'd wanted independence. She'd wanted to buy her own house, her own car and maybe one day, get married. But it wasn't on the top of her agenda. She'd wanted to finally live. But she was forced to get married as soon as she finished college. Of course, she'd thrown a tantrum. She'd created havoc. She swore she'd not get married. But, in the end, it all came down to respecting her parents and appreciating their sacrifices. She'd lost.

When she saw Ajay, sitting in the mandap dressed as a groom, her initial feeling had been hatred. She hated the man who stole her dreams from her. And she'd behaved in the only way she knew how – rude and insolent. She'd refused to adapt to the life of a submissive wife. She was educated. She was smart. Why should she be inferior to a man just because he married her? She loathed Ajay and his gentle manners.

He tried too hard to please her and it made her despise him more. At least if he'd treated her the same way it'd been easier for her to be herself. Then she became pregnant. Not once, three times. And her life was deduced to being a mother and a wife. Since Ajay was used to her tempers and rudeness, Menaka didn't bother improving. She had too much on her plate with three kids and the last thing on her mind was Ajay's happiness and her marriage. He was there, provided for her and the kids, and gave her a status in the society and that was enough. Never once did Menaka worry about her marriage, it had been immaterial. As far as she was concerned, her marriage had destroyed the life she'd dreamt of having. Marriage had rendered her helpless and useless.

Menaka looked at her face in the mirror again and shook her head. She realized she'd pushed Ajay away; she'd pushed him into another woman's arms and life. What scared her now was what if that woman was Devika? What if she'd pushed her husband into the arms of her sister? But, surely Devika wouldn't betray her? And what about Siva? Was her sister capable of cheating on her nice, sweet husband? Menaka straightened herself and started combing her hair. She washed her face and applied new make-up. She was going to get to the root of everything and she was determined to do it fast. For once she wanted to know what went on in everyone's lives under her roof. She wanted to know why her daughters behaved the way they did. And she wanted to know if Devika was sleeping with her husband. She knew there was a wedding on, but that was not going to stop her.

Chapter seventeen – Kaveri

Kaveri locked herself in the bathroom and sat on the toilet bowl, inhaling her third consecutive cigarette. But they were not doing their job. She wasn't feeling any better. Her nerves were twitching like they were being fried on a hot pan. She was anxious and very angry. Everything had backfired. Instead of making Jamuna look like a fool, she'd ended up looking like one. Oh, the audacity of it all! And her mother – since when did she switch sides? Kaveri felt alone, like she had many times as a child. She felt alone and unloved. At least when she'd been a child, she could run to Devika Aunty and be comforted. She wouldn't dream of doing that now. Devika Aunty had become one of them, one of her enemies since that morning, since Kaveri saw her aunt kissing her father out in the deck.

After the fiasco at breakfast that morning, Kaveri had confronted Raj and had accused him of not standing by her in front of everyone. Raj had shrugged and said it was her battle and he wanted no part of it.

"You're useless!" she had said.

"Not as useless as you are. What were you thinking, creating such a drama at breakfast? You looked stupid and childish, Kaveri. I hope you realize that," Raj pointed out.

"What do you care if I looked stupid?" Raj knew how to hurt her with words.

"Actually, I don't. I just thought you might." And he'd walked away.

Kaveri had wanted a smoke badly. But she didn't know where to go for a puff. She could go back to the bathroom downstairs but what if she bumped into Devika or her husband or someone else? They'd wonder what she was doing there. And she couldn't use any of the bathrooms upstairs since everyone was still in the kitchen and she was worried the cigarette smell might reach them. She did think of using her parents' bathroom, but what if Ajay showed up and saw her smoking. Not that she cared but she really was in no mood for further lectures. That was when she decided to go outside and walk to the back. She could stand near the deck, under the awning to shield from the rain. No one would see her there, not unless they were out taking a walk in the rain. So she'd put her raincoat on and had walked out the front door. Walking out the back door meant walking through the kitchen, and that only meant one thing – endless interrogation.

She had walked out in the rain and went to the side of the house to go to the backyard. But when she pushed the wooden gate open, she saw a couple of figures standing under the deck. They were facing each other and an umbrella was blocking their faces. A black umbrella that was wide enough to cover ten people under it. Kaveri inched nearer but not too close. She didn't want them to see her. Her first thought was Jamuna and Vikram. Maybe they were stealing some romantic moments together. *Pathetic*, thought Kaveri with a smug. Although, it could work on her behalf. She walked nearer until she could see the faces. But the miserable umbrella was still in the way. The couple was standing very close to each other.

Kaveri searched her brain for the best way to approach them without being noticed. She desperately wanted to see Jamuna and Vikram together – she wanted to say, 'I told you so' to everyone else. She wanted to expose them but first she needed to build evidence. And one was staring right at her on her face. All she had to do was walk into the kitchen and tell her mother to open the back door and have a peek at the deck. *If only I could get a glimpse of their faces*, Kaveri hoped, when, miraculously, the umbrella hit the grown. Bingo! She saw Vikram kissing Jamuna. Only, she realized with a thud in her heart that it wasn't Vikram…or Jamuna. It was her father! Kaveri stood absolutely still as if any movement on her part could alter the scene in front. And she knew who he was kissing although the person was facing her father – she recognized the light green salwar-kameez. It was Devika Aunty.

Kaveri stood staring at them – not comprehending. Rain water splashed at her feet, wetting her sandals and the end of her pants. She shivered as a cold breeze shot past her, but Kaveri was too stunned to move. Devika Aunty was kissing her father? She didn't understand any of it. The person who had warned her about Jamuna and Vikram was kissing her father? What was going on? Another strong wind splattered some rain water on her face, causing her to stagger backwards.

Quickly, but quietly, she had turned back and walked into the house. Still in shock, she'd somehow managed to strip her wet clothes and change into a pair of jeans and blouse – *who cares about dressing up anymore*, Kaveri had grunted.

She'd then walked into the kitchen just because she didn't have anywhere else to go. She wished desperately for Susan to be there. Susan was like her soul-mate, her true friend and companion. Kaveri entered the kitchen and felt like a stranger. The spicy aroma of cinnamon and cardamom brewing in the '*chai*' did nothing to ease her loneliness. She didn't feel like she was a part of this family, this family that was proving to be stranger by the hour. She didn't have anyone to talk to or hang out with. Her sisters ignored her completely. Her mother was too busy with the wedding preparation. Chandni Aunty was out of the question. And now, she didn't think she could even look at Devika Aunty's face.

Not knowing what to do, she'd walked into the family room. Vikram's twin brothers were playing some sort of a video game. They didn't acknowledge her presence. They were so into the game that nothing else seemed to matter to them. *At least they had each other*, sighed Kaveri. She grabbed a magazine and sat staring at the pages blankly. The image of her father kissing her aunt was stuck to her brain like it was glued there permanently. How long had this been going on? What shocked her the most wasn't that her father was having an affair but the person he was having it with. Kaveri didn't know her gentle, caring aunt was even capable of something as small as lying, and this was cheating! How could she do it? Anger suddenly crept on her with an alarming force. She clasped her fingers around the glossy pages of the magazine, crinkling the shiny, smooth surface.

What should she do? Kaveri wasn't sure. Or should she even do something? She thought of her mother but instead of feeling sorry for her, it was rage that she felt – rage and disgust. How could her mother let her husband behave so shamefully? And with her sister too? Was her mother that ignorant? Kaveri was sickened by what she considered as her mother's incompetence. Her mother had failed as a wife. If she had been a smart wife, she'd have known how to keep her husband within her grasp.

Kaveri didn't know how long she sat there. When she looked up, the twins were still playing the game. Their faces were stern as they peered at the screen while their fingers moved expertly on the control. If only she found pleasure in such trivial things, thought Kaveri, maybe she wouldn't feel so outraged all the time. Maybe she should learn from these two boys and block the world out. If only!

She then heard some other noise beside the shelling sound of the video-game. Someone was laughing. Sounded like one of her sisters. But who was the man? Why did he sound so eerily familiar? Intrigued, she'd walked to the kitchen. Although all the women had been there – including Devika, no one was laughing. Everyone was involved in some chore or the other. That was when Kaveri went into the living room and found her husband sitting with Jamuna. They were not laughing anymore, but talking. She stood, and watched as Raj reached for Jamuna's hand. And she lost it and had screamed at them. The earlier scene of Ajay kissing Devika had flashed in front of her eyes. And Kaveri wasn't going to let history repeat itself. She was not her mother.

But everything had backfired, once again. Kaveri inhaled deeply on the cigarette as her mother's earlier words replayed in her mind, "*Do you just get pleasure seeing your sisters get humiliated? First, you did it at breakfast. Now, here. Where are you going to cause a scene next, at the wedding?*"

What an excellent idea? Thought Kaveri as she stubbed the cigarette butt in the ceramic sink. She then threw the butt into the toilet and reached for another one. As she lit that one and started smoking, her mind began to work. Actually, it had just become very easy to humiliate her father in front of everyone. Although it meant putting Devika Aunty to shame as well. But at this point, Kaveri couldn't care less. If Ajay's demise caused Devika's downfall, then that was how it'd be. Suddenly the thought of seeing Ajay shrink in shame in front of everyone at Gangga's wedding exhilarated her. First, she'd casually mention Vikram and Jamuna, then enhance it with her father's affair. Sweet! Her mood changed instantly. Her cunning mind managed what the cigarettes failed to do. She was feeling jubilant. Kaveri didn't care if Gangga's wedding was interrupted by this scheme of hers or if her sister's day was ruined or if her mother was hurt. All that mattered to Kaveri was bringing Ajay down. And Jamuna with him.

Someone was knocking on the bathroom door.

Kaveri quickly quenched the half-finished cigarette and threw it into the toilet bowl with the rest. She rinsed her mouth, popped a gum into it and sprayed some 'Happy' on her and around the bathroom. She let the water run just to send a message that she was using the toilet. She opened the small window and aired the place for a few seconds, ignoring the knock that was getting louder. Finally, when she was convinced the bathroom was free of any cigarette smell; Kaveri closed the window and opened the door. Her mother-in-law was standing there; her face a quintessence of fury, with her sucked-in cheeks and eyes that looked like there were about to pop out of their sockets.

"Kaveri, what're you doing in here for so long?" her tone matched the look on her face.

"Sorry, I'm done now." Kaveri flashed Mrs. Dhillon a phony smile and stepped aside to let the older lady into the bathroom.

But in her excitement to shame Ajay and debase Jamuna, Kaveri forgot to flush the toilet.

Part Four – Two Hours Before the Wedding

Chapter eighteen – Ajay

"I hope this rain is a not a bad sign," said Ajay.

He was standing out under the car-porch with all the men – Vikram, Jason, Mahesh, Siva, Mr. Dhillon and Raj. In an hour they had to be at the wedding hall. Which meant they had to leave in half-an-hour. Since it was raining, they might have to leave ten minutes sooner. Ajay was arranging transportation for everyone.

"Of course it's not," Mahesh rebuked.

Ajay hoped it wasn't. When was the last time it had rained this badly in Vancouver? He knew rain was always associated with good luck – blessings from above. But too much rain could potentially ruin the whole event. As it was, the bridal car, which was adorned with flowers and ribbbons, was going to get drenched. And no amount of umbrellas were going to shield the guests from this rain. How was that a blessing?

"Ajay," Mr. Dhillon spoke. "Maybe we need to arrange for some umbrellas. A lot in this case. Maybe send of the boys to go around the house and gather as many umbrellas as they could."

Ajay wanted to *thank* him for stating the obvious but instead, decided to be polite.

"Good idea. Vikram and Jason – why don't you two do that. But before that, let's finalize transportation issues."

"My car will be full – with my wife, Raj and his wife," said Mr. Dhillon.

"Right. Mahesh doesn't have a car. How about if you guys split and Chandni can go with Siva, Devika, Priya and perhaps Jamuna."

"No, Jamuna can go with us," Vikram suggested, staggering everyone.

"You don't have a car, Vikram," pointed out Ajay.

"We'll go in Jason's."

"Right, I forgot about Jason. Well, that makes this easier. So, Jason, can you have Jamuna and can the twins go with you too?"

"Sure," said Jason, throwing a quick glance at his friend.

"Good. Okay, Mahesh, where shall we put you?"

"You can come with us, we can fit three people easily at the back seat," Mr. Dhillon suggested, hitting Mahesh on the back.

"But, Susan was going to come with us," Raj suddenly pointed out.

"Susan? She's not even here," Ajay looked annoyed. Where was Susan coming from?

"She will be here in a few minutes. She's taking a cab here," Raj looked sheepish as he spoke, almost shy.

"Why couldn't she take a cab to the hall?" Mr. Dhillon asked his son.

"Well I told her she could come with us."

"Raj, this is family affair, why are you including your friend in this?" Mr. Dhillon raised his voice.

"She's Kaveri's friend and I thought – well, isn't Jason a *friend* too?" Raj's voice was icy.

"Raj, you know what I mean." Mr. Dhillon cut his son short.

Ajay looked at the father and son and wondered what was brewing between them. But he had to stop whatever dispute they were having before it got out of hand. He had a wedding to worry about.

"Susan…Susan…" Ajay pondered loudly.

"Can't Mahesh Uncle go with you?" Raj asked Ajay.

"No, because Mrs. Mehra will be with us and she's got all the trays too. And Gangga will need to be comfortable in her bridal sari and ornaments, she can't be squeezed." Ajay thought a bit, and then he said, "Actually, it's simple. Since Jamuna will be with Jason, Mahesh can easily go with Devika and Siva."

"There you go, all settled. I'll tell Susan she can come with us," announced Raj happily.

"We'll leave in twenty minutes."

If Ajay thought it was strange for his son-in-law to be overly concerned about his wife's best friend, he didn't say anything. The men dispersed. Ajay, the last one out there, was about to enter the house when he saw a cab pulling up at the street. He watched as Susan got out and sort of ran into the porch, her long, blond hair waving in the breeze. She greeted him sweetly. Ajay was amused to see her dressed in a pale purple sari. She even had a *bindi* – red dot on the forehead – on.

"You look more Indian than an Indian," joked Ajay.

"Why, thank you. Is everyone inside?"

"Yes, and we're leaving in twenty minutes."

"Okay, good, I'm on time. Where's Raj?"

"Go inside, I'm sure you'll find him." Ajay moved aside to let Susan walk in. A light scent of something floral wafted toward him. He also noticed her mid-riff snowy white under her sari.

He'd known Susan for a long time. She was a frequent guest in his house when Kaveri still lived there. He never actually got to know her since she was never friendly. But one thing he remembered distinctly about Susan was her distaste toward everything that spelled 'Indian'. Kaveri and she would mock everything – from the food they ate to the clothes they wore. Kaveri would whine about how she wished she wasn't born an Indian, how she felt she didn't belong to the uncivilized, unsophisticated group of people and how she hated curry. Ajay always thought Susan was Kaveri's escapism. Susan was what Kaveri would have liked to be. And by having Susan in her life, it gave Kaveri a sense of superiority over him and her sisters. Susan taught Kaveri how to behave, speak and dress like a true Canadian. Susan took Kaveri to the Nickleback and Killers concerts. Susan invited Kaveri over to their house for Sunday evening barbeques. Susan introduced steak to Kaveri – which baffled Ajay and Menaka. It was a sin for Hindus to eat beef. But Kaveri rebelled and defied him all the way. And with Susan standing by her like a faithful coach, it made things easy for Kaveri.

Ajay could never understand Kaveri's hatred toward her culture and society. But whatever it was, she made her feelings clear. In fact, she swore she wouldn't marry an Indian man and become a dutiful Indian wife. But marrying Raj had been her choice, albeit a choice made to defy him.

What he couldn't fathom now was, why was Susan turning into

the Indian that she had despised so much? What had changed now that she was respecting their culture? Ajay was closing the main door behind him when something made him stop halfway. *Susan had asked for Raj, and not for Kaveri.* Ajay paused and felt momentarily unsettled. He hoped, for Kaveri's sake, that he was overreacting.

Chapter nineteen – Menaka

Menaka tied and retied her bright orange sari with glittery sequins all over it. But the sari wasn't sitting right. And the fact that her hands were unsteady didn't help either. She tried again but the sari fell around her clumsily, the long silky material gathering by her feet in a pile. Menaka stared at her image in the mirror. She looked awful. She'd been tying sari for as long as she could remember, why was she finding it such a difficult task that day? Surely one didn't forget how to tie a sari? She'd ask Mrs. Mehra for help, Menaka decided.

Menaka draped herself in a robe and descended the steps that lead to the kitchen. On the way she stopped at Jamuna's room and knocked on the door. She opened the door without waiting for an answer. Mrs. Mehra was applying something on Jamuna's face. Gangga was sitting on the bed – looking like a bride. She glowed in the red sari, the colour instantly adding brightness to her face. Menaka inhaled sharply; Gangga looked like she did thirty years ago, the same color sari, and the same hairstyle.

"You look lovely," she whispered to her daughter.

"Thanks, Mama. Aren't you supposed to be ready?"

"Oh, I can't believe you're getting married. Subash is a lucky man, you're very pretty." Menaka touched Gangga's cheeks and planted a gentle kiss.

Gangga stared up at her mother, uncertainty written on her made-up face. “I don’t know how lucky he thinks he is, Mama,” replied Gangga. Jamuna and Mrs. Mehra turned to look at her.

“Why would you say that?” Menaka asked. Kaveri’s earlier words about Subash not wanting to marry Gangga sprung to her ears. Was there something going on that she wasn’t aware of?

“For no reason. You should get ready. Papa said we’re leaving soon,” insisted Gangga.

Menaka looked at Mrs. Mehra and she was not even half-way done with Jamuna’s sari.

“How long will you be, Mrs. Mehra?” she asked.

“Should be done in ten minutes. Do you need help?”

“No, that’s okay. For some reason my sari’s got an attitude today. But I should hurry before Ajay loses his crazy mind.” Menaka turned around to leave when she came face to face with Devika. At first Devika had looked startled, but she recovered quickly and gave Menaka a meek smile.

“I’ll help you, didi,” she offered.

Menaka faltered. She wasn’t ready to share such proximity with her sister as yet and especially not in the same room. She wouldn’t be comfortable in Devika’s presence until she’d established the truth. But again, maybe being alone with Devika was exactly what she needed to learn the truth. She agreed although with an obvious reluctance and geared Devika toward her room.

As she watched Devika circle the sari around her, Menaka contemplated on ways to broach the subject. She studied Devika intently to see if her sister’s facial expression would reveal something. But Menaka couldn’t conclude anything based on Devika’s poker-face. Frustrated, Menaka let out a deliberate sigh.

“What’s wrong, didi?”

“Oh, nothing. Weddings are always a lot of work and stress. And this wedding is an unusual one.”

“Why is that?” Devika didn’t look at her sister as she spoke. Her hands and eyes were glued to the task at hand.

“Too many outbursts and revelations. Have you any idea why Kaveri has been so edgy and bitter?”

“No, I’ve been wondering the same.”

“Yeah, and Ajay’s no help. He seems to be caught up in his own pathetic world.” Menaka watched Devika closely as she spoke. But

Devika didn't display any form of emotion on her part neither did she show any interest in the matter of Ajay. Which was leery since it would've been only natural for anyone to ask more about Ajay and his pathetic world, at least out of curiosity if not concern. Menaka was dubious.

"Here you go, didi. All done," Devika announced. She stood back to look at Menaka. "You look very nice."

Menaka turned toward the mirror. She did look nice. She didn't think orange would suit her so well. It had somehow miraculously brought some life to her face. Devika was about to leave when Menaka turned to face her.

"Can I ask you something, Devika?"

"Sure, didi," her voice quivered slightly. And Devika was clutching the door knob as if impatient to leave.

"How's Siva, I mean…are you happy?"

"Yes, I am…we are. Why do you ask?"

"Just wondering. Well you must be happy if you thought you were pregnant right? Look at Ajay and I, I don't remember the last time we had sex." Menaka had deliberately mentioned 'sex' to her sister. She studied Devika's body language – nothing.

"I think we should go."

Menaka nodded. She glanced at herself once more in the mirror.

"Devika," she called out, still facing the mirror. "You wouldn't do anything to hurt me, would you?"

Devika didn't even pause to breathe when she spoke, "Never, didi. Your happiness matters to me more than my own."

Menaka stood staring at herself in the mirror for what seemed like a very long time. Then she turned around and braced herself to face the day. If it wasn't Devika, who was he screwing then? How she longed for another gulp of her scotch right that minute.

Chapter twenty – Kaveri

Kaveri took one last look at herself in the full-length mirror in her old room. The space was now converted into a general room by her father. He'd removed her bed and replaced it with a couple of leather chairs. There was a magazine rack full of the latest and out-dated magazines of all kinds. He'd build a book shelf against the wall and had filled it with books. Kaveri looked around the room and sighed to herself. Seemed like her father had managed to erase every memory of her childhood from that room.

Kaveri didn't actually plan on entering the room and be reminded of her father's abhor toward her. But that day it was used as the make-up and change room for the wedding throng. Chandni was there earlier beautifying herself, followed by Mrs. Dhillon. Kaveri had entered the room while her mother-in-law was still fixing herself. She'd tried to make empty conversation with her mother-in-law just to be polite. But Mrs.Dhillon had been rather terse with her. She hardly said a word or even looked her way. Kaveri had even complimented on the pastel green sari Mrs. Dhillon had on, although she personally hated pale green. It made the older woman look gaunter than she already was. But she got nothing in return, not even a thank you. Then the old lady had rushed out of the room. Kaveri had brushed her mother-in-law's indifference toward her aside and concentrated on getting ready.

Satisfied with the way she looked in her light beige sari with her white-gold accessories and matching beige bangles, Kaveri decided to go find Raj. She needed to know who was driving her to the wedding hall. She hadn't brought her car and if she didn't remind her husband, Kaveri was worried he might actually forget her – deliberately or otherwise.

She found her husband in the family room, sitting on the edge of the couch, facing…

"Susan?!"

What was Susan doing there? And why didn't she come looking for her? And what on earth was she wearing?

"Kaveri, there you are." Susan got up and kissed Kaveri on her cheeks. "I've been looking for you and Raj didn't know where you were."

"I was in the make-up room. But what're you doing here? You didn't tell me you were coming," her voice accusatory.

"Oh…I…" Why was she stammering?

"What?"

"I wanted to surprise you. I thought you'd be happy to see me."

"God, I *am* happy to see you, so happy!" Kaveri hugged her friend. Now that Susan was there, she wouldn't feel so left out. She didn't need anyone else when she had Susan.

"Phew, thank God. For a minute there you sounded pissed."

"*You kidding me?* I've been waiting to see you. You have no idea what has been going on in this place. God, I can't wait to tell you. Come, let's go somewhere private." Kaveri grabbed Susan by the arm and dragged her out of the family room. She didn't see Susan flashing Raj a desperate look. Neither did she see Raj shaking his head and dropping his hands around him as if defeated.

Kaveri sat with Susan in the make-up room and spilled everything that had been bottling up in her chest. She started with Jamuna and Vikram, then Gangga and Subash and finished with Ajay and Devika. Kaveri regaled her friend of how screwed up her family was. She spoke of Jamuna's relationship with Vikram with shame and distaste. And how when she'd found the pregnancy test-kit box in the bathroom, she'd thought it was Jamuna's. But it had only been Devika and her menopause. Then she rattled on about how Subash almost dumped Gangga on their wedding day because Gangga wasn't a virgin. If that wasn't enough to send Susan's head spinning, Kaveri started on Ajay and Devika's affair.

"Your dad's having an affair?"

"Yeah, with my aunt! And you'd think that mother of mine would at least suspect something, but no! My whole family's just messed up. And you know what else?"

"There's more?" Susan let out a big giggle.

"Yeah, I found Jamuna with Raj earlier, flirting like the slut that she is." Kaveri waited for Susan to shriek in disbelief or to exclaim with some smart comments. But Susan fell quiet. The earlier giggle sank with no trace. She'd gone very still and her pale face had turned paler that her long, dangly earrings and her heavy make-up looked almost daunting on her.

"Susan, are you all right?"

"What?" she looked spaced out but quickly gained her composure. "Sorry, I was thinking of something I…I…, something I forgot to do before I left."

"Oh, what?"

"Just…something. No biggie."

"Okay. Anyways, I was telling you about Raj and Jamuna. See, I found them sitting in the living room, holding hands and giggling like a pair of annoying teenagers in love. It was pathetic. Of course when I confronted him, he denied everything. One of these days I'm going to catch him red-handed with her and all hell's going to break loose, just watch."

"Could they not have been just talking?" Susan spoke in a small voice, as if she was trying to convince herself rather than Kaveri.

"No, I know a 'flirt' when I see one. And I know Raj. He'd been having his eyes on that woman since the day I met him."

"You never told me that." It was the way Susan said it, snappy, that took Kaveri by surprise. Kaveri was starting to get annoyed with Susan. Why was she behaving strange…like…like a jealous wife?

"Susan, what's gotten into you?"

"You tell me everything. I just find it strange you didn't tell me that part," now Susan sounded defensive.

"Why did it matter?" she shrieked – throwing Susan an exasperated look. It was her husband and her sister, what was it to Susan? Not enough with everything that had happened that day, Susan had to behave odd too?

"It doesn't. I'm only concerned for you, Kaveri. I don't want your husband to cheat on you."

"He wouldn't dare. I will not lose my husband to my sister like my daft mother did. I'm a smart, modern woman who knows how to keep her husband within her grasps."

Just then Menaka poked her head into the room and announced it was time to go.

Chapter twenty-one – Devika

Everyone was gathered at the front porch. Ajay had moved his car from the garage. Menaka and Mrs. Mehra ushered Gangga into Ajay's decorated car without letting the rain get to her. Devika thought Gangga looked stunning in her red bridal sari and adornments. Gangga gave Devika a calm smile before sitting in the car. Devika smiled back wondering why Gangga's eyes looked hollow, almost foreboding. Maybe Gangga finally had realized what a big deal this wedding was, that it was a life-altering union, thought Devika. In less than two hours, her whole life would be changed indefinitely. Just the mere thought of it was nerve racking enough, imagine going through it, Devika shook her head, silently praying for Gangga's married life to be better than hers.

Suddenly, the image of her own wedding danced in front of her eyes dauntingly. Her wedding had been life-altering in every way. It had changed her from an innocent, gentle, carefree girl to a mature, strong-willed and overwrought woman. Sometimes, when Devika mulled over her life, she didn't know whether to laugh or cry at the way karma had been playing with her. But one thing she knew and accepted was that her marriage to Siva had been God's will. It was her penance. She was being punished for sleeping with her sister's husband and for having his child. That was what made her marriage bearable. Under different circumstances, Devika would have collapsed like a wall without proper foundation. She would have left Siva a very long time ago. But she had to endure being married to him because she had to pay for her sins. It comforted her in a way. It made it easier to live with herself. It enabled her to look into her sister's eyes and lie.

But when she had told Menaka earlier that she'd never hurt her, Devika hadn't lied. It was the truth. She'd never deliberately hurt Menaka. If that had been her intention, she would've run away with Ajay long time ago in India, when she found herself pregnant with Priya. She didn't because Menaka's happiness was more important to her than her own. There hadn't been a second that passed by without Devika wishing she didn't fall in love with Ajay. But yet, there hadn't been a second that passed by without her counting her blessings for having Ajay in her life. What kind of a life would she have had without Ajay? How would she have tolerated being married to Siva? And of course, Priya made up for everything.

While she was busy reminiscing, Devika realized everyone had gotten into their respective cars. But where was Siva? She looked around and spotted Priya standing with her cousins. Devika walked over to Priya and asked if she knew where Siva was. Priya simply shrugged and didn't offer to go find him. She looked to see if she could seek Mahesh's or Chandni's help, but they were busy getting the twins settled in Jason's car. Frustrated, Devika walked back into the house. She didn't want to be late and she knew traffic would be heavy, especially with the rain.

It was when she was descending down the stairs to the basement that she thought of what Priya had said earlier – about Siva having an affair. Devika let out a small grunt at the thought of Siva having an affair. Not only did she think he was emotionally incapable of loving someone, she didn't think anyone would find him desirable. There was nothing about Siva that was attractive in a manly way. He was too soft and his dressing was too meticulous. There was no roughness about him. Which would all have been fine had he been passionate or loving. He was devoid of any humanly emotion. Like when she humiliated herself at the breakfast table that morning, he hadn't been the least bit curious. Other husbands would've been either devastated or flabbergasted if their wives had taken a pregnancy test. Did he not suspect anything? Did he not think what had prompted her to take the test? Did he not wonder whether she was sleeping with someone else since she wasn't sleeping with him?

Devika found Siva in the guest room. He was standing by the bed, staring out of the window. His thin shoulders looked relaxed. *What is he doing here?* Devika wondered and was going to call out to him when he spoke, not to her but someone else.

"If you keep on doing this, I'd be late for the wedding. I'll call you when I get back tonight."

He laughed. It was a laughter she'd never heard before or even knew he was capable of. It was a deep, sexy, flirtatious laughter. One that was full of life. Devika froze at the door. She knew she should turn back, turn away, but she couldn't. She stood listening.

"I'm wearing a traditional Indian costume. It's called a *Kurta*. It sort of looks like a pair of pajamas –with knee length shirt and baggy pants."

Another laugh.

"It's comfortable and I look good in it."

A bigger laugh.

"Maybe I will. It all depends on how you treat me."

Quiet.

"Of course I miss you."

Pause. Sigh.

"Okay, I really must be going."

Short pause.

"Yes, I know."

An uncharacteristic giggle.

"No, I will not"

Impatient sigh.

" Right. Now, I must go."

Pause.

"Tomorrow night. And please, just one favor – shave your mustache and beard before I see you. You know how much I detest seeing you that way. It pricks when we kiss. Ditto. Bye."

Click.

Devika wanted to turn around and head upstairs as fast as she could. But why did her feet feel glued to the ground? Why was her brain trying to make sense of what she had just heard? *And those last words…the words…oh, he can't be!* Devika gasped.

Then, as if in slow motion, Devika eyes widened in horror as Siva turned around and physically froze when he saw her. Both of them stood staring at each other, stunned, shocked, speechless and embarrassed. It was a strange moment, one that Devika wished she'd never have to relive. Devika tried saying something but it was as if her voice had abandoned her. She heard Siva clear his voice and wished there was some way she could just run out of the room.

But Siva spoke.

"How much did you hear?"

"Hear? What? Oh, you mean…the phone…," Devika felt her cheeks flush. Sudden tears escaped her eyes before she could stop them. Siva approached her awkwardly.

"Devika," Siva reached out to touch her but Devika took a step back.

"Everyone's ready to go." She turned around and ran out of the room, the *pallu* of her sari flapping behind her.

CHAPTER TWENTY-TWO – JAMUNA

SHE FOUND HERSELF HUDDLED at the back seat of Jason's car with Vikram's two odd looking twin brothers – Johan and Karan. (Who, by-the-way, were looking very uncomfortable and lost without their Nintendo). Jamuna for once would like to hear them say something, just anything. She'd never heard them talk, unlike their chatty big brother. She wondered how their voices sounded. How did they speak? Like nine-year-olds she was sure, but what did nine-year-olds talk about? She tried to think of something that might interest them, nothing came to her mind. How could she think when her mind was fully occupied with thoughts of her father and Devika Aunty?

For once that day, ever since she found out about the pregnancy, Jamuna wasn't thinking about it. What concerned her now was her father, and whether he was having an affair with Devika Aunty. Jamuna knew not to take every word that comes out of Kaveri's mouth seriously. But it wasn't Kaveri she believed. It was the look on Devika Aunty's face that had her convinced. Devika Aunty had looked guilty. Jamuna had always sensed the hostility between her parents, it wasn't news to her. She had always sided her father every time there was a domestic dispute between her parents. Her mother was known to pick fights over the smallest things. But now she wondered whether she'd been wrong, whether her mother wasn't the guilty one. Had she always known of Ajay's affair? Was that why they were so unhappy? Was that why Menaka often threw a tantrum and picked a fight?

Just when she thought she couldn't endure any more for the day, this surfaced. Poor Gangga, thought Jamuna. Her wedding day seemed like a mayday. What with Subash giving her grief over the virginity issue, with her pregnancy news, and Kaveri's endless dramas – and now this, her father having an affair. The sudden thought of her pregnancy made her hands fly to her stomach like reflex. She rubbed the almost concave surface of her belly, wondering when the bulge would start showing. Her eyes automatically fell on Jason at the driver's seat. Fresh stubble was obvious on his smooth cheek. She inhaled deeply to remind herself not to touch him – it was so easy to reach over and give him a peck. She longed to feel him, to be close to him.

But, right at that moment, Jamuna was dying to know what Jason thought and felt. He hadn't said a word to her. Even now, his eyes were stuck on the road ahead. He wasn't even talking to Vikram who was sitting next to him. Frustrated, Jamuna poked Vikram's shoulder with her index-finger. Vikram turned around.

"Vo Kuch Kaha?" *Did he say anything?*

"Kaun?" *Who*?

Jamuna pointed at Jason with her nose. Vikram let out a small laugh.

"Kuch bhi nahi." *Nothing at all.*

"Ghadar!" *Donkey or more appropriately - ass.*

Vikram grunted out another laugh and Jason's head swung to face him.

"Are you two talking about me again?" he said, turning back to look at the road.

Jamuna sat back in her seat.

"We were just saying how bad the weather is," said Vikram to his friend. "And besides, why would we talk about you?"

"I don't know. Why were you speaking in Hindi then?"

"Why not?" Jamuna butted in. "Why should everything be about you?" Jamuna said, letting out a steam.

"Yeah, looks like nothing's about me. Everything's about you and your family. I don't fit in the picture. You don't even want to try and squeeze me into the frame. I'm just not worth it, right?" Jason blurted out, his voice edged with pain.

"It's the frame that's not worthy of you," said Jamuna said softly.

"Bullshit! That's saying it politely!"

"Do you really think I don't want you in the picture? Is that what you really think?" Jamuna's voice quivered.

"What else am I supposed to think?"

"Maybe that the frame is too small and making it bigger would distort what's already in it."

"You don't want to distort that, but it's okay to hurt my feelings?"

"I knew you'd never understand my devotion to my family."

"What is there not to understand? You've made yourself clear more than once – they matter and I don't."

"I never said that."

"But that's what you meant."

"No – " Jamuna stopped when Vikram put out his hand and yelled, "Ooi! Enough with the domestics!"

Suddenly Jason pressed on his breaks. The tires screeched as the car came to an abrupt halt, with the inertia sending everyone flying forward in their seats.

"Damn it!" Jason swore.

Jamuna craned her neck to the front and saw all the cars were lined up on the road ahead. She glanced over at the back and saw Siva and Devika's car coming to a halt. Jamuna glanced at her watch and it was half-past-four. They were supposed to be at the wedding hall by quarter to five. They were running really late. Then slowly, the cars in the front started moving. Relieved, Jamuna sat back in her seat. She looked at her side and saw the twins sitting absolutely still. They were not even intrigued by Jason's sudden outburst. Meanwhile, Vikram speed dialled someone's number on his mobile. She heard him talking to her dad in Hindi. When he hung up the phone, he was shaking his head in disbelief.

"What?" Jamuna and Jason asked him in synchrony.

"Your dad has lost his marbles!" Vikram said to Jamuna.

"Why? What happened?"

"He stopped because a black cat ran across the road." Vikram threw his head back laughing. Jason let out a chuckle.

"Why is that so funny? That's a legitimate reason," said Jamuna defensively.

"Jamuna, you've always been superstitious. Don't believe in that kind of stuff." Vikram said.

"What is there not to believe? It's bad luck when a black cat crosses your path especially if you're going for an auspicious function."

"God, that's what *he* said," Vikram hit his forehead with the palm of his hand.

"J, you have to stop being so superstitious," advised Jason.

"I'm not superstitious," said Jamuna vehemently.

"Can we not start another domestic battle?" Vikram butted in before Jamuna and Jason went at each other's throat again. "Although, I do want to ask something," he paused. When no one said anything, he continued, "What're you two planning on doing about…you know…," he paused and looked back at his brothers.

"What?" asked Jamuna.

"About…well…the…"

"The bun in the oven?" asked Jason. Vikram nodded.

"All depends on the cook; all I ask for is a share of the bun when it's baked."

"I thought the cook wasn't worthy of your bun!" Jamuna said.

Silence fell. And it remained that way for the next few minutes. Each wondering of the right thing to say without getting the twins suspicious. Although Jamuna didn't think the twins even cared about their conversations. They'd been staring out of the window since they got into the car.

Then, just as she was looking, they turned toward her – in unison, catching her off-guard. Unsure of how to behave, she flashed them a wide grin. They didn't grin back, instead they spoke.

"We've seen your family picture," said Johan.

"The one in your living room," said Karan.

Jamuna's mouth fell wide open.

"We think you don't have to make the frame larger," said Johan.

"To fit Jason in," said Karan.

"You can squeeze him in," said Johan.

"Easily," said Karan.

"With no distortion." Finished Johan. Then they turned back to look out of the window as if nothing had happened.

Jamuna sat staring at the back of the boys' heads. *They had been paying attention – to every word.* And the way they spoke, it was as if they were one. They finished each other's sentence. It was as if they'd been practicing their conversation for weeks. But what shocked her most was what they said actually made sense – why couldn't she fit Jason into the picture without distorting the current image? Then she sighed, if only it was that easy. If only it really was a matter of the picture. She was about to say something back to the twins, when they turned to face her again.

"Also," began Johan.

"When the bun is baked," said Karan.

"Can we have some too?" finished Johan.

It was Jason who did it first. He burst into a loud, noisy laughter, followed by Vikram. As much as Jamuna didn't want to, as much as her insides were churning in turmoil and dread, she gave in. She laughed until tears ran down her cheeks. The twins gave them odd looks and quietly turned back toward the window, clearly concluding they were all either totally demented or gone completely mad!

Chapter twenty-three – Gangga

Gangga held on to her seat tightly, hoping and praying for some calamity to befall them so the journey would not only be delayed, but permanently halted. When her father had brought the car to an abrupt halt earlier, Gangga's heart had soared with hope. But it had only been a black cat. Still, Gangga had clutched her bosom in fear and anticipation as Ajay muttered a curse under his breath and pressed on the break. As he had waited for the cat to cross, he didn't put the car back on drive. Instead, he had sat staring at the road. Gangga thought it was a good thing he was only blocking cars from their own people who were following at the back. When Menaka had urged him to drive, whining about time constraint, he had given her an exasperated look.

"It was a black cat, Menaka," he had hissed.

"I saw that. Now, can we go?"

"Stop being so daft! Surely you know what that means, it's bad omen."

Gangga had held her breath. She knew he father was superstitious and to a degree, she was too. Maybe he would turn the car back. Maybe he'd call Subash's parents and tell them the wedding was postponed, or better still, cancelled. Oh, bless the cat, thought Gangga as she continued praying for, what she knew, was the impossible. Of course the wedding was not going to be cancelled. She and her wishful thinking!

"Mr. Sharma," Mrs. Mehra, who was sitting next to her, had spoken suddenly. "We should go if we want to make it for the wedding. There's still so much to do there. And we have to unload the trays as well. So what if the cat crossed? There's nothing we can do about it. Say a prayer in your hearts and let's continue. Nothing will happen to Gangga's wedding."

Gangga had watched as Ajay sighed and composed himself before putting the car back on drive. Damn, she had thought.

But now, as the car was moving along the slushy roads and they were nearing the wedding hall, Gangga felt like her insides were all in shambles. She felt queasy. Her blouse felt too tight around her chest. The ornaments felt heavy and uncomfortable. This was not at all what she had expected to feel hours before her wedding.

She remembered feeling exhilarated and on top of the world just the day before. And she'd been hopelessly in love with Subash. But here she was – hardly twenty-four hours later, feeling completely wretched. She wasn't sure whether she loved Subash anymore. Not after their last conversation, after him forgiving her for not being a virgin. The more she thought of it, the more confused she became. What angered her most was the fact that he never once mentioned about wanting to marry a virgin prior to this. If only they'd talked about it earlier, none of this would be taking place. She wouldn't be on the way to her wedding feeling like she was about to face death sentence. God, if not for her father, Gangga knew she would have told Subash to take his stupid 'virginity' and shove it where the sun didn't shine. But she couldn't see her father getting hurt or humiliated, which was exactly what would happen if there was no wedding. Ajay would be shamed in front of his relatives and friends and he would never be able to walk with his head held high again. And it would all be her fault.

Gangga slowly released the tight clutch of her fingers on the seat and took a deep breath in, telling herself to remain composed. Her wedding was less than two hours away, and after which, there was no turning back. She'd made her bed, and minutes away from lying on it. There was no one to blame but herself and there was no way out, but to go through with it. Gangga decided not to think of the future. She decided not to even think of the day after the wedding, or even the evening for that matter where Subash had planned on spending it at the Fairmont.

She couldn't imagine spending the whole night alone with him in a hotel room. She almost wished her parents had insisted Subash and her spend their wedding night at home. But they had given in too easily to Subash when he had asked their approval to scoop her away after the wedding. He had said it was more romantic to be on their own, in a honey-moon suite, on a rose-petal-spread bed instead of spending it at her parent's house. Gangga had been impressed. She had thought how unlike he was than the other men she had dated. Subash was modern, cultured and he loved her and respected her like an equal. But now, she didn't know what Subash thought of her or how he felt about her. She wasn't sure if he even loved her. All she knew was she'd been wrong about Subash.

As much as she had disliked the men in her life before, at least they'd respected her for what she was. Gangga closed her face with her hands. God, how was she going to spend the rest of her life with a man who'd lost all respect for her? And why on earth did she agree to an arranged marriage?

Gangga looked at her parents in the front seat. They were quiet. In fact, except for the time when the cat had crossed the road, her parents hadn't said a single word to each other. They looked tense and uncomfortable in each other's presence. Gangga had been noticing it the whole day. Maybe they had another fight. Gangga sighed, could they not fight for one miserable day? They fought on a regular basis. Could they not try to be civil with each other for one day – for her sake?

What did it matter, her whole future was screwed anyways. Her parents' fight wasn't going to make anything better or make the gnawing feeling in her belly disappear. But what was it that Kaveri had said earlier? That she didn't want to lose her husband to her sister like their mother did? What had she meant? Gangga looked over at her parents again. She knew Kaveri was a trouble-maker. She'd go to any extent to taint their father's reputation, but she'd always been fond of their mother. What had prompted Kaveri to make such accusation? The more Gangga pondered about it, the more it didn't make any sense to her. Gangga dismissed the idea as not only preposterous, but completely infantile. Trust Kaveri to come up with some obtuse, childish story just to make their father look like the villain.

"Here we are," Ajay's voice filled the chillied silence inside the car.

She looked out and found the car entering the gate of the wedding-hall. The parking lot was packed with vehicles. Gangga's hand moved to her stomach. She sat quietly as Ajay manoeuvred the car until it was under the front awning. Mrs. Mehra helped Gangga out and, together with Menaka, they lead her to the back door of the wedding hall. Gangga walked with her head bowed and felt like the biggest hypocrite alive. Why was she expected to behave demure for that one day? Gangga wished she could just turn back, run into the car and drive away…far, far away to a place that didn't exist on the map. To a place where no one judged her, where she didn't have to adhere to the stupid society and culture and rules that were a century old, where she didn't have to worry that her act might affront or hurt her loved ones. If only there was such a place, that'd be heaven, Gangga decided with a low grunt.

As soon as she started walking, a group of people she recognized and didn't recognize rushed toward her. There was so much noise, mixed with the loud sound of the rain and cars zooming outside that Gangga couldn't make sense of what everyone was saying. She figured they were praising her from their big, wide, smiles and large owl-like eyes. She couldn't focus. She craned her neck for some air. Her heart felt like it was on a treadmill set on full speed. She needed to breathe and felt her lungs contract tightly for air. She could feel her forehead perspiring and suddenly was overcome with great overwhelming emotion. Gangga wished she could rip everything that she had on off and dash out into the rain.

Within seconds, Gangga found herself being ushered into an empty room that contained only a few chairs and a full-length mirror. Mrs. Mehra eased her gently on one of the chairs facing the mirror as if she was an invalid. Her mother and Mrs. Mehra moved around her so slowly and quietly it made her sick. But being in the room, away from the maddening crowd was calming. She found she was beginning to breath, with each gulp of fresh air calming her senses. Mrs. Mehra and her mother finally exited the room, announcing on their way out how they had so much to do. Gangga sat facing the enormous mirror and concentrated on her breathing. *Breathe, Gangga, breathe.* She repeated over and over silently as if reciting a mantra.

The wedding was probably only for an hour or so, she could do it, Gangga consoled herself. One hour would pass in a whiff, quickly like a shooting star – gone before you know it. All she had to do was to just think of the wedding, and not of what would come after. She'd deal with things as they came, Gangga told herself and steadied her nerves. It was easy…but why was her heart still heavy? Why did she have this dreadful feeling in the pit of her stomach that she was about to make the biggest mistake of her life?

Part Five – The Wedding

Chapter twenty-four – Ajay

By the time Ajay had parked his car, the rest of the cars that were following him had also found their respective parking spaces. He watched as everyone dashed through the rain; some holding umbrellas; some with papers or booklets of some sort on top of their heads; and for the umpteenth time that day, Ajay cursed the rain.

Ajay tore through the rain with his hand shielding his head. His off-white, silk *Kurta* had blotches of wet spot on it by the time he was at the door of the hall. Ajay stood by the door and dusted the rain drops off his *Kurta*.

"Hey, Ajay," someone called out to him. He looked up and saw his old friends, three of them, standing facing him with grins as wide as hyenas.

"How's the proud father?" one of his friends asked and patted him on the shoulder.

Ajay smiled at them. "Proud. And wet. This rain's really starting to annoy me. But, come...let's go inside."

Ajay led his over-exited friends into the decorated wedding hall in the hope to divest himself of them soon. He had so much to take care of. The first thing he must do was go find the *panditji*. He ushered his friends through the throng that had gathered noisily inside the hall. A few people acknowledged him as he passed and pumped his hand while spitting out hurried words of congratulations. Ajay thanked everyone and tried to make a smooth escape without offending anyone.

Finally, after many thank-yous and congrats, he found himself at the mandap.

He looked back and saw the crowd settling in, everyone seating themselves in the perfectly arranged rows of white plastic chairs. He saw Vikram with Jamuna and Jason, greeting people and showing them to their seats. Ajay was glad. He had wanted to arrange Gangga's wedding on his own, with not much interference from Subash's side. He remembered for Kaveri's wedding The Dhillons had planned everything on their own. But with Subash it was different, since Subash's father – Arun, was a close friend of Ajay's. Arun had let Ajay plan the wedding as how he and Menaka wished. Which was nice since it was every father's dream to organize his daughters' wedding as lavishly as possibly. At Kaveri's wedding, Ajay had stood back and observed as a guest while the wedding ceremony took place, participating only when required. At Gangga's wedding, he was the man-in-charge.

Ajay faced the *mandap*. It stood on four pillars made of silver and red coloured bamboos, while the top was a hemispherical roof which gave it a palace-like look. Everything about a Hindu wedding has its meaning – as does the *mandap*. The four pillars represent the parents on both sides; parents who toiled hard to bring up their children. In the middle of the mandap, the *panditji* had erected washed bricks in a square and filled it with clean sand. He'd later build the holy-fire in the center of the brick square. No Hindu marriage is complete without the sacred-fire as the witness. Ajay envisioned Gangga and Subash walking around the fire seven times while pledging a lifetime of promises together and smiled to himself. Everything was happening according to how he'd wanted it, thought Ajay contently. He remembered for Kaveri's wedding, nothing had happened according to the traditional Hindu custom, even the four pillars of the *mandap* had been built with iron-pipes instead of bamboos. Didn't The Dhillons know it wasn't auspicious to use iron-pipes for wedding *mandaps*?

Ajay decided to check on Gangga one last time before she became a married woman. Why was it always so painful to see his daughters married? Even with Kaveri, Ajay had been overcome with emotion. But he'd never seen a happier bride than Kaveri. She had looked thrilled, as if it were some form of a victory. Ajay's only qualm was that she was married to a philanderer. If not for their stars matching perfectly, Ajay would have done all that was in his power to stop Kaveri's wedding.

And if The Dhillons hadn't approached him so humbly, he'd have even defied the stars. But, it was done; Ajay sighed and walked to the back of the wedding hall where the dressing rooms were located.

When he came to the back-rooms, Ajay pushed the door of one of the rooms without pausing to knock. But it was the wrong room. He'd expected to see Gangga with Menaka or Mrs. Mehra by her side. Instead, he had interrupted a couple in…well, in what looked like an argument. He couldn't quite see them since the woman was facing the man and hence facing away from the door. Ajay was about to pull the door shut when something made him pause – the sari the woman was wearing, it was strangely familiar. Why did he feel like he knew her? Then she spoke, and he knew.

"So, are you going to just stand there looking stupid?" it was Susan.

"Sue, darling, you've got it all wrong," came the man's voice. Ajay wasn't surprised, in fact had anticipated it – Raj's voice.

"Are you telling me Kaveri's lying to me? She *saw* you flirting with Jamuna!" Susan's voice was loud and angry.

At first Ajay was stunned. Was Susan defending Kaveri by confronting Raj of his indecent behaviour? Then rage took over – what was Raj doing with Jamuna in the first place? When Susan was done with him, Ajay would have his own session with his useless son-in-law.

"I wasn't flirting with Jamuna for heaven's sake," Raj protested.

"What were you doing then? Tell me." Ajay held his breath. He would like the answer to that question as well. Bravo Susan, he thought.

"Nothing. She was telling me some soapy story about her love life and I was simply listening. Come on, Sue, you know me better than that?"

"I *do*, and that's the problem!"

What came next was what threw Ajay off.

"Look, I will never cheat on you. We've been through this…many, many times. When are we going to get pass this? When are you going to start trusting me?"

Ajay's shock was immeasurable. At first he thought he'd heard it wrong. It took a while before the truth sank in, before he realized what Raj was saying. Why, that son-of-a-bitch! Ajay flung the door wider and marched toward the pair. Before Raj knew what hit him, Ajay grabbed him by the collar of his *Kurta* and back-tracked him all the way to the wall. He pinned Raj to the wall and fixed his deadly eyes on him.

"You useless piece of shit! How dare you cheat on my daughter? With her too?" Ajay glanced over at Susan, who looked like she'd seen a ghost – her pale skin at its palest.

"Look, Dad..."

"Don't call me that! How long have you been cheating on Kaveri? How long? Tell me before I pound you to pieces." At the sound of Ajay's threatening voice, Susan let out a scream and came forward to Raj's assistance.

"Mr. Sharma, let's talk about this please. It's not like what you think," Susan pleaded.

"Shut up, you two-faced-woman! Sleeping with your best-friend's husband, aren't you ashamed of yourself?" Ajay spat. Susan shrunk away and turned toward the door when she saw Kaveri standing there – alarmed and angry.

"Let go of my husband," said Kaveri, a little too calmly.

Ajay turned at the sound of Kaveri's voice.

"Kaveri, he's cheating on you...with her!" Ajay let go of Raj and pointed angrily at Susan. Kaveri didn't follow the direction in which his finger pointed; instead her gaze was fixed on him.

"So, is this it? Is this your way of trying to humiliate me in public?" she demanded.

Ajay stared at his daughter, not understanding. Raj steadied his rumpled *Kurta*. Susan slowly crept out of the room.

"Kaveri, I know you have a hard time believing me or listening to me for that matter, but please, this one time, believe me. Raj is cheating on you."

"Right, and with Susan?" Kaveri's voice was steady.

"Yes, with Susan. And why would I want to humiliate you? Is that all you think of me?" Kaveri deliberately ignored the hurt in Ajay's voice.

"You tell me."

"Kaveri, can we please put our differences aside for one day and concentrate on the problem at hand?"

By this time, much to Ajay's dismay and Kaveri's mirth, a small crowd had gathered outside the room. Among which were Menaka and

Devika. The rest were people who happened to be at the back room and stopped to listen. Ajay was glad his other relatives and children were not there, especially Gangga. God, this was supposed to be a happy occasion, but over and over, there were disputes, arguments, confrontations! It was like everything bad was waiting for this one day to spring to life. But why that day? Why on Gangga's wedding day? Why couldn't everyone wait for at least the following day to start with their nonsense?

"And what might that be?" he heard Kaveri ask. Ajay could see Kaveri clearly wanted to make a scene and he wasn't about to allow that.

"Nothing. If you'll excuse me, I have a wedding to attend to," he said politely and walked past Kaveri. But he didn't go very far.

"Not so fast, Papa," Kaveri's voice was loud and piercing. Ajay stopped and looked at his daughter, his eyes warning.

"Kaveri, not now," he kept his voice under control.

"Why not? Are you afraid?"

Ajay inhaled and was aware of the inquisitive gazes around him; gazes from people who'd love nothing but a bit of drama. "Why would I be afraid?"

"I would if I were you," Kaveri wasn't giving up easily. At this point Menaka pushed through the crowd and approached her daughter.

"Kaveri, you better stop this nonsense of yours," Menaka said. "Did I not tell you not to create any scene at the wedding? What has gotten into you? Whatever it is, we'll discuss at home."

Ajay was left dumbfounded – again. Of all people to come to his rescue, Menaka?

"Your husband just accused my husband of infidelity," Kaveri barked. "I saw him holding Raj by the collar and accusing him of sleeping with my best friend." The gathered crowd gasped. It was Raj's turn to look uncomfortable. He tried to stop Kaveri by putting his hand on her shoulder, but she shrugged him off.

"Like I said," Menaka spoke. "We'll have this discussion at home. Not now when there's a wedding on in less than an hour."

"I really don't care if there's a wedding on. This is my pride and dignity at stake here. I will not stand here listening to your husband throwing accusations at my husband. Just because he couldn't keep his hands off other women, he shouldn't assume every man to be like him!"

"Kaveri!" Menaka raised her voice.

Ajay's hands shook as he fought to remain calm. So Kaveri knew, he thought, then it was only a matter of time before the whole world did.

"Don't yell, Mama. It's the truth and you know it. You don't have the guts to deal with it or the will power to hold on to your husband. I *am* not you!" That did it. Ajay took a few brusque steps toward Kaveri and swung his palm across Kaveri's shocked face. The crowd's gasps grew stronger. Some women even had their hands covering their mouths. This wedding was turning out to be an event to remember.

But Kaveri didn't alter. Ajay's slap only managed to infuriate her more.

"I will not tolerate such insolence in front of my guest," Ajay hissed. "And I will not tolerate your rudeness toward your mother. You've disappointed me, Kaveri, today more than ever."

With that Ajay turned away from his daughter and made his way to the door. He saw Devika standing among the crowd, staring at him with alarmed expression. He avoided her eyes. He was at the door when he heard Kaveri's stinging words again.

"If I'm a disappointment, what will you say of your beloved daughter Jamuna?" As if in slow-motion, Ajay turned back to face Kaveri. What did she have cooking now?

"What will you say…" Kaveri spoke when Ajay didn't say anything, "…when you find out your darling daughter is sleeping with her cousin?" The room felt like it was swaying around him. Ajay had to put out a hand against the wall to steady himself. His mind went blank. He didn't even have to energy to slap Kaveri one more time. But, for the second time, Menaka came to his rescue.

"Besharam!" *Shameless.* "When are you going to stop accusing your sisters of unseemly behaviours? And how many people is Jamuna flirting with? First it was with your husband, and now it's with Vikram? Get a hold of yourself, Kaveri. You've managed to bring shame to this family just by being in it. I never thought I'd see the day where my daughter's determined to bring the family down – shame on you. I want you to leave this hall, now. I'm not going to let you ruin Gangga's day. You need to go and Raj, take her home."

"Right!" snorted Kaveri. "If there's going to be a wedding that is! I'm shocked at you, Mama. First, you couldn't hold on to your husband. Now, your children are taking you for a ride and you're just plain ignorant!"

"Enough, Kaveri," Raj interrupted. He held his wife by her elbow and directed her toward the door. The crowd parted automatically in the middle to let Raj and Kaveri through. Soon, everyone started moving away. But among the crowd, two small boys stood watching for a while longer: Johan and Karan, until someone instructed them to move along.

Ajay stood holding on to the wall while the throng dispersed. He didn't dare look at anyone in the face. The shame he felt was immeasurable. His eldest daughter had managed to embarrass him in front of his family and friends. Ajay bit his lips, his eyes felt moist. Did Kaveri really hate him so much she'd go to such extent to degrade him? And here he was trying to protect her from her philandering husband. He felt a gentle nudge on his shoulder.

"Come," Menaka urged. "Groom's party will be here soon. Brace yourself, please, for Gangga's sake."

"Is it all true, Menaka? About Jamuna?" Ajay's voice quivered.

"Is that how much you trust your daughter? Kaveri is on a rampage, she's determined to see you sink in shame. And she knows Jamuna is your weakest-link. She knows all she had to do is mention Jamuna and you'll collapse. You can't collapse now, Ajay. You need to be strong for Gangga."

Ajay nodded meekly. "Thank you, Menaka."

"For what?"

"For standing by me."

"It's Gangga I'm standing by."

"I never thought you'd..."

"I'd what?"

"I just never thought you cared about Gangga and Jamuna so much. You always seemed hostile toward them and you always favoured Kaveri above them. This is the first time I'm seeing you being brusque with Kaveri, what happened?"

Menaka was quiet for a while. She looked at Ajay as if she were seeing him for the first time. Then she shook her head.

"What?" Ajay asked.

"All these years and you didn't get any of it, did you?"

"Get what?"

"I didn't favour one daughter over the others, Ajay. I just paid more attention to her because you didn't. Gangga and Jamuna had your full attention and love, Kaveri had none."

"That's not true."

"That's the whole truth! All her life, she tried hard seeking your approval and your love, and she got nothing. Finally she'd reverted to revenge, maybe hoping that would get her some of your attention." Menaka said and quickly left the room.

Ajay remained in his spot, unmoving.

Chapter twenty-five – Gangga

Gangga was fidgety. She walked around the room in circles, trying to calm her nerves. It wasn't helping. She wished Jamuna would come. Or even her mother. And where was Mrs. Mehra? Wasn't she supposed to stand by Gangga until it was time to go out? Gangga wondered if the groom's party had arrived. Wasn't it time? What time was it? Gangga glanced at her wrist and realised she didn't have her watch on. With all her accessories that adorned her arms, there was no place for her watch. Where was her purse? Gangga looked around and all she could see was Mrs. Mehra's vanity-basket on one of the chairs. Then she remembered handing the purse over to her mother before getting out of the car. Damn, she didn't even have her cell phone with her.

The sudden knock on the door startled her.

"It's open," said Gangga, expecting to see her mother or Mrs. Mehra but instead two little black haired heads poked in. Gangga stared at them, momentarily stunned. Maybe they'd entered the wrong room and soon would realise their mistake and disappear, Gangga hoped. The last thing she wanted was a conversation (or a non-conversation) with the twins – Johan and Karan. But instead of going away, the twins entered the room and closed the door behind them. Gangga's eyes widened. The twins gazed at her strangely, as if they didn't recognize her. Then, they shrugged in unison and seated themselves on the empty chairs.

Gangga couldn't help not looking at them. They looked dorky in their traditional Indian costumes. And they didn't speak, they didn't need to speak. Gangga was sure they communicated telepathically with each other. Finally, after staring long enough, Gangga forced a smile. The twins didn't return her smile. In fact, they didn't even look at her. They were facing the floor with scornful faces. Gangga waited a few minutes for the boys to say something, but she knew she was wasting her time. She tried not to look at them, but she couldn't help it, they were distracting. Finally, to kill the silence, she said, "So, boys, how come you two are here?"

As if they were a pair of robots, the twins lifted their heads toward Gangga in synchrony. She waited for them to say something, but nothing. They diverted their eyes back to the floor. Gangga rolled her eyes upwards and sat on the chair that was facing the mirror.

A few minutes later, all of a sudden, the twins spoke.

"We were told to come here…" said Johan.

"To keep you company," finished Karan.

Gangga swivelled in her chair to face them.

"Oh?" she said, "Who told you?"

"Mum," said Johan.

"And Dad," said Karan.

"But shouldn't you two be seated with the family? It's almost time for the groom's party to arrive, isn't it?"

"Apparently we talk too much…" said Johan.

"And know too much," ended Karan.

"What do you mean? You guys hardly talk."

"That's what you think," said Johan.

"You don't know us all that well," said Karan. A sound resembling mock snigger emanated from the boys.

"Right," She said, pushing aside the desire to laugh. "So, tell me, what was it that got you in trouble? What were you talking about?" Not that she really cared or wanted to know, she just wanted to kill time and keep her nerves under control.

Karan and Johan threw each other unsure glances. Then they nodded as if in agreement. Gangga wasn't sure what to make of them. They really were a pair of queer boys.

"If you really must know…" began Johan.

"We were talking about the big fight in the next room," said Karan.

Gangga lifted a brow, "What fight?"

"The one between Kaveri didi..."

"And Raj Bhaiya,"

"And Ajay Uncle,"

"With Menaka Aunty."

Gangga looked from one twin to the other so fast she might as well be watching a game of tennis. The twins spoke fast and finished each other's sentence.

"What kind of a fight?" she was afraid to know. She swallowed a few times, hoping to moisten her throat that had suddenly turned dry.

"Ajay uncle was accusing Raj *bhaiya* of having an affair," Johan said.

"With Kaveri didi's best friend," said Karan.

"And Kaveri didi was accusing Ajay uncle of having an affair,"added Johan.

"With...we don't know," concluded Karan.

Gangga's throat felt parched. She opened her mouth to say something only to shut it back again. Obviously Kaveri was up to her nonsense once again, and this time she'd targeted Gangga's wedding as the best venue for it. But how did she manage to come up so much of crap? Raj having an affair didn't come as a shock to Gangga – but with Susan? Gangga made a point to ask Ajay after the wedding. But for Kaveri to accuse Ajay of having an affair was crossing the line. There was a limit to vengeance and Kaveri was obviously oblivious to it. Gangga looked at the twins and wondered how much of what they said was the truth. Did they even know what constituted an affair?

"How old are you two?" she asked finally, landing on safe ground.

"Nine," came the unanimous reply.

"And what do you know about 'affairs'?"

"That it runs in the family," Johan replied – poker-faced.

Gangga had to struggle to control the laughter that was threatening to burst out of her. She puckered her lips and thought of a decent believable response – none came to mind. She was still thinking when suddenly Karan spoke.

"Gangga didi," he said. "What does 'distort' mean?"

"Oh...hmm, well, it could mean a lot of things, depends on how the word is used, in what context."

"Jamuna didi was saying…" said Johan.

"That if she fit Jason into the family picture," continued Karan.

"It might distort the current image," said Johan.

Gangga wasn't clueing in. She studied the twins and tried to make sense of what they were saying.

"Although, we didn't think it will," spoke Karan.

"We've seen your family picture," said Johan.

"And they're a lot of empty spaces to fit Jason in," said Karan.

"That's why we're not quite sure what 'distort' means," finished Johan.

Gangga had to physically compose herself before she could speak. Talk about calming her nerves, the twins were having an adverse affect on her.

"Right," she finally said. "In this case, when they said 'distort', they meant to alter the current image. Naturally, Jason's presence in the picture would somehow alter the current image – don't you think?" Gangga hoped her answer would satisfy the twins. She didn't think she'd be able to handle any more questioning. Why was Jamuna discussing Jason in front of the twins?

The twins looked at each other and fell silent, much to Gangga's relief. She wished she knew what the time was. She felt like she was stuck in a cave with two very odd beings and all connections and communication with the outside world were hindered. She wished desperately for her mother or Mrs. Mehra to come in and save her.

"Do you think," Johan said thoughtfully. Gangga froze.

"That your husband would fit into the picture," said Karan.

"Without distorting it?"

Gangga swallowed a lump that had appeared out of nowhere down her throat. The twins were looking at her expectantly. She cleared her throat and opened her mouth to say something when the door opened and Chandni walked in.

"Johan, Karan, go and sit in the hall," she called at the twins. "The groom's party has arrived." The twins dashed out of the room like birds being freed from a cage – with not a moment of hesitation.

Gangga tensed. The groom's party had arrived. Subash was there. She should be happy, thrilled. Instead her body turned cold with dread.

Chapter twenty-six – Jamuna

Jamuna always found weddings to be such romantic, emotional moments. She cried at Kaveri's wedding and she knew she'd be crying as soon as she saw Gangga walking into the *mandap*. Jamuna was standing at the *mandap* herself, outside of it. The *panditji* had the fire lit-up. He was performing some prayers, his lips moving rapidly as if he was chewing on a betel leaf. Her parents and a few of her other relatives had gone to the main entrance to welcome the groom's party.

Jamuna didn't feel like welcoming Subash, not after all the hell he'd put Gangga through that morning. Jamuna felt that Subash had behaved badly toward Gangga. If Gangga didn't love him so much, Jamuna would've suggested she called the whole thing off. But, secretly, she was glad the wedding was taking place and that Subash hadn't stood Gangga up at the altar. Imagine the embarrassment Gangga would have had to bear otherwise.

Jamuna hoped Subash and Gangga would somehow work through their differences and live a happy life. She watched as the wedding guests were all turned toward the main entrance, anticipating the arrival of the groom. Good thing he didn't come on a horse or a donkey, thought Jamuna with a smirk. In a traditional Hindu wedding, grooms arrived on a horse or a donkey, but in Subash's case, he came in a tackily decorated BMW X-3. Jamuna craned her neck to see if she could have a peek at the entrance, but it was impossible with everyone crowding at the door.

While every head was turned toward the door, one head was watching her. Jamuna was turning her gaze away from the door when she realised Jason had his eyes fixed on her. Her heart gave a little leap. He was gazing at her with such intensity that it sent goose bumps down her spine. Jamuna tried to look away but she couldn't. Slowly and steadily, Jason walked toward her. He kept his eyes on her all the while. Jamuna panicked. What was he doing? Why was he coming up to her? Jason reached the *mandap*, eyes fixed tightly on Jamuna, leaned close to her face and whispered, "You look stunning." When suddenly, "No shoes, please!" the *panditji* yelled.

Jason stepped back from the *mandap* so fast he almost tripped. Jamuna gave him a wan look.

"You can't wear shoes inside the altar, it's sinful," Jamuna explained.

Jason slipped his shoes off. "Sorry."

"What're you doing here?" whispered Jamuna. She darted her eyes around the wedding hall to see if anyone was looking.

"I came to say how beautiful you look in that sari. I don't think I'd ever seen you in a sari before, very becoming."

Jamuna found herself blushing. "Thanks. You should go."

"Can we talk?"

"What? Now?"

"Step out with me for a while, I really must talk," Jason tried taking Jamuna by the elbow. She moved away.

"The groom's here, I can't leave now," Jamuna hissed.

"Please, it'll take two minutes, I beg you."

Jamuna saw the desperation in Jason's eyes and gave-in, making him promise that it would only be two minutes. They made their escape through the back door and stopped under the awning. The rain was coming down with a new vigour. Jamuna stood against the wall and Jason hovered over her, blocking the rain from getting to her. Jason was so close to her that Jamuna could feel his warm breath on her cheeks. She lowered her eyes from his face and fixed them on his chests. She was too close to him for comfort and she was worried someone might see them together. She knew Jason was looking at her, she could feel his blue eyes piercing into hers, but she refused to meet his gaze. For she knew, if she did she'd let her feelings for Jason show and Jamuna didn't think that would be prudent, given their circumstances.

"J," whispered Jason and touched his forehead to hers. "I've missed you so much."

Jamuna winched as a wave of emotion hit her. She felt Jason's love for her and felt both comforted and wretched. She leaned forward and let him hold her. She felt close to tears. Why on earth did she have to go and fall for a white guy? What was she thinking?

"You didn't say a word to me the whole day?" she said softly.

"I didn't want to upset you. How're you feeling?" Jason brought his hand forward and placed in gently on her tummy.

"Sick and afraid and..."

"And?"

"Happy. I'm going to be a mother," Jamuna let the words sink. Jason brought her closer and buried his face in the curves of her neck.

"You're going to be the mother of my child, I'm so proud of you, J."

"Are you sure?" she teased him. "I thought I wasn't worthy..."

Jason covered her lips with his. He kissed her briefly and passionately and when he released her, she was panting. Then he looked into her big eyes and said, "You're the only one I want to have my child with. Sorry I said all those things, I didn't mean any of them. I was upset. You don't know how you've made me feel. God, J, I can't imagine a life without you."

"What're we going to do?" whispered Jamuna. The prospect of not having Jason in her life suddenly terrified her. But at the same time, the idea of defying her father and marrying Jason terrified her more. She didn't want to lose Jason and she didn't want to lose her family by marrying Jason.

Jason held Jamuna away from him and spoke with chilling seriousness, "I already told you what I want and where I stand when it comes to us. I will sit under that temple or whatever you call it, wearing what looks like a pajama suit with no shoes on if it means I'll get to spend the rest of my life with you. That's all I want to say, J. The rest is up to you. Whatever you decide, I just hope you'll not keep our baby from me. I love you, J, more than life itself. The question is do you love me enough to defy your family and your culture? I don't want to take you away from your family. I just want to be a part of them, a part of you. You have to decide if I'll fit into the frame or not."

"Jason," said Jamuna but Jason interrupted her.

"I think my two-minute is up. I also think the groom's already at the altar."

Before Jamuna could say more, Jason walked back into the wedding hall.

Chapter twenty-seven – The Wedding

Subash shook his sleepers off his feet and bent his head to enter the *mandap*. His parents and relatives were close behind him. The *panditji* started with his *mantras* and in the midst of it said, to no-one in particular, to go get the bride. Menaka rushed ahead and called Jamuna to accompany her. Mrs. Mehra followed them as well and a few other girls who suddenly materialized into the scene, including Priya.

Gangga looked up when the ladies entered the room, all excited and loud. Jamuna ran to her and hugged her tightly.

"Didi, are you excited?"

"I don't have to be since you lot are," said Gangga.

Mrs. Mehra rushed to her side and started fiddling with her sari and make-up. Menaka planted a kiss on Gangga's forehead, exclaiming how pretty she looked and how lucky Subash was – again.

"Mama, you're repeating yourself, and really, I don't think Subash considers himself all that lucky," said Gangga.

"Well he should!" said Menaka. "Oh, I can't believe it. Jamuna, you're the only one left after this, then I can take a long vacation. Mrs. Mehra, we should really discuss about that boy you know from that good family."

"Yes...yes, of course. I think he'll be good for our lovely Jamuna," Mrs. Mehra shook her head like a hen.

Jamuna glanced over at Gangga with a *I-told-you-so look* on her face. The wedding wasn't even over yet, and they were already discussing Jamuna's wedding. Gangga flashed her sister a knowing smile.

"Come...come, it's time," Menaka held Gangga's hand and led her out of the room, followed by the rest of the ladies.

Gangga felt like a mannequin-in-sari being ushered forward forcefully by her mother. She walked mutely, her eyes on the floor. Although there were all sorts of people's voices in the background, Gangga could still hear the heavy rain outside. It gave her no comfort. Her internal turmoil matched the reckless rain outside – persistent and irrepressible.

When Gangga entered the wedding-hall, she saw Subash sitting yoga-style on the floor in the *mandap* in front of the priest. He looked different in his cream-colored *sherwani* (long jacket) and *churidars* (fitted trousers) with a turban on. He looked...he looked like an Indian prince, charming. Gangga was surprised Subash didn't have flowers dangling down from his turban to cover his face like most grooms normally did during Hindu weddings.

Subash lifted his head briefly when he sensed Gangga's presence but he didn't let his gaze linger on her. He darted his eyes away fast as if the sight of her tormented him. Gangga felt her heart pumping harder and her steps slowed significantly that Menaka had to nudge her forward. She was made to sit on the floor next to Subash. She fixed her eyes on the mini campfire in the middle of the mandap, with bricks arranged around it. Its flames roared upward in bright yellow and orange, creating a cloud of black smoke to linger in the air above.

Gangga watched the fire and felt more and more unsettled. The fire was sacred. And the promises made in front of the fire in a Hindu wedding were unbreakable. Gangga wanted to glance over at Subash – to see if he'd look at her. But it was not proper for the bride to boldly look at her husband during their wedding – so she was told repeatedly by her mother and Mrs. Mehra. They had reminded her over and over that she had to behave like a bride. But she really wanted to look at Subash.

She knew it was too late to turn back but she was hoping for some kind of assurance from him. She was hoping he'd at least smile at her or acknowledge her with a nod. That was all she wanted. She was about to dart her eyes sideways toward Subash when the priest ordered them to stand.

Gangga stood facing Subash and as she'd dreaded, he wasn't looking at her. His eyes were fixed stubbornly on the fire. Gangga's insides started to churn. *God, please don't make me throw up,* she prayed.

After that, things happened quite fast. Everything took place smoothly and very quickly. She was handed a flower garland and asked to place it around Subash's neck.

And yet, he wasn't looking at her, not even when he had placed the garland around her. The garland was meant to signify their acceptance of each other as husband and wife and Gangga felt like she was being insincere since in her heart, she was finding it very hard to accept Subash as her husband.

But she felt like a bigger sinner when the *Kanya Daan* ceremony took place. '*Kanya*' in Sanskrit means a virgin and '*Daan*' refers to donation. This ceremony involved Gangga's father who was giving his virgin-daughter away to Subash. Gangga shook slightly as the *panditji* placed a conch that contained gold, betel-nut, flowers and fruits on her right hand. Subash was made to support her hand with his right hand. Meanwhile, Menaka and Ajay placed their left hands below Subash's hand and their right hands on top of Gangga's hand. All the while, *panditji's* lips were moving as mantras flowed out of his mouth.

The mantras were alien to Gangga's ears. A couple of times she looked up when her parents' names were mentioned, Everything else was French – or on this case, Sanskrit to her. But she couldn't help feeling wretched with guilt. She wasn't a virgin and here was her father, performing the rituals of giving his virgin-daughter away with the fire-God as their witness. Gangga prayed with all her might that she'd be forgiven. She wished she'd told her mother the truth; maybe then this ritual could've been avoided. It was too late now. She was a sinner. How was she to ever look back at her wedding day without feeling guilty? She wouldn't be able to even celebrate her wedding anniversary without a taint of guilt attached to it. Was this how weddings were supposed to be? Feeling shameful, Gangga looked up at Subash and found him staring at her. His eyes glinted accusingly. Great! Gangga looked away.

The rituals that followed next were vague to Gangga. She didn't hear anything the *panditji* was saying and didn't feel anything. She shut everything out. She decided the only way to live through the miserable wedding rituals was to block her mind out of everything. The only way she could be strong and endure the torturing moments was to be totally emotionless – void like a vacuum.

Before she knew it, she was standing next to Subash and her mother was tying the end of her sari that fell over her shoulders to the end of Subash's *kurta* into a small, tight knot. Gangga realized what would take place next. The knot symbolized the sacred wedlock and the proceeding ritual was going to eternally bound Gangga to Subash as his wife – it was the '*Saat Phere*'or '*The Seven Rounds*' – where she walked around the fire seven times with Subash leading her and pledging a lifetime of promises together. Gangga stood in agony as preparations for '*Saat-Phere*' took place around her. The *panditji* was still muttering some *mantras* under his breath. He was also explaining to them about the ritual and its importance. Gangga listened half-heartedly. It didn't matter anymore, none of it mattered – the wedding, the sanctity of it, and the eternal bond that came with it – when there was no love and especially, when there was no respect. Gangga felt like she was doomed as Subash's wife.

With the fire, her parents, her sister, her relatives and hundred other people as witnesses, Gangga walked around the fire with Subash on the lead. The *panditji* spoke before he chanted the first mantra:

"I ask you, Subash Mehta and Gangga Sharma, to concentrate upon these seven vows as you make the seven rounds." He then recited the first mantra for the first round around the fire which translated to, "May you be blessed with abundance of food."

First round completed, Gangga continued with the second round and *panditji* chanted, "May you be strong and complement each other."

At the end of the second round, Gangga felt she was cheating not only herself but everyone else present. She looked at the crowd in front of her and her eyes settled on Jason who was standing not far away from the *mandap*. Jason wasn't looking at her or at the ritual that was in progress; instead his eyes were glued on someone over Gangga's shoulder. Gangga looked back and saw Jamuna standing close by her at the *mandap*. She smiled when she saw Gangga's eyes on her.

Gangga felt Subash moving and followed him but not before darting Jason another look. It wasn't that he was looking only at Jamuna in that large throng that amused Gangga but it was the way he looked – his eyes were soft with love, it was as if she was the only thing that mattered to him. *Panditji* was chanting the mantra for the third round, "May you be blessed with prosperity."

Gangga walked around the fire mechanically. She couldn't shake the look in Jason's eyes from her head. That was what she had felt for Subash initially, until that morning. But all that had changed. She couldn't contemplate ever looking at him with the same affection and love she'd seen in Jason's eyes. And she was sure she'd not get the same look from Subash.

And when the *panditji* chanted the fourth mantra for the fourth round, "May you be eternally happy," Gangga stopped abruptly halfway. Eternally happy? She looked over at her parents in front of her, standing a safe-distance from each other. Her father had a forlorn, confused look on his face while her mother looked impatient, as if waiting for her wedding to be over. But that wasn't the problem – the problem was Gangga didn't want her marriage to Subash to end up like her parents'. They hadn't found their eternal happiness with each other and Gangga knew in her heart, she'd not find her happiness with Subash.

Just then her eyes fell on the eager faces of the twins, Johan and Karan, and their earlier question came to mind. '*Will Subash fit into the frame?*' and Gangga knew the answer then. Subash, not realizing Gangga's halt, continued walking until he felt his *kurta* that was tied to Gangga's sari being pulled. Intrigued, he turned around and saw Gangga staring at him with a bizarre look in her eyes.

The *panditji*, who was chanting the mantra, looked up from where he was sitting, slightly annoyed at what he clearly considered an infringement and asked Gangga if there was a problem. Gangga pulled her eyes from Subash and faced the crowd. Jamuna was by her side in an instant, as was Menaka and Ajay.

"Beta, is something wrong?" Ajay asked her.

"Didi, what is the matter?" Jamuna probed. Gangga remained quiet but her eyes were welling up dangerously. Menaka held Gangga's shoulders and whispered, "Gangga, what is it?"

Gangga was close to tears but she remained calm. The throng in the wedding-hall suddenly became alert. All eyes were on the *mandap*. Even those who were not paying any attention to the boring, mundane ritual of a regular Hindu wedding earlier became vigilant. Slowly, people started whispering among each other with all sorts of presumed speculations – the bride was in love with someone else, she was pregnant, she was having cold feet, or she was…until Subash lost his cool.

"For heaven's sake, will you tell what's wrong?" he yelled.

Ajay, taken aback with Subash's loud voice, laid a calming hand on him but Subash shook it off. That was all that Gangga needed to gain new strength. This man didn't even have the decency to be respectful toward her father, how would he make a good son-in-law? She wasn't weak and she certainly didn't want to seem vulnerable in front of Subash. And how dare he yell at her in front of everyone? By this time, Subash's parents, who had been sitting close to the *mandap* , approached them. Gangga sucked in her breath and gathered courage for the hell that was about to befall her. She walked to the center of the *mandap* so she could be visible to everyone. Meanwhile, the *panditji* was getting impatient.

"Sharmaji, baath kia he?" *Mr. Sharma, what's the matter?*

"Zaara rukhye, panditji." *Wait for a while, panditji.*

Ajay turned to Gangga, "Gangga, the auspicious time is passing, what's wrong? Are you not feeling well?"

"Gangga," Subash's angry voice boomed loudly. "I don't have time for this, now out with it, so we can complete this…this…round."

"I don't think you'd fit in the frame?" Gangga spoke finally, eyes on Subash.

"What?"

"I'm sorry, Subash. But the more I think of it the more I can't fathom you within the frame – you'd not fit in without distorting the image."

"What on earth are you mumbling about? What bloody frame? Will you start walking so we can finish this?"

"I can't complete the circle, not with you when I know in my heart that you will punish me for the rest of my life for not…for not… meeting certain expectations of yours," Gangga paused and looked at Subash before turning to her father, her eyes glistening with tears. "Papa, I'm sorry, terribly sorry to have to do this to you. I can't go through with this wedding."

The loud gasps that emanated from the crowd sounded like dogs howling. Gangga felt like placing her hands over her ears to block the 'ahh's' and 'uuhhhs' from the disbelieving throng. She'd just given her relatives something to talk about for the next ten years.

"Gangga?" she heard her father's controlled voice addressing her. "Did something happen? Until yesterday, you were really into this wedding. What happened between yesterday and now?"

"Reality, Papa…reality happened and the truth is, Subash and I are two different people with totally different ideologies in life. We'll never make it. I can't go through the sacred rituals of this wedding with the man that I don't love, not anymore."

The gasps had turned into whispers, loud whispers. Subash's father, who was listening quietly all the while, suddenly threw his walking stick dramatically across the floor of the wedding hall from the *mandap*. A few nearby people scooted out of the way as the stick tumbled down the platform and landed on the floor with a loud clout. "Ajay! What crap is your daughter going on about? Tell her to stop this nonsense and finish this wedding. We really have no time to be sitting around listening to her 'reality' and 'truth' bullshit!"

Before Ajay could respond, Subash took the flower garland from around his neck and flung it across the *mandap*. Then he roughly untied the knot that tied his *kurta* to Gangga's sari. With everyone, except Gangga, calling out his name in an attempt to stop him, he descended the few steps that led to the wedding hall from the *mandap* while at the same time taking his turban off and flinging it to the side. Everyone watched as Subash walked into the middle of the hall before turning abruptly toward the *mandap*, as if he forgot something.

"Gangga, go ahead and screw your life up, see if I care. I was doing you a favour by agreeing to this wedding. Let's see which decent man is going to marry you now!" he turned around to leave before turning right back around. This time he addressed the audience. "Oh, and did I mention she's not a virgin? Despite that, despite the fact that she's a slut I was willing to marry her, you know why? Because I felt sorry for her, because I knew if I didn't marry her, she'd grow into an old maid! But this is what I get in return, this!" Subash threw his hands around him in a helpless manner. "She chose to embarrass me in front of my family and friends!" Then to his parents, "Let's get out of here and you folks, please feel free to eat before leaving."

Part Six – That Evening

Chapter twenty-eight – Ajay

Ajay sat on one of the chairs in the room Gangga was in earlier with his hands cradling his head. In front of him stood Gangga, Jamuna, Menaka, and Chandni. Chandni's husband, Mahesh with Siva, Devika, Priya and Vikram, decided to stay out of the family confrontation and helped to clear the tables and chairs in the wedding hall. The twins were put to work as well. Mrs. Mehra had rushed out together with the throng about half-an-hour ago, leaving the family to tend to their predicaments. The Dhillons left briefly as soon as Subash walked out of the wedding hall, without so much of a word of support to their in-laws.

"Papa?" Ajay heard Gangga's voice and lifted his head to look at his daughter; his eyes were strained, his face gaunt with anguish. "Papa, please forgive me. I never meant to hurt you, but I didn't have any other choice. I couldn't marry Subash. Would you rather I married him and lived in hell? Papa, that's what it would've been marrying to Subash – a living hell!"

"If you didn't love him," Menaka spoke instead. "Why did you wait until the last minute? Why didn't you say something before? You let us go through the whole wedding preparation and you waited until the last minute, half-way through the wedding before saying something. What were you thinking, Gangga?"

Ajay watched as Gangga dropped her gaze to the floor. He was glad

Menaka was doing the questioning since he really didn't trust his voice right at that moment.

"I'm sorry, Mama. I know how much this hurt you and Papa and everyone else. But I didn't do it deliberately. I knew all preparations had taken place and I didn't want to embarrass Papa and you in front of our relatives. And I know I've done exactly that but I had to do it. It was while performing The Seven Rounds that I realised I didn't love Subash and that he'd not fit into the frame."

"What stupid frame are you going on about?"

"The family photo – the twins asked me a valid question earlier, would Subash fit into the family photo without distorting the current image. At that point, I found their question ridiculous, but as I made the rounds around the fire, I saw them and realised Subash would not fit into the photo. He'd not get along with everyone because he's not a very likable person. And I was right, did you not see how he pushed Papa's hand away just now in the *mandap?* He can be insolent when he wants to be and I discovered that a little too late."

"Gangga, you knew Subash for a few months now and you liked him just fine," Menaka said. "Why the sudden change of heart? You looked in love with him, you were all for marrying him, I don't understand."

"I guess I have to tell the truth," Gangga's voice sounded muffled. Ajay waited patiently thinking nothing that Gangga had to confess could shock him more. The damage was done, and the post-mortem process didn't in any way lessen the degree of the damage, it merely gave it a better understanding. "Subash actually became indecisive about marrying me earlier this morning. He found out that I wasn't a virgin and hung up on me, saying he wasn't sure about the wedding anymore. And when he called back, he told me that by going ahead with the wedding, he was actually doing me a favour. How can I marry him after that?" Gangga sounded defeated.

Ajay's heart sank. How did he make a mistake in choosing Subash for Gangga? Where did he go wrong? But Menaka wasn't satisfied with Gangga's answer.

"He *was* doing you a favour, Gangga," she said. "Which decent guy is going to marry you now? And what are you going on about love? This is not some fairy tale you're living in, and there's no such thing as falling in love and all that nonsense. You get married to the man we pick because we know he's right for you. And by him wanting to marry you despite the fact that you're not...well, pure anymore, I think we chose the right guy for you but you had to go and mess it up."

Jamuna, who'd been quiet all these while, spoke suddenly, "But, Mama, he didn't love Gangga didi. If he loved her, what did it matter if she was a virgin or not, why would he even contemplate otherwise? And if he respected her, he wouldn't degrade her the way he did."

"You two need to get your head examined! What's this love nonsense all about? I told you, this is real life, not some fairy-tale!"

"Well, Mama, I don't want to be in a loveless marriage!" Gangga retorted. "I've lived with Papa and you long enough to know what a loveless marriage does to couples and I don't want my marriage to suffer the same consequences. I'd rather not be married!"

Ajay felt like Gangga had slapped him.

Menaka snorted, "You're a disgrace!"

"No, she's not," Jamuna retaliated. "She just did what she thought was right. Do you want her to be stuck in a loveless marriage where her husband could use his power and superiority against her anytime he wished, where he had the upper hand?"

"She brought that upon herself, didn't she?" Menaka argued back.

"Well, if you think she's a disgrace, what would you think of me?" Jamuna asked boldly. Ajay felt his adrenalin pumping. Something told him the worst was not yet over.

"Are you going to tell us you're corrupted as well?" Menaka could never bring herself to use the word 'virgin'.

"Very, and I'm also pregnant," Jamuna said it so casually and poker-faced that everyone, including Ajay, thought she was joking at first.

"Jamuna," Chandni interrupted, "We're discussing serious matter here, please don't joke at times like this."

"Who said I was joking?" Jamuna joined Gangga in gazing at the floor as she said this. Ajay stood up, pushing his chair back with such vehemence that it fell backwards. His face was contorted in confusion and anger. He looked from Gangga to Jamuna as if he didn't recognize them. There was so much pain written all over his face that everyone in the room felt sorry for him. He opened his mouth to say something but clamped it shut when he couldn't think of anything to say. Then a loud, shocking wheeze-like puff emanated from Menaka.

"Good God!" Menaka exclaimed loudly. "*Besharam*!! Kaveri was right all along...you have been fooling around with Vikram, haven't you, you shameless girl!"

Ajay felt dizzy and sweaty...what more was there in stock for him? How much more of this day could he endure?

"With Vikram?" Chandni's voice was like someone pounding on his ear-drums, loud and agonizing. "What do you mean with Vikram?"

"Kaveri's wrong, Mama," Gangga said. "Vikram had not been fooling around with Jamuna. For heaven's sake, their related!"

"Thank God," came Chandni's relieved voice.

Jamune started sobbing, "Is that how low you think of me, Mama?"

"You don't want to know what I think of you, both of you! I'm disappointed, terribly. I don't know where to put my face or how to face people after this," Menaka was dramatic.

"Mama, it'd be nice if you asked how Jamuna's doing – you know, being pregnant and all," Gangga's turn to defend her sister.

"Gangga, I don't think you should talk! And as for you, Jamuna, you're a bigger disgrace. Dear God, what will I do now?" Menaka started pacing. Ajay was sure she'd love to have a swig of her scotch, and come to think of it, so would he. Ajay knew he had to step forward and say something to his two daughters, but he was still at loss for words.

"Menaka, there's really one option here," Ajay heard Chandni addressing Menaka.

All heads turned toward Chandni. "Well, I know someone, a doctor...who'd assist in such matters..."

"Chandni, what're you suggesting?" Ajay finally spoke.

"Well, Ajay, what else is there to do?" Chandni asked back. "Do you want everyone to find out and lose face? There's only one thing to do, take her to the doctor...how many months are you..."

"I'm not aborting this baby," screamed Jamuna suddenly. She was clutching to her stomach and sobbing. Gangga ran to her and held her close.

"Well, you certainly can't have it, not in my house!" decided Menaka. "I'm not having a bastard in the family. Jamuna, you don't have a choice."

"Mama," Gangga said, "You're not going to make Jamuna abort

this baby. She can have it in my apartment, but she's not going to get rid of it."

"She's most definitely not having it!" Menaka yelled. "Who's going to marry her now? As it is, I have you as the old-maid; I can't have another daughter not married and staying under my roof. God, what calamity has befallen us? This is all your fault, Ajay. If we hadn't left India all those years back, this wouldn't have happened to us – our children would not have turned out this way! You've ruined it all for us, Ajay...you've ruined it!"

"It was ruined the day I married you, Menaka," Ajay's voice was heavy with emotion. "Don't blame the country for it, blame us."

"Why would I blame me? I don't remember doing anything wrong."

"You agreed to marry me. What goes around comes around, Menaka. You married me even though you didn't love me, and although I tried to love you, I couldn't. We were trapped in a loveless marriage we couldn't get out of and became victims of. And instead of learning from our mistakes, we're trying to impose the same thing on our children. Our children are paying for our sins, Menaka. Don't you get it, it's all karma." Ajay saw Menaka staring at him as if he'd lost his mind.

"Speak for yourself, Ajay. I'm not the one who destroyed our marriage. This is bullshit! You can stand there and defend your girls all you like, but please don't put any blame on me. I may not have been a good wife to you but I've always been a good mother to these children. I've had enough for one day. I'm going home and pour myself a stiff drink!" Ajay was surprised Menaka admitted to drinking in front of their daughters. Maybe she didn't realise she'd said it. He watched as she walked out of the room. Chandni approached Ajay and tried to talk to him but he dismissed her, asking her to leave him alone with his daughters. Shrugging off with defeat, Chandni left the room. Ajay pushed a couple of chairs toward the girls, indicating them to sit.

Gangga opened her mouth to say something, but Ajay put his hand up and stopped her, "Let me talk, you girls have said enough for one night." He paused and walked around the room. He wasn't trying to decide what to tell his daughters, but merely trying to gather his thoughts and deciding on a tactful manner to approach them. He stopped walking abruptly, pulled a chair forward and sat facing them.

"When did you find out you were pregnant?" he asked Jamuna.

"This morning."

"So the test-kit Kaveri produced at the breakfast table was yours and not Devika's?"

Jamuna nodded. She had remorse written all over her face. Ajay shook his head in disbelief. Devika, as usual, had placed his children's best interest before hers, despite the embarrassment that befell her. But why didn't Devika say anything to him when he had confronted her?

"We don't know why Devika Aunty took the blame; she didn't know it was Jamuna's. Maybe she guessed it was one of ours," Gangga said, breaking into his thoughts.

"She took the blame to protect you. But did she know the truth?" he asked.

"We didn't get a chance to talk to her," Jamuna said.

"I think you owe her an explanation and an apology," Ajay said and the girls nodded vigorously.

"Now, the bigger question and one that had been driving me insane – "

"It's Jason," Jamuna said before Ajay could go on.

Ajay rubbed his hands over his face and found them shaking. Jason? Jamuna was having Jason's baby? A *gora*?

"He's a good man, Papa," Gangga said. "He loves Jamuna very much. There's nothing wrong with him."

"Nothing wrong with him?" Ajay hollered. "Not only is he white, he got her pregnant! And what is he doing about it? How dare he come into my house and mess with my daughter's life? And pretending to be helpful and all...such a cheat!"

"He's not a cheat, Papa!" Jamuna said defensively. "And he wasn't pretending to be helpful, he *was* being helpful. Why do you blame it all on him, I'm at fault too – I slept with him too."

Ajay grunted something unintelligible under his breath.

"He does love Jamuna, Papa. He even asked her to marry him," said Gangga.

Ajay looked unconvinced. "He did, did he? So are you marrying him?"

"No, because I know how you feel about it," said Jamuna.

"Oh, now you think of my feelings! What happened when you were with him? Would've been nice if you had thought of my feelings then!"

Ajay knew he sounded harsh, very unlike him, but he was livid. He didn't expect this from his daughters, especially not from Jamuna.

"I'm sorry, Papa," Jamuna started sobbing again. "I know I've let you down. I will not marry Jason but at the same time, don't tell me to get rid of this baby, I will not do that either."

"God, Jamuna, how did it all come to this?"

"I don't know..."

"She fell in love, Papa," Gangga spoke. "She fell in love with the wrong guy by your book. But it doesn't have to be that way, you can change it."

"What're you talking about?"

"The only reason Jamuna doesn't want to marry Jason is because she thinks you won't approve of him. Let her marry him, Papa. At least let one of us be happy."

"This is insane! I'm not having a *gora* in my family."

"You go on about not wanting a white-guy in your family – when the white-guy is a hundred-times better than the two Indian guys combined – Raj and Subash! Why the stereotype, Papa?" Gangga asked.

Ajay stared at the floor of the room speechlessly. Gangga's word made complete sense to him, yet he couldn't bring himself to say yes to Jason. Feeling completely drained and tired, Ajay instructed the girls to go back to the house. He had one more person to see before he went home. He left his daughters and walked into the wedding-hall.

He noticed the hundreds of chairs being stacked on top of one another by Siva and Mahesh, with the help of the twins. Vikram was sweeping the floor with Priya and Devika. He scanned the hall and spotted Jason, who was on his knees, clearing things away from the *mandap.* Ajay took a few brusque steps up the stairs leading to the *mandap* and stood patronizingly in front of Jason. He held Jason by his collar with one hand and pulled him up. Jason, looking baffled, staggered to his feet clumsily.

"You no good son-of-a-bitch!" Ajay said vehemently. "How dare you enter my house and mess with my daughter?"

Everyone working down at the hall paused on their tasks and turned toward the *mandap.* Vikram ran up to Jason's side instantly. He tried interrupting but Ajay ordered him to keep his mouth shut.

"You pretended to be good and helpful, when all the while you've been screwing my daughter."

"I love your daughter, Mr. Sharma," Jason squeezed his words in before Ajay could continue with his bantering.

"Bullshit!" Ajay yelled. "What do you know about love? What do any of you about love? Let me tell you something, you don't go around getting innocent girls pregnant in the name of love, that's what you call uncontrollable, disgusting lust!"

"Mr. Sharma..."

"I'm not done speaking! So, tell me, Mr. Love – what do you intend to do about this situation?"

"Jamuna knows where I stand and the end decision is hers. I'm sorry."

"Sorry? Jason, you're this close from getting beaten to pulp," Ajay brought his index finger close to his thumb and displayed it in front of Jason's face.

"Uncle Ajay, please calm down," Vikram interrupted.

"Stay out of this, Vikram."

Vikram spoke regardless, "Jason is not the kind of guy you think he is. He really loves Jamuna and wants to marry her, only she's not too sure."

"And why is that? If she really loves him, and is having his baby, why does she not want to marry him? What kind of a love is that?"

"She loves me, Mr. Sharma."

"Bullshit!"

"But she loves you more."

Ajay froze in stunned silence. For the first time, Ajay saw above his anger and noticed Jason's tear glistened eyes, soft with love and his heart twisted in wretched guilt. Slowly, he eased the hold on Jason's collar. He didn't need any more proof. Any idiot looking at Jason could tell he was consumed by love and misery.

"Uncle Ajay..." Vikram started to speak when Ajay shook his head resignedly.

"I'm going home."

Everyone in the hall watched as Ajay walked unsteadily out of the wedding hall, his shoulders drooped, his head bowed.

CHAPTER TWENTY-NINE – DEVIKA

DEVIKA HAD TO CONTROL every molecule in her body from running to Ajay and holding him. She couldn't see him looking so drenched in misery. Her heart went awry at the sight of him. She watched him leave the wedding hall and fell backward into a nearby chair. From Ajay's confrontation with Jason, Devika knew the pregnancy test had been Jamuna's. She could only imagine what Ajay would be going through. She sat there as everyone else slowly returned to their original task of clearing the wedding-hall. Devika shook her head when she thought of the wedding that didn't take place. Why did she not see it coming? How could everyone in the house have missed the turmoil Gangga had been struggling with?

Devika got up to continue with the sweeping but her heart and mind were not at ease. She felt in desperate need to see Ajay and comfort him. His pain was too deep to be endured alone. That was when she decided to go look for him. When she was sure no one was paying any attention to her, Devika slithered out of the hall quietly.

It was dark outside and cold. Although it was still raining, the velocity of it had lessened. Devika looked up toward the sky and saw the heavy, dark cloud slowly descending further away in the horizon. She was sure by the next day the cloud would have been replaced by clear, blue sky. She only hoped the turmoil in the Sharma's residence would subside as well. She was concerned for Ajay and Menaka.

"Devika?" She swung around and saw Ajay standing at the far end of the building, under the awning, smoking a cigarette.

"I thought you'd left," she said once she was standing close to him.

"I knew you'd be coming out looking for me," Ajay inhaled deeply on the cigarette.

"Where did you get the cigarette from?" Ajay didn't smoke.

"I have my stash for days like this."

"I want to hug you."

"I'm dying for a hug from you."

"Ajay, what's going on? How did everything become so warped?"

Ajay sighed and puffed out heavy smoke from his lungs, "Karma, Devika. It's all karma."

"I don't get it."

"What goes around comes around…my children are paying for my sins."

"Oh, Ajay…"

"It's true. I've been cheating on their mother for as long as I can remember. My whole bloody marriage is a lie! I couldn't love Menaka even when I tried. But I guess I didn't try hard enough. And I shouldn't have cheated on her…all throughout our marriage. I've wronged not only her, but you too. I've complicated both your lives, I've messed things up for both of you."

"No, Ajay…"

"I'm sorry, Devika. It was wrong of me to want you the way I did, the way I still do. Whatever happened today, I deserve it – the embarrassment, the humiliation, the disgrace…you name it, I deserve it! I've failed as a husband and as a father."

"Ajay, you're being too hard on yourself."

"Am I?" Ajay let out a cynical snigger. He studied Devika for a while and asked, "You lied to me about the pregnancy-test-kit. I don't want to know why, all I want to know is, are you happy?"

Devika darted her eyes away from Ajay's face. Everything glistened with a hint of golden color under the moonlight like newly polished brass. The heavy rain earlier was only a slight drizzle now. She thought of the new, clear day the rain was going to leave behind – the fresh, untainted day. That was what Ajay needed – a fresh, new start with the fresh, new day. He needed a change in his life and it couldn't involve her. If Ajay even got a whiff of how her life was with Siva, he wouldn't leave her be. And really, how did she tell him that her rival was not another woman? Devika was not over the shock yet, but Ajay's words made perfect sense to her. It *was* karma. She'd always known her marriage to Siva was a form of punishment for sleeping with her sister's husband, but only now did she realise the degree of that punishment. She was married to a homosexual! She wanted to laugh out loud.

"Devika?" Ajay's voice brought her back to the present.

"Yes, I'm very happy."

"Good, I want you to be happy; I wouldn't have it any other way."

"I have a request."

"Hmmm?"

"Give my sister another chance, please? What would she do if you left her?"

"I was thinking of the same thing. I owe her that much."

"I think I should leave tonight." Devika turned around to go.

"I'll always love you," Ajay said just as she was walking. She didn't turn back to look at him for she was afraid he'd see the tears that were pouring down her cheeks heavier than the drops of rainfalls.

Chapter thirty – Kaveri

Kaveri put her legs up on the ottoman and reclined herself on the couch she was sitting. She was glad to have left the wedding early, albeit unwillingly. And she was even more glad to have Raj rush back to the wedding after dropping her off. He had to drive his parents back home after the wedding. Kaveri took a sip of her red wine. She hadn't confronted Raj on the earlier incident at the wedding. They didn't say a word to each other on the drive back home. Raj had been unusually quiet. He didn't even lecture her on her misbehaviour. In fact, He had been too quiet for Kaveri's liking.

As much as Kaveri wanted to believe her husband, something was gnawing at her, like an unidentifiable itch. She had defended Raj in front of everyone and had called her father a cheat – in front of everyone. Shouldn't he at least thank her for it? Shouldn't he praise her and call her a good wife for having faith in him? What bothered her beyond reason was her father accusing Raj of having an affair with Susan, why Susan? If he wanted to frame Raj, could he not have picked someone else, someone whom Kaveri didn't know? Why would he use Susan's name? Kaveri had always known her father's hatred toward Raj and his dislike toward Susan, maybe that was why he'd linked the two names together – two birds with one stone. But it still didn't make any sense. Did Ajay really think that Kaveri would fall for his word and then what? Leave Raj? And Susan? That was crazy.

Kaveri sipped her wine and thought of Susan. She'd noticed Susan's sudden interest in wanting to be Indian. The way she dressed, the way she wore bangles instead of bracelets, like she used to. She even wore a *bindi* quite regularly although Kaveri told Susan it looked weird on her forehead, like a colourful sticker. And wasn't that what Susan had said when she had seen Kaveri wearing a *bindi?* So what had changed? Also, more importantly, when Susan had come to the house earlier, why didn't she come looking for Kaveri?

The gnawing feeling was getting harsher and Kaveri gulped down the rest of her wine. She poured herself another glass and dialled Susan's cell number from her home phone. Kaveri never used the home phone; she felt there was no privacy when the whole household could hear her conversation. But she was too lazy to walk to her room for her cell and, anyway, there was no one else at home. The phone rang once before Susan's voice boomed in.

"Thank God, I've been waiting to hear from you. I even tried your cell so many times, why didn't you answer? Are you in big trouble, sweetie?"

"Why am I in trouble?" asked Kaveri, wondering what Susan was so anxious about. Susan had gone completely quiet. Then she forced out a laugh.

"Oh...Kaveri...I was just worried...about you..."

"How did you know it was me? I never call you from this number," Kaveri felt the room spinning. Of course Susan recognized the number... but, of course! Realization dawned on her like a judge's harsh verdict! The truth and nothing but the truth.

"I...I just guessed...I've been thinking about you and well I assumed it was you." Another sheepish laugh. *Fuck!*

"How long, Susan? How long have you been screwing my husband?" Kaveri barked, pressing a finger to her temple that was starting to throb mercilessly.

"I don't know what you're talking about..."

"This explains everything – the sari, the bangles, the stupid dot on your forehead...you're such a fucking hypocrite, Susan!"

"Look, now, Kaveri...stop throwing accusations at me..."

"Oh, shut the fuck up, you crazy bitch!" Kaveri threw the phone into its cradle and took a long swig of her wine.

She filled her glass back again, this time right to the brim and sat looking at the dark burgundy liquid. She was expecting tears to pour down her cheek, but none came. In fact, she felt oddly calm. Was she relieved? Had she always hoped for something like this? Or was she in so much shock that she was not capable of crying?

When Kaveri heard the front door opening, she didn't move from her spot. She realised she was drinking and she also realised her in-laws would probably be coming in with Raj but she didn't care. Kaveri didn't drink in front of her in-laws, Raj had forbidden her. It was apparently disrespectful to consume alcohol in front of her in-laws. But she was too tired to care. She heard Raj's voice emerging from the front foyer and felt her body trickle with anger. When he entered the living room, Kaveri stood up and swung the glass of wine in her hand onto the face of the person she thought was Raj. Only, it wasn't Raj, it was her mother-in-law. Mrs. Dhillon, with wine dripping from her thin face, walked forward and slapped Kaveri across the face. Her second slap for the day.

"Bathtamiss." *Insolent.* She hissed. "How dare you! Not enough with your smoking, you've started drinking as well? And that too, in my house?"

"I'm sorry. Mummyji, I thought it was Raj."

"And that makes it all better?" asked Mrs. Dhillon. "Why would you pour wine on Raj's face?"

"Because he's been cheating on me…with Susan," Kaveri said, looking at Raj. She expected some kind of a drama from The Dhillons, either accusing her of being irrational or confronting their son on the matter. They did neither. Instead, Mr. Dhillon started bulleting her with words.

"Is this how the *bahu* (daughter-in-law) should be behaving?" he asked. "Your Mummyji said she found cigarette butts in the toilet bowl this afternoon when she went in after you, and now I find you drinking. Are all you Sharma girls without values?"

Kaveri didn't know why Mr. Dhillon was attacking her sisters but it infuriated her.

"Papaji, did you not hear me? Your son has been cheating on me with my best friend," Kaveri pointed a shaky finger at Raj.

"Well, of course he'd be having an affair being married to the likes of you," snorted Mrs. Dhillon. That stung and the tears that refused to flow earlier started falling down Kaveri's cheeks in abundance. Had her in-laws always known about Raj?

"Are you blaming me for your son's behaviour?" she finally asked.

"If you were a better wife, why would your husband go after another woman? And, looking at you now, I think I just proved my point. If only I'd known about you Sharma girls before, I wouldn't have insisted on this marriage," said Mr. Dhillon with a dramatic shake of his head. Throughout their conversation Raj kept quiet as if he'd suddenly forgotten how to speak. He sat on the couch and stared into oblivion.

Kaveri looked at her husband and knew that she was on her own on this battle against her in-laws. What she didn't understand was her father-in-law's regular reference to the Sharma girls. "What do my sisters have to do with this?"

"Look, she doesn't know what happened today," Mrs. Dhillon's sarcastic laugh pierced into Kaveri's heart like a piece of sharp blade. "Your sister left the *mandap* halfway through the wedding – she refused to marry Subash."

"What? There was no wedding?"

"There was no wedding!" tittered Mr. Dhillon. "It was all pathetically pitiful – such shame, *rama*...If I were Ajay Sharma, I'd run away from this country! Let's see who'd marry Gangga now!"

Mr. Dhillon's words sank into Kaveri painfully. Wasn't this what she'd always wanted – to see her father shamed in front of his relatives and friends? Why then was her heart in so much pain? And Gangga left the wedding halfway? Not able to withstand the accusations thrown at her and the infamy against her family, Kaveri ran out of the room in tears.

She lit a cigarette and took a long inhale in her bedroom when Raj walked in. He took one look at her and shook his head in disgust.

"Did you not hear anything my parents said?" he murmured in an attempt to keep his voice down. "Put that thing off before they smell it."

Kaveri continued smoking as if Raj hadn't spoken.

"Kaveri, put that thing off."

"You know what's funny?" Kaveri asked, still puffing on the cigarette. "I was so careful not to end up like mother, but here I am – in the same situation she is."

"Whatever, put that thing off before I snatch it from you," Raj ordered. Kaveri took another long puff and deliberately blew the smoke onto Raj's face.

"Kaveri!" Raj bawled while flapping his hand in front of him as if swatting a fly. Kavery laughed a bitter laugh.

"You're pathetic! But do you know what makes me different from my mother?"

"I don't and I really don't care!"

"Oh, you will when I tell you," Kaveri stubbed the cigarette butt on the wooden vanity table and took pleasure as Raj's mouth opened wide in shock. "I'm leaving you, Raj."

And he laughed. He laughed long and hard that Kaveri wished she'd stubbed the cigarette butt on his face instead.

"That's the best joke I've heard tonight. You don't have the guts to leave me, Kaveri! What would you do? You don't work and even if you did, you're only qualified to be a miserable cashier! You don't have a car, you don't have a house…you don't even have your parents on your side! So, tell me…if you left me, where would you go? Face it, Kaveri – you need me more than I need you and that's why we're going to look past this incident tonight as if it never took place. As for Susan and me, you don't have any say in it."

Kaveri met Raj's gaze for the longest time until he decided to turn around and walk out of the room. She took out another cigarette and lit it. Then she took her cell phone and dialled a number. She almost gave up when Ajay's voice finally came into the phone.

"Yes?" was all he said. Ajay sounded groggy and unpleasant.

"Papa, it's me, Kaveri," how could she remain so calm? Maybe it was the nicotine.

"Are you calling to gloat? Isn't this what you've been wanting? To see me wither in shame?" Ajay's words stung. It was true she'd wanted him degraded but at that moment she didn't feel at all good about it.

"I didn't call to gloat, Papa," her voice started to waver.

Ajay didn't reply immediately. But when he did he asked whether she'd called for Menaka.

"No, I wanted to talk to you. I just want to say you were right all along."

"About what?"

"Raj…and Susan."

Silences ensued. Kaveri broke it first. "I'm sorry, Papa, for not believing you."

"How did you find out?" Ajay's voice was softer.

"It doesn't matter. I do have a question – you were almost beating Raj up when I found you. Why were you so upset?"

"He's cheating on my daughter, am I supposed to be happy about it?"

"Do you really care?" Kaveri struggled to keep her voice steady, but failed miserably.

"Kaveri, you are my daughter – I care about you and your two sisters more than I care about anyone else in this world. I don't know why you're under the impression I don't love you, and I'm sorry to have made you feel that way. But I love you and anyone messes with you, they mess with me."

Kaveri started sobbing. "I'm leaving Raj, Papa."

"How can I help?"

"You don't care that I'm leaving him?"

"I care about you more than I care about your marriage."

"But what would I do, where would I go?"

"It breaks my heart to think that you even have to wonder when you have me. As long as I'm around, you'll always have a place to live… remember that."

Kaveri didn't trust her voice to speak.

"And you know something else? You've given me the best bit of news for today."

Part Seven – Ten Months Later

Jamuna

Jamuna paced in her apartment restlessly. She kept looking out of the window at the parking lot below as if waiting for the mailman to bring important news. She didn't expect to see anything clearly from the tenth floor but the sweet sense of anticipation thrilled her. She then walked to the balcony and pushed the sliding door opened before stepping out. She looked out and saw the busy street below with vehicles and pedestrians bustling about on the hectic Saturday morning. Jamuna always looked forward to the weekend, when she got some help around the house and mostly, she anticipated Ajay's faithful visits. But that day was a special day. She was on a mission. One that involved Ajay.

The baby's slow cry forced her to step back inside. She glanced up at the clock on the wall before going into the baby's room. He'd only been sleeping for an hour, thought Jamuna distractedly. She wondered whether he needed a change. She entered the baby's room and was welcomed by the soothing smell of baby talcum and milk. She smiled and made cooing sounds as she gently picked up her baby and planted soft kisses on his forehead. He smelled sweet and his skin felt like a soft toy against her face. He stopped groaning as soon as Jamuna held him. Everyone said her baby was a mellow one, he didn't throw screaming tantrums when he was hungry or wet – he'd whimper and as soon as she held him, he'd calm down, it was as if that was all he really needed – to be held by her.

Jamuna checked his diaper and decided to change it. Once that was done, she brought him outside to the living room and settled comfortably on the rocking chair by the fire-place. She eased the flap off her feeding-bra and gently attached the baby's mouth to her nipple. As he started sucking, she leaned back on the chair and rocked the chair lightly to and fro. Jamuna couldn't believe it had been ten months since…well, since the fated day.

The day Pandora's box was opened and all evil escaped into the Sharma's household. The day that re-wrote all their destinies and altered their fates. What a day that had been. But Jamuna was glad for that day. If not for that rainy day, she wouldn't be there, sitting on a rocking chair, in her own apartment, holding her precious baby…her baby, Jeremy Sharma Broughton.

Jamuna ran her fingers through Jeremy's thick, curly, auburn baby hair and caught the shiny glitter on her ring finger. A smile passed Jamuna's lips and lingered as she looked at the ring – her wedding ring. Even now, after almost ten months, she sometimes had to pinch herself to make sure she wasn't dreaming. How had it all happened? And how easy it had been, to get married to Jason? It had been too easy – nothing like she had feared or dreaded. And the person who made it all happen – her father. She owed Ajay her life. She wouldn't have what she had if not for Ajay. She knew she'd still have had Jeremy not matter what, but Ajay was the one who gave her Jason permanently in her life.

She still remembered the day after the non-wedding. She was with Gangga in her room – eyes swollen from crying and lack of sleep, when Ajay walked into their room. Gangga and her had flinched when they saw him in his sad, pathetic state. He looked like he hadn't had a wink of sleep and the dark green stubble on his cheeks with the tousled hair confirmed their suspicion. He had walked wearily into the room and to their shock , had fallen to his knees. Jamuna and Gangga staggered to their feet in an instant and had run to his side, thinking he wasn't well. But when Ajay had looked at them with tear glistened eyes, they had got on their knees as well and he had hugged them both fiercely.

"I'm sorry, my children," he had cried. "I have failed you."

"Papa, please don't," Gangga had protested. "You have not at all failed us. We're the ones who should be on our knees, apologizing – we've let you down."

"Yes, Papa," Jamuna had agreed. "We've let you down, especially me. I don't know how to ever look at your face again without feeling guilty."

"You have nothing to feel guilty about, and please, don't stop looking at me," Ajay had said, holding them closer. Once they had all calmed down, they sat on Gangga's bed. That was when Ajay had told them his plan.

"I just spoke to Vikram this morning," he had begun. "Apparently they didn't get to clean up the wedding-hall after all last night. Once I left, I guess they became disheartened and left as well. So, except for the chairs, everything else is as it was..."

"Oh, Papa, we'll help you clean up," Gangga had offered.

"I don't want it cleaned – at least not until tomorrow."

"Why not?"

"All these years, I've lived a life I didn't want – with your mother. I tried and tried to make amends and to find a spot for her in my heart, but I couldn't. I often wondered how our lives would have been if we were not compelled to marry each other. Would she have been happier? Would I have married the one I truly love? I don't know and the thing is, I'd never find out. That opportunity was taken away from me by my parents when they asked me to marry Menaka. But we still made it through – we have three beautiful children. You three are the best part of my marriage to your mother. And, as you probably know, or have guessed – I've cheated on your mother, all throughout our lives together. She knows and for some reason, had been putting up with it, until now. Your mother has decided to leave me..."

"No!" Jamuna let out a scream, closing her mouth with her hand.

"You can't let her go, you can't! Please, Papa, you can't," Gangga had begged.

"I tried..." Ajay started to speak when the door of the room opened and Menaka walked in.

"He can't stop me, I've decided to go," said Menaka. Jamuna and Gangga had rushed to her and she had thrown her hands around them. Jamuna didn't know how Kaveri ended up being in the house that morning, but she found her standing by the door as well.

"You can't leave, Mama, please," Jamuna had begged. Menaka eased the girls from her and sat next to Ajay. She'd taken Ajay's hand in hers and had smiled into his eyes. Jamuna remember giving Gangga a surprised look at Menaka's obvious display of affection toward their father – when was the last time their parents held hands?

"You father and I spent the past thirty-two-years giving you girls good lives. Despite our differences and struggles, we've always wanted to give you the best. So much so that we've overlooked one most important thing – the thing that destroyed us – our marriage. We tried to impose the same tradition on you girls without realising what that tradition did to us, it caused us our lives. Your father and I have not once been happy with each other. We've never been close and intimate throughout our marriage…until now."

"Then why do you have to still go?" Gangga asked.

"Because, we've realised that we can love each other as best friends, but not as husband and wife. I can love your father, but only as a friend. I couldn't love him all these years because I couldn't be a wife to him. I found myself hating him for marrying me and deducing my life to being a wife and a mother. I had dreams before that. I wanted to be successful, to have a career, to be independent. But all that was snatched from me in a heartbeat when I married your father. I held him guilty throughout all these years. But that was wrong of me. He was a prisoner of our marriage as much as I was. Instead of understanding the predicament we were in and trying to find solutions, I pushed him away. I don't blame him for having an affair, although I wished he didn't. I do know now of the other woman in our lives, but as much as I don't wish her any harm, I also don't ever want to see her again. Her betrayal hurts more than your father's and as I have forgiven your father, I can never forgive my sister. But I can't continue with this life, I can't continue being Mrs. Menaka Sharma. I think it's time I lived my own life."

"But, Mama, where would you go?" Gangga had asked.

"I'm going back to India."

"Your mother wants to fulfill her dreams – she wants to become independent and finally live her life, and it'll be wrong of me to hold her back."

"But what're you going to do in India?" Jamuna asked.

That was when Kaveri spoke, "Mama and I are going to open our own business."

"You're going too? What about Raj?" asked Gangga.

"I've left Raj. Please don't ask the details – it's too tedious and really, I'm not in the mood to discuss him."

Jamuna had wanted to laugh at Kaveri's melodramatic speech. Only Kaveri could handle a separation so nonchalantly, like she did everything else in her life. Jamuna could never be as brave as her. She could never leave her husband and think it was something tedious…that was their differences; Kaveri was in the end very much like Menaka.

"What kind of business?" Gangga asked.

Menaka explained, "My father, your Dadaji, has a small sari store that he'd owned after he got Devika and Imarried off. I'm thinking of taking over and expanding on it."

"I'm selling this house," Ajay said. "And I'm giving every penny of it to your mother."

"You don't have to, Ajay."

"I want to. I have my own place and I don't need the money from this place. You need it more than I do."

"Selling the house?" Gangga had gasped. "What about Jamuna?"

"And Vikram?" added Jamuna.

"Well, that brings us back to the beginning of this conversation, before we got side-tracked," said Ajay.

"What? About cleaning the wedding-hall?"

"Yes, we were thinking, your mother and I, since the hall is all ready for a wedding, and the *mandap* is still up…and if you're sure Jason wouldn't mind sitting in it, with a turban and wearing a pyjamas, with no shoes of course – then, why not put it to good use and get the two of you married?"

And that was how her wedding had taken place the next day of the non-wedding, with almost no relatives and a few close friends. Jason had indeed sat in the *mandap*, with a pyjama-like kurta and no shoes. He had anyhow refused to wear a turban. But it had been perfect. He had been perfect. Jason's parents had arrived the following day from Kelowna. At first Jamuna had been sceptical and afraid of how his parents would react to their son marrying an Indian girl. But The Broughtons had embraced her into their lives with open arms. Jason had told them about Jamuna and they knew everything about her. They made it all look so simple and uncomplicated that Jamuna felt she belonged with them instantaneously.

A week after Jamuna's wedding, Menaka and Kaveri left to India. Vikram decided to rent a room in Vancouver and had moved out there. Ajay had moved into his Langley apartment, and Jason had rented the apartment in Surrey since it was closer to Jamuna's work and his. Ajay and Gangga had stood by Jamuna and Jason all through their journey in securing their lives together. Jeremy was born two months ago. And Jamuna had decided, it was finally time to do what she'd been meaning to do ever since Menaka left to India for good.

The oven beeped, reminding her of the chicken she was roasting. She looked down at Jeremy and found him fast asleep. Jamuna placed him in his crib and was pulling the room door shut quietly when she felt a pair of arms circling her around the waist. She turned around and found her nose brushing with her husband's.

"Shhh...I just put him down," she whispered.

"Oh...good, finally get to have you for myself," Jason said as he planted little kisses all over her face. Jamuna pushed him away laughingly.

"We have company coming for lunch and I still have lots to do."

"Damn...just when I thought I could have some time alone with my wife! Remind me again why we're having this get together?" he followed her into the kitchen and helped her take the chicken out of the oven.

"For Papa, you know that."

"Right...for him to have his happily ever after. When will you realise you're not God?"

"I'm not playing God. I just want him to be happy. Plus, he gave me my happily ever after, I'm just paying him back."

"Come to think of it...he did, didn't he? If you had it your way, we'd never be married."

"Stop it already, you know I was a basket case. I couldn't decide or think for myself and you know how worried I was of destroying everyone else by marrying you? It wasn't because I didn't love you..."

"It was because you loved everyone else more..."

"Not more..."

"More!"

The door bell interrupted their little dispute. Jamuna threw a kitchen towel at Jason playfully and went to answer the door. She opened it to see Devika standing there, with a bouquet of flowers, looking pretty in her light blue sari and her hair let down. Jamuna hugged her aunt, praying she was doing the right thing.

DEVIKA

WHEN SHE SAW JAMUNA, she was overcome with a sense of loss and emptiness. Looking at Jamuna she was reminded of the big, gaping void in her heart that could never be filled again – and of the pain that would never heal, like a permanent scar. How had it all happened so fast and so drastically…and all it took was one day…one rainy day!

Jamuna led her into her little apartment and Devika looked around appreciatively. Jamuna and Jason had done well for themselves. The apartment, albeit was small, spoke their love in every corner. Pictures of both of them together adorned one wall, followed by photos of his and her family and they'd dedicated a whole wall for Jeremy alone. Devika looked around to see if she could spot the baby, but Jamuna told her she'd just put Jeremy down for a nap.

Devika had seen Jeremy only once, when he was born. Circumstances and fear had kept her away from the Sharma family since. She made sure she didn't interfere with their lives and especially with Ajay and Menaka again. Ever since the evening of the non-wedding, Devika had stayed away from Ajay. When she found out Jamuna was getting married on the same *mandap* the next day, she'd mustered all her courage and showed up for the wedding with Priya. It had been the most difficult and embarrassing moment of her life. She knew by then everyone had learned of her affair with Ajay and it made her feel cheap and unwanted, not less like a whore. She remembered standing by the *mandap*, while Jamuna got married and feeling like an outsider. No one spoke to her – not Jamuna, Gangga or Kaveri. Menaka didn't even look her way, so much for talking to her. But she had wanted to be there for Jamuna and she didn't care if she was basked in mortification. It was one of the prices she had to pay for her sins.

"Hello Devika." She turned around and saw Jason standing with an apron around his waist and an oven-mitten on one hand. He came forward and hugged her.

"Jason darling, how lovely to see you," she kissed him on the cheeks.

"And you look stunning. Do you know you're the reason I really married Jamuna?"

"Oh, why is that?"

"Well, I figured if she looked like you when she reaches your age, then I've got it made!" Devika slapped him lightly on the arm and laughed.

"Shut up, you brute!" Jamuna interjected. "The only reason you married me was because you can't live without me."

"So you think!"

"So I know…have we forgotten all the begging and you're-my-life sonnets?"

Devika laughed at the pair of them. Looking at them it dawned on her how close they became to not being with each other. If Gangga did end up marrying Subash, Jamuna may never have ended up with Jason for Ajay and Menaka would never have realised their mistakes. Bless Gangga and her non-wedding.

"Is Gangga coming?" she asked suddenly, interrupting Jamuna and Jason.

"Yes, with her new boyfriend," said Jamuna.

"What new boyfriend?"

"She's been dating this guy for a few months now. She met him while organizing an event; actually she was organizing it for him. Jason and I have met him once. I thought it'd be nice to have him here, so you can all meet him."

Devika had wanted to ask more of the guy when the words 'you all' sprung to her ears.

"Who else is coming?" her voice was cautious, lest she arose any suspicion. She prayed Menaka and Ajay wouldn't be coming. She'd have to leave if they did. She could not face them…not in a million years!

"Hmmm…just a few other people – Vikram and his twins, he's babysitting them this weekend and they're very keen to know what came out of the oven!" Jamuna gave Jason a strange look and the two burst into silly giggles. Devika watched them with amusement mingled with envy. When was the last time she'd shared a loving laugh over a private joke with anyone?

"How come Priya didn't come?" asked Jamuna.

"Oh…she…she's got her exam next week and she's busy, but she did ask to send you her love," lied Devika. Priya had said no such thing.

"She's sweet. Okay, Jason we need to get everything ready. Devika Aunty, can we leave you for a while to get lunch going?"

"Of course, darling. Is there anything I can do to help?"

"Yes, just sit down and rest, I'll get you a drink soon." Jamuna and Jason disappeared into the kitchen, leaving Devika by herself.

Devika walked from wall to wall, admiring the photos. She found it uncanny how Jason and Jamuna looked so compatible together, like they were made for each other. It was like their love shone from their eyes right to their hearts. Devika didn't know of many people who were blessed with such love. Devika noticed a photo of Priya's with Gangga and Jamuna, it looked like it was taken right after Jamuna's wedding. That was the last time Priya had seen her cousins as well. That had been Priya's choice. After the incident at Gangga's wedding, Priya was intimidated by the girls, especially Kaveri. When she saw Gangga walking out of the *mandap*, she'd been taken aback. And the next day when Jamuna married Jason, Priya had become completely disheartened.

"Poor Uncle Ajay," she'd told Devika after Jamuna's wedding. "Everyone had been so mean to him. It was like none of his daughters respected him."

"We don't know the real story, beta. Best to stay out of it," Devika had warned her gently.

As much as she felt bad for Ajay, she was proud of the decision he took and was proud of him for standing by his daughters. She only wished Priya was lucky enough to get the same kind of support from her father. But Priya was unlucky when it came to both her fathers. Her real father was in no position of accepting her as his own and the father she'd known all her life had left them for good.

It hadn't been Siva's decision to leave. It had been Devika's request that he left. The Sharma household only knew how much Gangga's non-wedding had changed their lives, but they didn't know it had changed Devika's life as well.

Devika had planned to drive back to her house that same evening and had gone straight to the basement below. She was packing her suitcases when Siva walked into the room.

"We need to talk," he said. Devika didn't look at him. She wasn't sure what to say to him, so she continued putting her clothes away as if he hadn't spoken.

"Devika, I know you know. So, please, can we talk?"

"What do you want to talk about?" she had asked finally.

"Us, what do you want to do?"

She looked up at Siva and saw his worried look. No wonder he'd been so miserable living with her all these years, Devika mused bitterly.

"How long have you known?" she asked him.

"As long as I could remember."

"God, Siva, why did you marry me then?"

"I had to, I had no choice. My parents would've killed themselves if they found out their only son was gay! I had to do it for them. And I thought marrying you could change me, somehow make me straight."

Devika had laughed acidly, "It's funny how tradition could kill ones spirit and render them helpless."

"But I have no regrets, Devika. You gave me everything plus a daughter – although, of course I know she's not really mine, but you gave me the status of a father. I was accepted by the society because of you. I seem normal to them, not an outcast."

But Devika didn't hear anything beyond 'of course I know she's not really mine.' If he had always known, why did he…? That explained his attitude toward Priya. He couldn't love her knowing she was never his.

"What do you want me to do?" she heard him ask. That was when Devika decided she'd rather be a divorcee than remained married to a gay man. Siva deserved to be happy, to be free. She didn't know how she'd walk with her head held high, but she couldn't remain in a marriage that would destroy not only her, but Siva as well.

"I think we should go our separate ways," she said finally.

"We don't have to."

"Yes, we have to. If I were you I'd want to spend the rest of my life with the one I truly love. But since I can't have that, I want at least you to have it. Be happy, Siva, God knows, you deserve it." Siva had hugged her and cried. Devika had held him and remember thinking how stupid of her for not have noticed – he even cried like a woman. And when she released him, the shock registered on his face compelled her to look at the back and she found Priya standing by the door, the twins on tow.

Siva awkwardly excused himself and had made his escape. Devika didn't meet Priya's gaze. The twins entered the room and sat on one of the beds with their Nintendo Games.

"Why are you here with Johan and Karan?" Devika asked Priya.

"Chandni Aunty wanted me to watch them while she took her bath."

"Oh… I see, have you finished packing?"

"Mama? Who's daughter am I?"

That had been the hardest moment of Devika's life. She was not only speechless but embarrassed. It was not easy for a mother to tell her daughter that her father was not her real father, no matter how bad of a father he was. Devika never did tell Priya who her real father was and she knew they'd drifted apart slightly since that day. Siva moved out as soon as they got back from Jamuna's wedding, with a brief pat on Priya's head. Since that day, Priya had devoted all her time to her school work and spoke to Devika when only necessary. Devika tried to get closer to her, but it was like something had snapped in Priya, it was as if she had shut everyone out of her world. She almost reminded Devika of the twins, consumed by her school work and friends. Although Priya had never brought up the question about her real father, Devika knew that was the only thing that would restore the lost love between them. But she couldn't do it to Ajay and his family. Devika couldn't cause Ajay's family any more pain than she already had. If Menaka found out about Priya, Devika was sure Ajay's marriage would fall apart. For the sake of his marriage, Devika had to endure the animosity that had settled between Priya and her.

Gangga

Gangga slipped on her favourite dress and attached a pair of pearl earrings to her ears. She pulled her hair up and held it high with a pin with a few tendrils falling around her neck enticingly. She smiled at her image in the mirror to camouflage the anxiety within but failed. Who was she fooling? Gangga felt as nervous as a five-year-old on her first day of kindergarten. Of course she knew it was foolish to be nervous; it wasn't like this was her first day out with Aman. She'd been out with him before, many times on serious dates. But this was the first time Aman was going to meet her family. But that wasn't her only anxiety. Jamuna was threading on thin ice that afternoon and it gave Gangga butterflies in her tummy every time she thought about it.

When Jamuna first approached her with what Gangga considered an insane idea, Gangga had been baffled. She understood Jamuna's wish to see their father happy, but what Jamuna was about to do was not only interfering but risky. She tried talking her sister out of her crazy plan, but Jamuna was steadfast on her desire to see Ajay happy. Gangga prayed her sister was not disappointed.

The honk outside made Gangga scamper around the room for her shoes and handbag. She also grabbed the wrapped presents for her nephew. It was a celebration for him that day after all. Jamuna's reason for having them over was to celebrate Jeremy's safe arrival into this world – of course, that was only part of the reason.

Gangga ran down the steps of her apartment on her heels and

her heart almost stopped beating when she saw Aman standing by his black, 3-series BMW. He looked like a model who'd just walked out of a magazine, handsome and sleek. Gangga was so glad she had her best red dress on. Aman planted a not-too-brief kiss on her cheeks and murmured how sexy she looked. Gangga leaned closer and inhaled the fresh smell of bath soap and musky aftershave.

"I hope your sister doesn't serve dessert tonight," he said as he opened the car door for her.

"Why? Surely you're not on a diet?" laughed Gangga.

"Because I'd like to have you..."

"Aman..." Gangga hit his arm with her handbag.

By the time they hit the road, Gangga had forgotten all about her anxiety, until she reached Jamuna's apartment.

Ajay

"Damn this traffic!" Ajay murmured and hit the steering wheel lightly with his fists, an act which caused him to smile involuntarily. Devika always said he was a very patient man that when he actually grumbled about something, it had to be something really bad. Ajay didn't usually complain about the traffic, but that day he was in a hurry and he was already late. Traffic in the Lower Mainland was not uncommon, but he wished he'd left his apartment in Langley earlier that morning. Jamuna specifically told him to be at her place by lunch and glancing at the digital clock on his car, Ajay knew it was nearing lunch time in the Broughton residence.

Ajay had been dropping on Jamuna and Jason so often in the past few months that it almost felt like his second home there. But he couldn't refrain himself, he constantly found himself being pulled like a magnet toward Jamuna's apartment. Jeremy, his grandson, had become someone so crucial to Ajay's happiness that if Ajay didn't see him at least three or four times a week, he felt incomplete – and incomplete he was.

Life had become so empty for Ajay that sometimes he wished he'd never met Devika. If not for Jamuna and Gangga, Ajay would have quit his job and gone on a long tour somewhere. But the two girls had been by his side at all times, looking after him and behaving like mothers. As it was, the girls had lost their mother, who'd taken off on them. He didn't want to leave them as well, especially when Jamuna had just delivered. Menaka was planning on coming to see Jamuna and her grandson, but that wouldn't be happening anytime soon. Since the sari business was new to her, she needed more time to learn and get organized. Although, looking at Jamuna, it didn't seem like she was missing her mother at all.

Menaka's decision to leave him, albeit was a surprise, was the best thing that happened to him. He was glad to see Menaka go and he was happy she finally was going after her dreams. It hadn't been easy for Ajay to learn that Menaka had been holding grudges against him all these years for marrying her and ruining her future. But it also gave him a consolation knowing that he wasn't the sole criminal in their marriage and that he was as much a victim as he was a felon. Ajay was also glad the house finally sold two months ago and he was able to transfer the profit to Menaka's account in India. She had called, frantic with gratitude, from India and had regaled him of her business which was flourishing magnificently. And apparently Kaveri was a true entrepreneur. She'd dedicated her spirit into the sari business and was doing a wonderful job in promoting it. It was strange in an uncanny way how things unfolded for all of them. Kaveri, who had always struggled hard to belong in Canada and who tried so hard to become a true Canadian, had finally found her sense of belonging, her niche among the Indians in India. She'd at last found herself and accepted the Indian blood in her. If Ajay had known earlier, he'd have packed her off to India long time ago. But, all was good.

Ajay was still affected by Gangga's decision not to marry Subash. Or her decision not to get married at all. She seemed content being single or being on dating-mode. He hoped eventually she'd settle down and have her own family like Jamuna. Although he had reached a point in his life where he really didn't care who his children were married to, the orthodox side of him still wanted them to be married. He still believed that his daughters' lives would be complete once they were married and he also felt like he'd sleep a little better at night knowing his daughters were looked after. Of course, as far as Kaveri was concerned, he doubted she'd ever get married. If she couldn't find a decent man in Canada, he very much doubted she'd find a half-decent man in India, especially one that would marry a divorcee. But Ajay wasn't worried about Kaveri, for if she was anything like Menaka, then she'd be happier not being tight down by marriage.

He worried about Gangga since age was catching up on her and he worried about his other daughter – Priya. Ajay hadn't been in touch with Devika or Priya in the last ten months or so. He knew Devika had visited Jamuna when Jeremy was born but that was the last he heard of her. He wished things were different between them, that they had at least planned on staying friends, but he realised that was impossible.

All his daughters had learned of his relationship with Devika. He could only imagine how hard it was for Devika to stay away from the nieces she'd helped to bring up. As much as he felt bad for Devika, he couldn't do anything to change the situation. He sometimes cursed the day that opened all the evils of their lives into the world. At the same time, he was glad for that day – he'd be still married to Menaka otherwise and living in hell. His only qualm was not having Devika in his life and not being a part of Priya's life anymore. He had wanted to provide for Priya like he had his other daughters. That didn't seem possible any more.

But he was determined to somehow get in touch with Priya and be a part of her life again. Of course, that didn't involve looking for a suitable boy for her. He saw how that turned out with his other daughters. Ajay vowed to himself never to interfere in his children's love lives any more. They were all adults with rights to live life as they wished. That was one thing he'd learned through Gangga's non-wedding day – never to interfere or play God anymore.

Ajay reached Jamuna's apartment the same time Vikram arrived with his brothers – Johan and Karan. Ajay greeted Vikram with a fond handshake and rustled the twin's heads as they headed toward Jamuna's apartment.

"Mr. Sharma, come on in," Jason answered the door for them. Ajay pumped his son-in-law's hand and handed him the red wine he'd brought along.

"You have to stop calling me Mr. Sharma, dear boy."

"Sorry, what to do, *adat bangaye*." It's become a habit. Ajay laughed at Jason's attempt with Hindi.

"Not bad at all," he said, hitting him on the back gently.

"Dude, is Jamuna giving you Hindi lessons now?" asked Vikram, laughing at his friend.

"Not really, but she says that word to me so much, it's stuck. That's the only word I know."

"That's a start," said Vikram, putting his arms around his friend and following him into the living room. "So, you called us over, what's for lunch?" Then he lowered his voice in a whisper, "Feed my brothers last if you want the rest of us to eat at all, they're a pair of Hoovers!"

Ajay walked into the kitchen and found Jamuna, who hugged and kissed him with unconditional fondness.

"Is your sister coming?" asked Ajay.

"As far as I know, unless she changed plans on me last minute."

"And with Gangga, that wouldn't be the first time," said Ajay jokingly.

"Papa, surely you're over that?"

"Sure I am. Where's my angel?"

Jamuna hesitated. Just then the door bell rang again and Gangga's voice loomed into the living room. Ajay and Jamuna headed to the living room and were introduced to the handsome Aman. Ajay shook Aman's hand apprehensively. It wasn't the way Aman looked that concerned Ajay, but it was the name. From where he came from, Aman was a Muslim name. Ajay prayed in his heart Gangga wasn't dating a Muslim man. It was one thing to accept Jason; it was totally a different thing to accept a Muslim man as his son-in-law.

"So, where's everyone?" Gangga asked.

"Are there more people coming?" Ajay asked Jamuna. He wasn't aware Jamuna had planned an elobrate lunch with a lot of people.

"No...not really...err...Papa?" why was she stammering? Ajay cocked his eyes and studied his daughter suspiciously. Gangga jumped in and asked about the baby as if she was digressing from the topic.

"Actually, Papa, why don't you go check on the baby while we get dinner ready?" suggested Jamuna. Ajay shrugged and walked toward the baby's room, but not before noticing the look Gangga was giving her sister – as if something was brewing.

AND THE END

AS SOON AS AJAY vacated the living room, everyone gathered together in a circle and started whispering as if thieves in conspiracy.

"Jamuna," Gangga said. "Do you think it's going to work?"

"What's going to work?" asked Aman.

"I hope so, didi," replied Jamuna, ignoring Aman.

"I just hope it doesn't backfire – you and your dreams to change the planet!" grunted Jason.

"I mean well," protested Jamuna.

"She means well," agreed Gangga. "Although, what makes you think Devika Aunty is going to agree?"

"I was thinking of the same thing," added Vikram.

"What's going on?" asked Aman.

"If she loves him, then nothing will stop her," said Jamuna, ignoring Aman again.

"But she's married, and they have a kid," said Jason. "I doubt this is going to work."

"What's not going to work?" asked Aman.

"I haven't thought that far," said Jamuna. "I just wanted to bring them together one last time. The rest, we'll leave to fate."

"And destiny?" asked Jason.

"Yes, destiny...*kismet*," said Gangga.

"I don't believe in *kismet* bullshit!" said Vikram. "But I hope, for your sake, this works out."

"For crying out loud," screamed Aman. "What the hell is going on?"

All heads turned toward Aman and everyone started laughing at Aman's confused, flushed face.

What were his daughters up to now? Ajay thought to himself as he gently pushed the baby's room door opened. But when he entered the room, Ajay stood rooted for what was in front of him took all his breath away – there, sitting on a rocking chair in a corner, gently feeding Jeremy with a bottle, was Devika. She looked up absently at the sound of the door opening. At first her eyes widened in shock, then she darted them away from Ajay uneasily.

"Devika?" Ajay's voice came out a soft whisper. "What're you doing here?"

"I came for Jeremy's party," replied Devika, in equally hushed tone. "I didn't know you're going to be here. Is didi here too?"

Ajay sensed Devika's restlessness. She looked uncomfortable. She thought he was still with Menaka. *She thought he was still with Menaka?*

"Menaka left me," he said and Devika gasped. "She left me ten months ago, the day after Jamuna's wedding."

"Oh...Ajay. I'm so sorry."

"Don't be. She's happier now than she had ever been."

"Is she really?"

Ajay nodded.

"Where is she?" Devika's voice was still small.

"She's gone back to India, with Kaveri."

"To India? But why?"

"She's taken over your father's sari shop and is turning it into a big successful business. Kaveri's her PR person. And I've never seen my daughter and my ex-wife this happy in all my life. I've been bad for them, and I'm only thankful I realised it sooner than later."

"Oh, Ajay...you're wrong. They didn't appreciate you for what you are. It's their loss, Ajay. Did didi ever find out it was me?"

"Yes..."

"Will she ever forgive me?"

"Why do you care?"

"She's my sister. I guess now even my father wouldn't be talking to me any longer. God, Ajay, I've burnt all bridges with my family."

"It's all my fault, Devika. I'm sorry."

"It takes two to tango. I wish things were different, I miss everyone. You don't know how thankful I am for Jamuna and Gangga. They've allowed me back into their lives and I'm grateful. I've lost everything else, Ajay."

"What do you mean you've lost everything else?"

Devika looked at him as if she'd said something she shouldn't have. Jeremy chose that moment to grumble. Devika took the milk bottle away and propped the baby up. She patted him lightly on the back in an attempt to burp him. She was so deep into her task that it almost appeared as if she was avoiding Ajay's question. Ajay was about to question her again when suddenly the twins rushed into the room.

"Here he is," said Johan.

"He's so tiny," remarked Karan.

They sat by the end of the rocking chair and observed the baby as if he was a science specimen under experiment. They looked at his tiny fingers and marvelled at their minuteness.

"Everything's so small," observed Johan.

"Like a toy," said Karan.

Devika pursed her lips together and concealed a smile. The twins were an amusing pair. Ajay, on the other hand, was not at all amused. He found the twins presence intrusive. He really wanted to talk to Devika. He sensed there was something she wasn't telling him.

"Where's Priya?" asked Karan, lifting his eyes away from the baby.

Devika jolted as if caught off-guard. "She's…she's got some reading to do…"

"Is she still sad?" asked Johan.

"Sad?" Devika asked. "Why should she be sad?"

"Isn't she sad?" asked Karan.

"When she heard Siva Uncle is gay?" asked Johan.

Ajay felt like he'd swollen needles. His heart felt like it was being poked by the needles, sharp and painful. What were the twins rambling on? And why was Devika looking so pallid suddenly?

"Karan, Johan, the baby needs to sleep, why don't the two of you run along? We'll be out shortly," Ajay said firmly. He ushered the twins out of the door but not before Karan turned around and asked very matter-of-factly, "Uncle Ajay, what does 'gay' mean?"

Ajay had to literally shove the twins out of the baby's room. He turned around and faced Devika.

"Do you have something to tell me?" he demanded.

Devika gently placed Jeremy in his crib. "You know how those two are. They must've somehow learned the word and decided to use it."

Ajay would have believed her if only she didn't look so nervous and almost guilty. She wasn't looking at him as she spoke.

"Do you want to tell me?" he demanded again, this time harsher.

Devika paused and held on to the side of the crib. "Ajay, please..."

"Why did the twins say that? And why is Priya not here?"

But Devika ran past him, grabbed her handbag from the living room and with everyone gaping at her, ran out of the Jamuna's apartment in tears. Ajay came out of Jeremy's room and before he could say anything or stop Devika, she was gone.

That was when Ajay realised everyone else was standing around watching as one would a drama serial. Embarrassed, he plopped onto a nearby chair and brushed his hair away from his face, a habit when he was distressed.

"Papa," he looked up and saw Jamuna standing by him, her hand on his shoulder. "Go get her."

"What?"

"Yes, Papa," Gangga was by Jamuna's side. "Go get the love of your life."

"I can't. I won't spoil her life. I just...I can't." Ajay's eyes clouded and something vague and distant flashed in them. He looked desolate as if he was in mourning.

"Uncle Ajay," Vikram approached Ajay and pulled a chair to sit by him. "Devika Aunty is separated from her husband, ten months ago."

Ajay turned to look at Vikram blankly, as if not comprehending him.

"The day after Gangga's wedding, or non-wedding, Uncle Siva left their house. There's more to the story, but suffice to say you won't be ruining anything."

"Why didn't she say anything to me?"

"For the same reason you didn't say anything to her when Mama left," said Jamuna.

"You both wanted to protect each other and save each other's marriage," said Gangga.

"If that's not true love, Mr. Sharma," Jason butted in. "Then nothing is."

"Go get her, Papa," urged Jamuna.

"Why?" Ajay finally faced the young people around him. "Why are you all so…so…eager?"

"Because all your life, you placed our happiness before yours," said Gangga. "We want you to finally have your happily-ever-after."

"You deserve it all, Papa," said Jamuna.

Ajay gathered his daughters, Jason and Vikram in a big bear hug. "I'm the luckiest person alive to have you in my life." Then he stood up abruptly, flashed them a wide, shy grin and rushed out of the door.

Aman, who had been watching the drama in front of him, cleared his throat and asked, "Does anyone want to fill me in on what's going on here?"

Gangga opened her mouth to say something but Jason preceded, "Dude, if I were you, I'd think twice before I dated anyone from the Sharma family."

"Jason!" yelled Jamuna, "What are you doing with me then?"

"Of course, I was too late, but Aman, dude, there's still time for you."

Gangga rolled her eyes skyward. "Don't listen to him, Aman. He's full of it. Now, shall we have lunch? I'm starving."

"Me too, where's the food?" asked Vikram as he headed to the kitchen, and the rest followed. Aman was the last in line.

"I still don't know what's going on," he murmured to himself.

The twins who were sitting in front of the TV looked at each other and shook their heads in unison.

"I never want to be a grown up," said Johan.

"They're all complicated, confused bunch of people," agreed Karan. Then they turned back toward the TV and tuned the world out.

Ajay found Devika sitting in her car dabbing her eyes with tissue. He opened the car door, pulled Devika out with force and as her eyes widened in surprise, embraced her roughly. Devika resisted at first, but not for long. She hugged him back and buried her face in his chest, sobbing her heart out.

"You stupid, stupid woman," said Ajay passionately.

"I just wanted you to be happy."

"When will you realise my happiness is with you?" Ajay gently inched her away from him and bent down and kissed her on the lips. It was a brief kiss, but it was the most meaningful of all their kisses. It was a kiss that finally sealed them together for life.

The End

CPSIA information can be obtained at www.ICGtesting.com
Printed in the USA
LVOW072321160911

246637LV00001B/18/P